DIG DEEP MY GRAVE

This Large Print Book carries the
Seal of Approval of N.A.V.H.

A VIV AND CHARLIE MYSTERY

DIG DEEP MY GRAVE

CHERYL HONIGFORD

THORNDIKE PRESS
A part of Gale, a Cengage Company

Farmington Hills, Mich • San Francisco • New York • Waterville, Maine
Meriden, Conn • Mason, Ohio • Chicago

Copyright © 2018 by Cheryl Honigford.
A Viv and Charlie Mystery.
Thorndike Press, a part of Gale, a Cengage Company.

LIBRARY OF CONGRESS CIP DATA ON FILE.
CATALOGUING IN PUBLICATION FOR THIS BOOK
IS AVAILABLE FROM THE LIBRARY OF CONGRESS

ISBN-13: 978-1-4328-5549-9 (hardcover)

Published in 2018 by arrangement with Sourcebooks, Inc.

Printed in Mexico
1 2 3 4 5 6 7 22 21 20 19 18

For Kate

CHAPTER ONE

June 11, 1939

Oakhaven had been a magical place for her once, Vivian thought as the boat sped toward the wooded shore of Geneva Lake. But that had been long ago. The towering Victorian mansion looked the same as she remembered — beautiful, enormous, daunting. She pulled her eyes away, squinting in the bright sunlight glinting off the water. She held her wide-brimmed summer hat to her head with one hand and reached out with the other to touch the tops of the waves skimming past. The water was ice cold, and her fingertips tingled as she pulled them toward her again. It may have been a sunny day in June, but the deep water never warmed much in southern Wisconsin, not even when summer was in full swing.

She glanced sidelong at Charlie. "Nervous?"

He shook his head, his dark-blond hair

blowing back from his forehead. He might deny his nerves, but the way his fingers tightened around the brim of the panama hat clutched to his chest told the real story. His other hand, resting on her waist, pulled her closer toward him on the padded bench seat. Vivian followed his narrowed gaze: first to the tidy, uniformed driver of the speed-boat, then on toward the looming bulk of their destination on the far shore.

Of course Charlie was nervous, she thought. He would meet her extended family for the first time today. Heck, Vivian was nervous, and she'd known them her whole life. She supposed she was nervous *because* she'd known them her whole life. They were an imposing bunch — and Oakhaven an imposing place.

It was her mother's family's summer estate on Geneva Lake, the Newport of the West. Julia Witchell, then Julia Markham, had spent her girlhood summers here among high society, far away from the suf-focating air of the city. When Julia's father died, not long after her mother, the owner-ship of Oakhaven had passed to Julia's older sister, Adaline, and her husband — as did the Markham meatpacking dynasty.

The success of the family meatpacking business is what had made the ownership of a sprawling Victorian summer estate possible. Oakhaven sat on three green acres among the likes of the Wrigleys and the Schwinns — Chicago's upper crust. There were only thirty-one estates sprinkled around the twenty-plus mile shoreline of the lake. It was a privileged life, and the family did not take their standing here lightly.

The house came into closer focus as the speedboat approached — the gingerbread facade rising over the wide green expanse of lawn that ran to the water's edge. Guests in white muslin milled about near the wraparound front porch, drinks in hand. The garden party was already in full swing. *"A place of wide lawns and narrow minds,"* Vivian thought. Who'd said that? Hemingway? She swallowed and glanced sidelong at Charlie. She was by no means ashamed of her handsome private eye — quite the opposite, in fact — but she hoped the minds of her extended family had grown substantially wider than she remembered them being. If not, it might be a rough afternoon for both of them.

Charlie whistled through his teeth, his eyes still trained on the mansion looming ever closer. "All of that from sausages?"

Vivian smirked. "Well, Chicago *is* hog

9

butcher for the world."

Charlie returned the smile, but one eyebrow remained quirked in either disbelief or alarm. Likely both.

Vivian's maternal grandfather had owned a swath of the vast Union Stock Yard in the final quarter of the last century. Markham Meats had competed with the likes of Armour and Swift. The whole idea of her mother's family gaining their wealth and status from such a lowbrow business amused Vivian. Her mother was insufferably elitist, as were her mother's sisters. And all of that wealth and superiority came from something so gauche and thoroughly midwestern as butchering hogs. But that was the American way, wasn't it? Fathers got their hands dirty so their children would never have to. Vivian's mother and her mother's sisters had led privileged, sheltered lives: private boarding schools, coming-out parties. Her mother's eldest sister, Ethel, had even married an English aristocrat.

Charlie looked off down the shore at the other estates visible through the thick canopy of leaves. He leaned down and spoke directly into Vivian's ear so he could be heard over the roar of the engine and the waves smashing against the hull.

"We really couldn't have driven?" he said.

10

"Surely, there are roads up here. It's the twentieth century, for heaven's sake."

"Oh, we could have," Vivian said, shouting into the wind. "There's a service road behind the cottage, but Aunt Adaline prefers her guests to arrive across the lake by boat. It's more dramatic this way."

Charlie lifted his chin toward the quickly advancing shoreline, brows knit together over his nose. "And *that's* what you call a cottage?"

She smiled and squeezed his forearm lightly. "Oakhaven has no insulation and is not habitable in the winter. So yes, a summer cottage."

Charlie snorted but said nothing more.

The boat shifted into a lower gear as they approached the pristine-white wooden dock.

Vivian knew she was asking a lot of Charlie. This was so far removed from the world he'd grown up in and what he still knew every day. She loved him for doing this for her. She loved him for a lot of things. She wrapped both arms around his middle and squeezed.

"*Oof,* what's that for?" he asked.

"For being such a good sport." She rested her cheek against his chest for a moment before pulling back to look up into his handsome, sharp-angled face. "I owe you one."

"You owe me more than one," Charlie said. Then he bent down and kissed the tip of her nose.

Vivian had spent almost every summer on Geneva Lake as a girl, but she hadn't been to Oakhaven since she'd started working as a secretary at WCHI radio four years ago, when her summers had been consumed with sorting, typing, and filing. Then her acting career had taken off, and she'd found herself costarring in the detective serial, *The Darkness Knows,* as well as multiple other dramatic engagements on any given day. She no longer had the leisure time for lolling about in sailboats or sipping iced tea on shaded verandas. She tilted her face up to the bright June sunshine and closed her eyes. She missed the idleness sometimes. Not often, but sometimes.

Charlie helped her from the boat and then paused, head cocked. "What's that noise?"

Vivian paused to listen, noticing the monotonous whirring drone underneath the music and conversation. She looked off toward the acres of woods at the back of the property.

"Cicadas," she said. "The seventeen-year

kind. I read something about their return in the paper this morning. You've never heard them?"

Charlie shook his head. "Don't get many cicadas in the city, I guess."

"Disgustingly fascinating little creatures," she said, thinking of how she'd pick the cicada's empty shells from the trees and drop them in her cousin David's hair. She'd been eight at the time. Still, inexcusable behavior, according to her aunt Adaline.

"I think that racket would drive me batty."

"Well, welcome to the country, Mr. Haverman," Vivian said, smiling up at him.

This was supposed to have been an intimate family gathering, but there were at least a hundred people milling about the lawn, and Vivian recognized almost no one. She was the sole representative of the Witchell branch of the family today, as her mother was in Washington, DC, with her companion, Oskar. It had been half a year since Oskar had entered their lives, and Vivian still had trouble defining his relationship with Julia. *Companion* was as good a word as any, she thought.

Despite Vivian's initial misgivings, Oskar had been all sorts of good for her mother. Julia Witchell had — dare Vivian even think it — loosened up in the past six months.

She smiled at regular intervals now. She laughed. Vivian hadn't seen her mother this happy in years. Vivian's younger brother, Everett, would agree, but he couldn't be here today either. He was studying for his sophomore-year finals at Northwestern.

Vivian looked up at Charlie. She could tell nothing of his feelings from his stony exterior. Perhaps it wasn't fair to throw him into the lion's den like this, she thought. But their relationship was serious. Charlie was in her life for good, or so she hoped, and she wanted her family to know him. She snaked one arm around his waist. Her eyes drifted over the crowd again and stopped at the fountain on the opposite end of the lawn and her cousin Constance.

"Ah," she said. "Let's make the introductions to the heirs of the Markham meat-packing dynasty, shall we?"

Vivian's eldest cousin stood near the splashing copy of the Manneken Pis, a statue of a naked little boy peeing into the fountain. The famous original stood in Brussels. Vivian's grandfather had wanted the original, of course, but it turned out that there were some things in the world that couldn't be bought.

Constance was ten years Vivian's senior. Physically, she took after her father, Vivian's

Uncle Bernard, with her dark, wiry hair and long face. Still, Constance had an austere sort of beauty, even if she did lean a bit toward malnourished. In fact, every time Vivian heard advertisements on the radio for Ironized Yeast and the pill's ability to add life to flagging constitutions, the ads always brought to mind images of Cousin Constance.

"Hello, Vivian," Constance said. One corner of her pale lips lifted as her eyes flicked to Charlie.

"Constance, it's been too long," Vivian said. It hadn't, she thought, but that was what one said when one saw relatives after a prolonged period. "This is Charlie Haverman," she added, putting her hand lightly on Charlie's forearm. "Charlie, this is my cousin Constance Lang Ames."

Charlie held his hand out to Constance, and she shook it. Her smile didn't touch her dark eyes. "Pleased to meet you," she said. "Vivian so rarely brings anyone home to meet the family. You must be something special."

There was a slight pause before Charlie answered, "I'd like to think so."

"Where are Gil and the boys?" Vivian asked.

"Oh, Gil's in Paris for business, and the

boys have already gone off to their summer camp in the Adirondacks." Constance's husband was rarely in the same city as his wife, much less the same room, and she'd been shipping her sons off to somewhere or another since they were five years old.

"Are you staying here for the summer then?" Vivian said.

"Only for the next two weeks. Then I'm off to Europe to meet Gil for the remainder," she said and took a sip of her cocktail. Her eyes focused on something over Vivian's shoulder.

"Viv! Mother told me you were coming, but I didn't believe her."

Vivian turned to find her middle cousin, David, striding toward them. David was a year older than Vivian. He was handsome, tall, and strong with the ruddy features of his mother. The sunlight glinted off his red-gold hair — a shade lighter than Vivian's. Of her three cousins, she'd always been closest to David. He was sharp-witted and lively, always good for a climb into the trees or a canoe race across the narrows. David had been training at helming the meatpacking company since birth. Uncle Bernard would pass the torch soon, and David would inherit everything. Vivian couldn't be sure he actually liked the idea of running a meatpacking company, but he *did* like his father's attention.

David had a young woman with him — a slight and willowy creature with long, golden-brown hair framing her face like a halo. She clung to David's side, looking up at Vivian and Charlie through long, pale lashes. She reminded Vivian of the silent screen star Mary Pickford — all doe eyes and veiled innocence. This girl wasn't beautiful so much as striking. Ethereal, Vivian thought. As though if she were touched, the girl would shatter into a thousand pieces.

"Vivian, this is Lillian Dacre," David said, putting his hand proprietarily on the young woman's arm. He leaned toward Lillian and added in a loud whisper. "And that's Vivian, the cousin I told you about. We got into all sorts of trouble as kids." He turned his attention back to Vivian. "Remember that time we took the rowboat out after Father told us expressly not to?"

"And then we sprung a leak halfway across the lake and had to swim back to shore fully clothed." Vivian winked at David and extended a hand to the young woman. "Pleased to meet you, Lillian." Then she leaned in and whispered, "I don't think you have any idea of what you're in for with this lug."

Lillian smiled at the friendly dig and then lightly grasped Vivian's hand in her own. "Charmed," she said. Her blue eyes darted to Charlie, and she gave the back of her hand to him as if being presented at court, wrist bent, palm down. Charlie stared down at it, bewildered. After a moment's hesitation, he clasped her fingers in his and gave her hand one determined pump. Vivian stifled a laugh. This girl was a real hothouse flower, she thought. David had always fancied the earthier sort, the kind of girl that bronzed in the sun and beat him at tennis. His tastes seemed to have changed drastically.

"How long have you been seeing each other?" Vivian asked David.

David looked sidelong at Lillian and raised one eyebrow. "Oh, it's been ages . . . What, a month?"

"Three weeks," Lillian corrected with a shy smile.

"Best three weeks of my life," he said.

They gazed at each other for a long moment, clearly oblivious to everyone around them.

Vivian cleared her throat. "Three weeks and already meeting your parents, David?"

18

she said. Talk about the lion's den. David was pushing this poor girl in headfirst.

In response, David grabbed Lillian's left hand and held it out to Vivian. A large, round diamond winked at her in the sun from Lillian's ring finger.

Vivian gasped. She glanced from David to Lillian and back again. "Well, I guess congratulations are in order, then. Three weeks is quite the whirlwind courtship."

"What can I say? When you know, you know, right? You got to follow your gut." David gazed at Lillian and smiled.

Vivian glanced at Charlie. They locked eyes for a brief moment before she turned her attention to the happy couple again with a broad smile.

"Congratulations," Charlie said, holding out his hand to David for a shake. "To both of you."

"Where did you meet?" Vivian asked.

"Funny thing, that. I had gone to a party — Garner Hayward, you know him? Well, I went to his party, dreadfully boring, and then I heard this angelic voice speaking to a waiter in French. I turned, and there she was. I couldn't take my eyes off her. I haven't taken my eyes off her since."

"Stop, David. You're embarrassing me." Lillian murmured in the tone of voice that meant *No, go on. I love it.*

He patted her hand on his arm and turned back to Vivian.

"Enough about me and my blissful happiness. How's the radio biz?"

"Wonderful," she said. And it was. Things were going well in her career indeed. *The Darkness Knows* was at the top of the Crossley ratings in its time slot — Thursdays at eight o'clock. She and her costar, Graham Yarborough, had just appeared in a nationwide magazine campaign for the show's sponsor, Sultan's Gold cigarettes. In fact, they'd just completed a photo shoot that might be the cover of the next *Radio Stars* magazine.

"I hear you might be moving on up to the pictures," David said. "You'll be costarring with Clark Gable soon."

Vivian smiled. "We'll see. I'm heading out to Hollywood tomorrow for a number of things, but a screen test with MGM is one of them."

The studio was thinking of making a movie from *The Darkness Knows.* The sponsor, Sultan's Gold cigarettes, was so happy with the show's two leads that they were heavily lobbying MGM to transfer them both to the big-screen version. It was a huge opportunity.

"A screen test. Gosh!" Vivian's youngest cousin, Gwen, stepped forward, eyes wide. She stood gaping at Vivian.

Gwen was eight years younger than Vivian and had been a sort of mascot for her, the kid sister she never had. Gwen had always followed her around like a puppy, and Vivian welcomed the unrestricted love and adoration. It was hard to come by. Despite all of that, Vivian felt a twinge of guilt. She hadn't seen Gwen in at least two years.

Vivian held Gwen's arms out to her sides and gave her an appreciative once-over. She was lovely. Big, brown eyes and chestnut hair, with a hint of early summer bronze to her skin. "Just look at you! Gone and become a young lady on me."

Gwen flushed. *Caught between child and woman,* Vivian thought. She must be what? Seventeen? *Seventeen,* Vivian thought, her stomach flipping involuntarily at long-buried memories. What a pill Vivian had been at that age. She narrowed her eyes at the girl. Was Gwen half as much trouble as she had been? She watched Gwen's dark eyes shift toward Charlie and widen with interest — saw her long, painted eyelashes flutter. *Perhaps she is,* she thought.

"Oh, I'm sorry," Vivian said. "Charlie Haverman, this is the baby of the family,

Gwendolyn."

Gwen held out her hand. "You can call me Gwen, and I'm no baby."

"I can see that," Charlie said. He flashed a devastatingly charming smile at her as he took her hand.

Two spots of color appeared on the apples of Gwen's cheeks. "I was just trying to rustle up a game of croquet," Gwen said. "Any takers?"

"I'll play," David said. "Viv?"

"I'm not sure we should. As *I* recall, the last game of croquet I played with you became so heated that we almost came to blows," Vivian said.

"We never."

"Prone to fisticuffs in his younger days, this one. Someone's never quite gotten the hang of losing," she whispered to Charlie loud enough for David to overhear.

David rolled his eyes toward the blue sky.

"How about you?" Gwen asked Charlie. "Will you join us?"

Charlie looked down at Vivian.

"How about a drink?" he said. Doubtless he'd never been anywhere near a croquet mallet and was not about to start now.

CHAPTER TWO

Vivian's mallet met the ball with a satisfying *thwack,* and she watched as the ball sailed through the wicket. She glanced over at Charlie, and he smiled at her.

"Nice shot," he mouthed.

Charlie must have run into Uncle Bernard at the bar because now he stood among a circle of middle-aged balding men on the periphery of the croquet field. Uncle Bernard was in the middle of some sort of diatribe, and he jabbed his finger in the air perilously close to Charlie's nose as he spoke. To his credit, Charlie didn't flinch. Those lovely blue-green eyes of his remained on Vivian, and she saw the sardonic smile flicker at the corner of his mouth. He looked so dashing in his all-white seersucker suit, she thought. It had been the devil of a time getting him to agree to wear it — he was a man more prone to gray serge. But she'd convinced him that it was just for the afternoon, and she'd promised that no one of his regular acquaintance would lay eyes on him. In fact, Vivian thought he was the most beautiful thing on this lawn, females included. So beautiful that she was considering tossing her croquet mallet aside and laying more than her eyes on him.

Charlie winked at her as if he could read her lecherous thoughts before his eyes shifted back to Bernard. Uncle Bernard was known for his strong opinions — about anything and everything. But he was especially fond of railing on about how he felt Roosevelt was mucking everything up for the upper classes with what Bernard called his "New Deal rigmarole."

Gwen came to stand beside Vivian. She twirled her croquet mallet in her hands. "I'm so very proud of you, Vivian," she said. "A radio star."

"Thank you. I meant what I said before. You've grown into a lovely young woman, Gwen."

Gwen smiled her thanks.

"I'm sorry I haven't been in touch," Vivian said. She did feel terrible about leaving Gwen in the lurch like that. Vivian remembered very well what it had been like to be Gwen's age. She'd had so many questions, and no one she trusted to give her advice without judgment. Vivian's mother would never have understood, just as Vivian was sure Gwen's mother wouldn't. They were products of another time.

Gwen shrugged. "You've been busy," she said. There wasn't any resentment evident in her voice. "How long have you been seeing Mr. Haverman?" Vivian saw Gwen's eyes shoot toward Charlie and light with appreciation.

"About six months, I suppose."

"Is it serious?"

Vivian smiled. "Why else would I subject him to all of this?"

Gwen smiled in return. Then she stopped spinning her mallet and leaned toward Vivian. "I have a surprise for you," she said. "I'm not sure it's appropriate anymore but —"

"Your shot, Gwen!" David called.

Gwen glanced at her older brother and then back at Vivian. Gwen had always been dramatic. No telling what her surprise might be, but odds were it wasn't terribly important to know right now.

"Go ahead," Vivian said. "We'll catch up later."

She looked over at Charlie again. All and all, he was doing quite well, so far. And her relatives were behaving. Not as she'd feared they would, like Vivian had brought them one of the hoi polloi for their amusement.

Vivian hadn't seen any of her mother's family since the truth had come out about her father. Julia Witchell had known something of what her husband had been up to, as Vivian had suspected. Oh, not the details, not that he'd plotted to have men killed, but she'd known he'd trucked with unsavory characters. She'd known all along. Julia had also known that the copious amounts of money he had made from his association with those unsavory characters had, in large part, bought her that grand house on the Gold Coast. But Julia had played the dutiful society wife and she hadn't asked any questions — mostly, Vivian suspected, because her mother hadn't wanted to know the answers. Vivian looked around at the members of her mother's extended family. Certainly, they'd all known what Arthur Witchell had been. And they'd all kept quiet.

David won the match and raised his fist in the air in triumph. Vivian conceded his victory and laid her mallet against one of the wickets. She approached Charlie and the small cluster of older men.

"War within the year," her uncle said, nodding his head vigorously. "There's no stopping Hitler. He's said he wants Poland, and he'll take it."

Vivian saw Charlie grimace, but he didn't disagree. There was no point. What her uncle had said was true. War loomed on the horizon. The question wasn't if America would get involved, but when.

Vivian tried not to think of such things, but her mother's involvement with Oskar Heigel had impressed the plight of European Jews onto her mind. She noticed the tiny articles on the sixth and seventh pages of the newspaper, hidden among the lesser news. Germany was taking away the Jews' dignity, their rights as human beings. Just recently, a boatload of Jewish refugees had been turned away from Cuba. There was very little sympathy anywhere in the world for them. Oskar was trying to garner some. He was in Washington right now lobbying congressmen, senators, and anyone who would listen on the Jewish situation.

"I just hope we stay out of it," Bernard continued. "We can't afford another war. Though we did make a killing during the last one with those government meat contracts."

Vivian winced at her uncle's inelegant phrasing. *Made a killing.* She glanced around at the dour middle-aged faces that ringed the circle around Bernard. All of them were too old to have served in the Great War and too young to have sons who had either. That was the particular luck of their generation. Likely, they had very little personal connection to the war itself, beyond having made a fortune off other people's suffering.

"I say we just stay out of it, but if Roosevelt has his way, we'll find ourselves in the thick of that mess," one man said.

"Well, you know, those Jew bankers have him in their pockets," another said.

Vivian's eyes darted up to meet Charlie's as she felt the heat rise to her face. Surely, her uncle knew about the new man in her mother's life — the very *Jewish* man. She turned and looked pointedly at Bernard.

"You know, Father Coughlin just made that very point the other evening on his radio program," Bernard said.

Vivian snorted through her nose. *Father Coughlin, that bigoted, loud-mouthed fool.* Although he was a Catholic priest, Father Coughlin's audience consisted mainly of well-to-do Protestants with very narrow beliefs about who should be considered true Americans. The men turned to look at her, and for a moment, she was terrified that she'd actually spoken aloud. But their expressions were merely curious, not outraged.

"Ah, something in my throat," she said. "I think I'll find the punch bowl."

Charlie made a move to come with her, but he was stopped by Bernard's large hand on his forearm. "Now don't run off so quickly, young man. I'd like to hear about this private eye business."

Vivian shot Charlie an apologetic look. He shrugged, resigned, and quickly brought his hand to his temple, cocked in the shape of a gun. *Save yourself,* he mouthed.

So she did.

Vivian whirled on her heel and headed in the opposite direction. Her uncle was a blowhard of the first variety. She'd like to believe he meant well, but she couldn't think of one instance where he had done something from the goodness of his heart. He was all about money and power and image. Besides, she couldn't abide war talk. This was a garden party. You shouldn't talk about invading countries and killing people at a garden party, no matter how pressing the idea.

She decided to clear her head with a walk in the forest. Adaline and Bernard owned three acres of wooded land behind Oakhaven in addition to the lake frontage.

Most of it was wild and overgrown, but there was a nice path through the first half acre. Or at least there used to be. Vivian had walked it all the time as a girl, pretending she was an explorer in the virgin forest. She'd imagined the Potawatomi Indians living here long ago off the land, gazing at the calm blue waters of the lake.

Vivian headed in, the thick mat of damp leaves squishing underfoot. The sounds of the party hushed as she entered the forest proper, drowned out by the tuneless drone of the cicadas. That drone became a whirring screech here among the trees. A clamoring mass of the crawling creatures clumped on the tree nearest to her, single-minded in their effort to mate and die. They molted when they emerged from the earth, and empty brown shells littered the ground and stuck to the tree trunks all around her. She pulled an empty shell from a tree trunk and drew it close to her nose for inspection. It was a perfect replica of the creature itself — even its feelers were molded in the brown shellac-like shell.

The air itself was stagnant and thick. It had been a wet spring, and she could smell the fungus and the squishy things growing just under the fallen oaks.

Suddenly there was movement, a rustling

of leaves as someone stepped from the clump of wild raspberry bushes to the left of the path in front of her. A very large someone.

The man stood in the middle of the path, blocking her way forward. His face was in shadow. Vivian could still hear the sounds of the party behind her underneath the cicadas; life and safety were just beyond the trees. That gave her small comfort. Still, she was uneasy at the looming bulk of this man and his sudden appearance. It was almost as if he'd been waiting for her to come along. She clenched her hands at her sides, preparing to put up a fight if necessary.

"Hello, Viv," the man said. "It's been a long time."

The bass voice was familiar. Something about the sound of it started a reflexive tingle at the base of her spine, but still, she couldn't quite place it. He moved a few paces closer, and as he did, the shaded face came into view.

Vivian's breath caught in her throat.

"Hap," she said. That one raspy syllable was all the sound she managed to produce. Seeing him again after so many years was like a punch straight to the solar plexus.

She hadn't seen Hap Prescott, hadn't spoken one word to him, since the night

31

eight years ago when everything had ended so abruptly between them. He'd disappeared, and her mother had yanked her back to the Gold Coast for her senior year of high school. That summer here had been a passionate, tumultuous whirlwind. At least for her.

It had become clear in the intervening years that Hap had not felt the same. He'd never been in contact, never apologized for the way he'd left her. He'd never explained why he'd disappeared without a word. Vivian had come to understand in the years since that she'd only been a convenient diversion for him, and she'd come to the conclusion that they had never really had anything in common other than boredom and proximity. But they'd certainly had that in spades that summer here at Oakhaven, hadn't they?

She reminded herself of all of that now, lest she find herself enthralled by his charms once again. Even though she'd only been in his presence for a few seconds, she could feel her skin prickling with the memory of those stolen moments so many years ago. He'd made her feel so alive, so grown up. She'd attached such hopes to him. She'd been so hopelessly naive.

What was he doing here?

Vivian scrutinized his face, hoping to find it irrevocably altered by the passage of time. But Hap Prescott was as handsome as ever. He was older, of course. Little wrinkles played about the corners of his eyes, as if he'd smiled too much or spent too much time in the sun. Though he must be just shy of forty by now, there was no gray in his shining mink-colored hair. His eyes were still the same crisp, disarming green of fresh grass. He smiled at her now with warmth and presumption — as if he'd seen her just yesterday. As if he hadn't ripped her heart from her chest all those years ago and stolen away with it.

"You look marvelous," he said as his eyes traveled down the length of her frame and back up again.

She dipped the wide brim of her hat to cover the traitorous blush that rushed to her cheeks. Despite what her head told her about how ill-suited they were, her body remembered exactly what this man had been to her once upon a time. "H-how long have you been back?"

"Three months," he said.

She looked down at her clenched fists. She'd crushed the cicada shell in her surprise, and she spread her fingers and let the pieces fall to the ground. Then she lifted her chin so that she could meet his eyes. She would not look away. She would not let him know that he'd ever meant anything to her.

She opened her mouth to ask where he'd been, but there was the chance that it would come out all wrong — like she'd been waiting on tenterhooks for his return. But she didn't need to ask. She'd known where he'd gone when he disappeared, if not why. All she'd had to do was drop a casual reference into conversation with Adaline and Bernard now and then to get information. Hap had gone off to Europe when he'd disappeared so suddenly. He'd lived the life of the idle rich on the French Riviera for a time and then gone on to the Swiss Alps for a while longer. Then there were those ridiculous rumors, the ones Gwen had whispered, her childish face aglow with awe. Those rumors that painted Hap as some sort of revolutionary hero.

"I heard you were off fighting Franco," Vivian said. The Spanish Civil War had ended just a few months before. Hitler and Mussolini's ally, the fascist Franco, had finally crushed the Republicans after nearly three years of brutal warfare. The war had been something of a cause célèbre with certain Americans, those who sympathized with the socialists, communists, and anarchists of the motley Spanish Republic. Thousands of them had traveled to Spain to fight for a cause that was not theirs either to foster high ideals of equality and brotherhood or to borrow a little excitement. *The latter is right up Hap's alley,* Vivian thought. *He'd do anything for a little excitement.*

Hap frowned slightly, and a cloud passed over his expression before he looked back to meet her eyes again. "I was in Spain for a time flying supplies," he said. Then he shrugged as if to imply aiding military rebels was an ordinary endeavor — just something he did to pass the time. Maybe it was for someone like Hap.

"That's . . ." Vivian struggled for the right word. *Foolhardy? Reckless? Incredibly stupid?* "Brave of you."

Hap glanced at her sidelong, a smile slipping back onto his face. After all, she'd always been impressed with his feats of derring-do in the past. There was a hopeful lift to his eyebrows now, a light in his eyes. She could almost see the thoughts marshaling in his head. They could go back to the way it had been between them that summer eight years ago — as if nothing had happened. He wanted that. He wanted *her.* Renewing what they'd had would be like slipping into a warm bath. Except that Vivian wasn't that girl anymore. She'd matured, moved on. And despite that echo of long-dormant passion, she could never forget how he'd treated her at the end.

And besides, there was Charlie now. Charlie was good. Charlie was honorable. Charlie was who she wanted.

Hap moved closer to her, so close she could feel the heat of his skin against hers. "And while I've been gone, you've been making something of yourself, eh? Next stop Hollywood?" he said.

She only nodded. Her throat felt like it was coated in dust. He whistled with admiration. "I always knew you'd do something big, Viv. You always had that extra something special." He ran his fingertips lightly up her forearm, raising gooseflesh in their wake. Then he leaned down toward her, his lips brushing her temple as he spoke. "You know, I still think about you. About us. How good we were together."

Vivian stepped backward and pulled her arm from his grasp.

"I'm with someone," she said.

His rakish smile remained, though his eyebrows drew together in incredulity.

"That dime-novel detective?" His head cocked to the side as he studied her. So Hap had been keeping tabs on her as well, she thought. He hooked two fingers under her chin and lifted it.

Vivian forced herself to meet his gaze, if only to prove that she could do it and not falter. She saw lust in Hap's green eyes. Lust and calculation and a certain knowing calm behind it all.

He thought he could snap his fingers, and she would melt into a puddle at his feet. The Hap of her memories had been suave, dazzlingly charming, and full of amusement, but there was a hardness to him now. The smile on his lips did not reach his eyes. This Hap was only wearing those qualities like a mask. Perhaps it was what he had seen in Europe, in Spain with the rebels, she thought. Perhaps it was that he realized he was very near forty with nothing to show for his life thus far. His once-effortless charm had twisted and become a sharp thing. Or perhaps she'd imagined all of it to begin with.

"I know we parted . . . on bad terms, and I regret that. I'd like a chance to try to explain. I think you'd like that too." His voice was low. He leaned down toward her then, lips parted, and Vivian sidestepped him with a jerk of her head.

"I have to go," she said. She turned and

started toward the house without waiting for his reply, the leaves squishing under her heel, the whir of the cicadas in her ears.

Hap didn't follow. He didn't call after her. Knowing, of course, like she did that he'd have another chance to win her over. No doubt he thought he would. He thought Vivian was still that confused, angry, rebellious girl who had been putty in his hands that summer. He thought he would always get what he wanted.

Well, he's wrong, she thought. *He's wrong.*

CHAPTER THREE

Vivian's skin prickled as if she'd been standing too close to a bonfire. Hap had always done that to her. That prickly feeling used to make her smile, used to make her breath come fast with anticipation. She should feel nothing, she reminded herself. He'd disappeared and hadn't contacted her for eight years. Then again, maybe he truly did want to explain what had gone so horribly wrong that summer. And, God help her, she wanted to hear it. She needed to hear that explanation.

Vivian sat alone in the quiet garden on the side of the house far from the party. She let the sun warm her skin until she calmed herself, until she stopped wondering how Hap had come to be here. Then she climbed the porch steps at the side of the house and made her way slowly around the wraparound porch. Charlie was leaning against the railing at the front, facing away from her. *Such a strapping man,* she thought. And all hers. How did she ever get so lucky?

She'd been surprised by Hap, that's all. He'd startled her, and all those unresolved feelings from her past had bobbed to the surface. Vivian knew now that any lingering feelings she had for Hap were nothing compared to what she felt for this man in front of her. She stepped to Charlie's side and leaned against the railing next to him.

"Hello there, handsome," she said, nudging him with her elbow. "Come here often?"

Charlie didn't smile at the joke.

Vivian cleared her throat. She opened her mouth to suggest an early departure when Charlie interrupted. He pointed toward the far side of the lawn, eyes narrowed.

"Who's that man to you?"

Vivian followed Charlie's glare, and her smile faded. "Oh, that's just Hap," she said, careful to keep her voice light. Her stomach clenched reflexively at the very recent memory of his fingers on her arm, his breath on her temple. The thought ran round and round in her mind like a dog chasing its tail: *It's not over. No matter what you think. It's not over.*

"And what is 'Just Hap' to you?"

Vivian turned to study Charlie's expression. It was as hard as his tone was icy. He

40

was angry. With her. About Hap Prescott. *How on earth had Charlie heard about Hap Prescott?*

"He's an old friend, I suppose," she said, trying to sound breezy. Her fingers closed around the porch railing. She looked out over the lawn as she spoke. "No direct relation of mine, you see. Or anyone's, really . . . Uncle Bernard's ward, I suppose you'd call him. I haven't seen him in years."

She glanced sidelong at Charlie. All of that was a carefully curated version of the truth. Charlie narrowed his eyes as he continued to stare out onto the lawn and spoke without looking at her.

"Let me rephrase the question, then. What *was* he to you?"

Vivian felt the heat rise to her cheeks. Her eyes inadvertently darted toward where Hap was standing talking to Gwen. As she watched, Hap leaned down and whispered something into the girl's ear. Even from this distance, Vivian could see Gwen's coquettish blush. *Hap, the cad,* she thought bitterly. *Up to his old tricks.* Maybe that's what this was all about. Charlie had heard a rumor of their long-ago relationship, and his jealousy had carried him away.

"Charlie, that was a long time ago. Long before I met you." She chose her words

41

carefully. She smiled, looking up at him through lowered lashes. But she could see that her flirtatious charm would have no effect this time. He was well and truly steamed. She sighed and lowered her voice, leaning in toward him. "I mean, you didn't think that before you I'd never . . . Well, that you were my fir—"

Charlie held his hand up and silenced her with a grimace. "Of course I didn't, Viv. But someone like him?" He glanced back toward Hap and Gwen.

Vivian was glad to see that Constance had now joined their discussion, wedging her thin frame between the two of them. "I was young and stupid then," she said. She was thinking more so every minute.

"And 'then' was . . . ?"

"The summer after my father died."

Charlie's blue-green eyes tracked Hap as he moved through the crowd now, the furrow between his brows deepening.

"God, Viv, he had to have been in his thirties even then."

The words *Don't be silly* almost tripped off her tongue, but she stopped them. She didn't want Charlie to think she was defending Hap Prescott with her careless, flippant remarks. And she wasn't, was she? Of course not. She narrowed her eyes at Hap across the lawn. He *had* been at least thirty years old then. Jesus, she thought. He hadn't seemed that old at the time. He'd just seemed worldly, mature, a man who knew his mind. A man who'd wanted her as much as she'd wanted him.

Vivian exhaled through her nose. She could feel her own ire growing. "I know exactly what you're thinking. I wasn't a kid, and he didn't prey on me, Charlie."

He turned to her, eyebrows raised. "Then what he said was true?"

Vivian's stomach clenched. She felt her hands grow cold. So that's how he'd found out, she thought, from Hap himself. When had that happened? She hadn't even known the man was here herself until ten minutes ago.

"That depends on what he said," she responded carefully.

Charlie's jaw was set. "He congratulated me on catching such a prize. And then asked me if you were still a spicy little minx."

Vivian blinked. *A spicy little minx?*

"And he made it known that he had shared — what did he call them? — 'a couple of good tussles' with you himself."

Vivian felt like she'd been sucker punched. All of the air rushed out of her lungs.

Her mind worked furiously on how to repair this situation. The language Hap had used was disrespectful, but she couldn't deny the crude truth in them. If she'd acted out before her father died, then she'd really kicked it into high gear after he was gone — especially that summer here at Oakhaven when she was seventeen. Though it was immensely insulting to characterize her affair with Hap as a couple of "good tussles."

But something told her that admitting this wouldn't exactly make the conversation with Charlie any easier — or allay any of his jealousy. No doubt Hap wanted Charlie to know that he'd beaten him to the punch and was a presumptive rival for Vivian's affections now that he was back. And he likely hadn't expected Charlie to share their conversation with Vivian herself. The presumption in all of it made her suddenly, intensely angry. How dare he?

"I should've clocked the son of a bitch," Charlie said.

"No!"

Charlie's expression darkened.

"I mean, not that he didn't deserve to have his nose broken," Vivian said. "But you were right not to cause a scene. You'd have been sent packing . . . right back to Chicago."

44

"Maybe not such a bad idea." Charlie looked off into the distance.

Vivian stayed quiet. She knew enough about Charlie and his temper to know that saying anything in an attempt to smooth things over would only serve to stir him up.

"Look, Viv." He paused, exhaled, and then turned to face her. "I don't care what you may or may not have done in the past . . . or who you may have done it with. But I don't especially enjoy having it thrown in my face at a goddamn garden party."

Vivian knew that the unspoken undercurrent of his statement was that he regretted even being at that goddamn garden party in the first place. Which, of course, was her fault. She'd dragged him here, if not kicking and screaming, then certainly under duress. He'd come solely to make her happy, and now she felt miserable about making him feel so miserable.

"I know. I'm sorry." She put her hand on his forearm and was relieved when he didn't immediately shake it off. "I didn't know Hap would be here, and I certainly didn't know he'd . . . stir up the past. He's a fool."

"Well, if that fool says one more thing about you, or so much as glances in your direction, I'll shut him up for good." A surprised laugh escaped Vivian's mouth, but

Charlie's eyes were cold. "I won't have you spoken about in that way."

His voice was low and menacing. If she wasn't careful, if she didn't deflect this anger and keep the two men on opposite sides of the lawn at all times, then this garden party would turn out to be a god-awful mess after all.

She scanned the crowd, noting that Hap was standing with David and Lillian. Then she grabbed Charlie's arm and tugged him in the opposite direction. When Charlie's temper was up, it was best to distract him from the issue at hand. She turned on her heel, stopping just in time to keep herself from knocking over a spindly woman in a loud, flower-print dress, holding a large and sweaty Gin Ricky. Vivian stopped short, Charlie bumping into her back like a falling domino.

"Oh, hello, Aunt Wilhelmina," she said, pasting a smile to her face. "Lovely to see you."

The woman's mouth gaped slightly as she glanced from Vivian to Charlie over Vivian's shoulder. She narrowed her watery eyes at him and shook her head. How long had she been standing there? Had she heard any of their conversation? *No, of course not,* Vivian thought. Aunt Wilhelmina was ninety-three and deaf as a post. That scowl was just her permanent expression.

Constance appeared and took the older woman's arm. "There you are," she said to Wilhelmina. She glanced at Vivian and Charlie with one dark eyebrow raised.

Vivian sidestepped her great-aunt and Constance without a word, pulling Charlie along with her. Bar the breach of etiquette, she thought.

They needed some time alone. She needed to explain all of this to Charlie. She needed, in a way, to explain it to herself. She pulled him gently past the swarm of partygoers to the back of the estate where the towering oaks and poplars turned the yard into a cool glade. She ducked into the oriental pagoda under the shade of a giant, overhanging burr oak. It was an elaborately carved wooden structure with a steep, peaked roof. Charlie's eyes flitted over the intricate carvings along the roof's edge: dragons and birds and large flowers with sweeping, pointed petals. It was exotic and not in keeping with the Victoriana gingerbread of the main house. It was dark inside and blessedly cool.

"This was originally the Siam pagoda from the Manufactures and Liberal Arts Building at the '93 Columbian Exposition,"

Vivian said, answering a question he hadn't asked.

Charlie's dark-blond eyebrows still met over the bridge of his nose in a scowl. Vivian wasn't sure he'd heard her, but she kept on anyway. Anything to take his mind off Hap and what he'd said. Anything to smooth that wrinkled forehead out again.

"My grandfather bought it after the fair and carted it wholesale up here. That was en vogue at the time — to pillage exotic objets d'art from the exposition. The Ceylon teahouse was disassembled and put back together just down the shore from here." She motioned vaguely to the vast wooden building on the bluffs to the east. She was blathering, but she couldn't stop herself. "It's now the Maytags' summer home. Quite nice. I was there once about five years ago. They have special things built into the walls to keep snakes from slithering up them. Handy in Ceylon, I suppose, but hopefully not so useful here in Wisconsin . . ."

Charlie had turned away from her, and her heart climbed into her throat.

"Charlie, for God's sake, tell me what you're thinking." She wasn't sure she wanted to know, but she was unable to bear the tension any longer.

48

Charlie exhaled and ran a palm down the pole nearest him. He glanced at her and then away. "What I'm thinking is that when you bring me to things like this, I'm reminded of how very different we are." He craned his neck to gaze up at the elaborate, soaring pointed roof of the pagoda. "Summer cottages on the lake. Siamese pagodas in the backyard . . ." he said with a rueful shake of his head. He looked away from her, his voice low as he said the rest. "And I'm afraid that you'll come to your senses one day and give me the heave-ho."

Vivian almost laughed. She couldn't help it. But then she realized how serious Charlie was, and her stomach dipped. Did he really think she'd leave him for some stuffed-shirt bank president if she only got the chance? Good lord, did he think she actually wanted someone like Hap, after the way he'd treated her? She moved forward and put both palms on Charlie's chest and stared deeply and unblinkingly into his beautiful aqua eyes.

"*You're* on my level, Charlie Haverman."

He looked down at her, his expression solemn. "I don't have any money, Viv."

She sighed and bit her lip so she wouldn't smile at his sincerity. She knew he would take her amusement precisely the wrong

49

way. Of course she knew he didn't have any money, and she didn't care. Why would he ever think she would?

"Money makes absolutely no difference to me," she said.

And that was true, but perhaps not exactly in the way Charlie thought she meant it. Money, to a large degree, didn't matter to her because she was currently in possession of more money than she could ever use in her lifetime. She'd inherited her father's secreted, mostly ill-gotten fortune on her twenty-fifth birthday this past January. She had more than enough money for the both of them.

Not that she'd told Charlie about it. It had been five months since she'd acquired a small fortune, and she hadn't been able to break the news yet. Every time she tried, something like this would come up. Something to remind both of them just how different they were, and she knew the money would only cause a rift between them.

Charlie wasn't the type to be overjoyed at the prospect of becoming one of the idle rich, a playboy type who could sit back while his woman held the purse strings. That was an impossibility in the dynamics of their relationship, and Vivian knew that. She just had to work out a way to let him know about her inheritance without hurting his ample pride and ruining everything between them in the process.

"I don't have any social standing," Charlie said, his tone taken on a teasing lilt.

Her hands snaked up his chest to latch together at the base of his neck, where her thumb rubbed lightly up and down among the closely shorn hair at the nape. "Ask me if I give one whit for social standing."

"Any standing then? Because I've never had any standing as far as I can tell." He smiled then, and she sighed with relief and kissed the tiny dimple that formed at the corner of his mouth. Then she lowered her head and nuzzled into his chest. She inhaled the spicy citrus of his aftershave and waited a moment for the turn in Charlie's mood to really take hold.

"How about we just let bygones be bygones?" she said softly, glancing up at him.

"As long as Hap Prescott is a bygone."

"Of course he is. He's been a bygone for years. You, however" — she trailed a fingertip down the side of his cheek — "are right here in my arms." She stood on her tiptoes and planted a long, slow kiss on his mouth.

After a long moment, Charlie pulled away. "Viv," he said, his voice husky.

She settled her chin on his chest and

looked up at him. "Yes?"

"Marry me."

Vivian sighed, holding his gaze for a moment longer before lowering her forehead to his chest and closing her eyes. She felt the *thump thump thump* of his heart — rabbit-quick under his shirtfront. *Why'd he have to go and do that? Why'd he have to ruin such a perfectly perfect moment?*

"Oh, Charlie," she said finally.

He pulled away from her.

"Don't 'Oh, Charlie' me," he said. He turned his back to her to lean on the rail of the pagoda. "I'm going to keep asking until you accept."

He would. She knew he would. He'd asked her three times now, and it was growing increasingly more difficult to turn him down gracefully. She loved Charlie and she didn't want to lose him, but she didn't want to be anyone's wife. Not now, and maybe not ever.

The proposals had started out as a joke, as things did with Charlie. "Behave, or I'll make an honest woman of you," he'd said in that growly voice that made her stomach turn inside out. The first time, Vivian had brushed it off with a giggle and by distracting him with a rustle under the bedclothes. But it was hard to ignore it when he'd repeated it the next morning. Then he'd started asking her seriously.

Maybe she should just accept. After all, an engagement was not a marriage. An engagement could last interminably, and maybe in time she would change her mind about marriage. If anyone could change her mind, it would be Charlie. He was practically living at her coach house anyway. What would change?

In fact, since that "Hollywood's Unmarried Husbands and Wives" article had come out in *Photoplay* discussing star couples like Clark Gable and Carole Lombard acting as marrieds without the benefit of vows, the station's brass had been pushing her not so subtly toward the altar herself. They'd had their sights set on her costar Graham for her, of course, but a series of diplomatic negotiations had convinced the powers that be that she and Graham were not destined to be more than friends and costars. Thank heavens that Graham felt as strongly about it as she did. Still, she knew she couldn't avoid marriage forever. After all, it wasn't good publicity for one of the station's stars to be shacking up with anyone. The public wouldn't approve if the truth about her and Charlie came out, and she knew it.

It was just such terrible timing. She was

off to Hollywood tomorrow evening. This trip to Hollywood was big. She knew Charlie didn't begrudge her her dreams, but she also knew — though he'd never admit it — that he was terrified that she wouldn't come back. He was probably imagining that she would take the Super Chief to Los Angeles, ace the screen test, and be contracted to MGM on the spot. Then her movie career would take off, and she would forget all about Chicago. Forget all about him. Of course, she knew that would never happen, but no matter how she tried to allay his unspoken fears, his hackles still rose when the subject was approached. And when his hackles rose, he tried to pull her closer and did something silly like propose.

"Charlie . . ." She stepped forward and placed one palm lightly on his back. She felt him tense under her fingers. "You know I love you."

"Do I?" He turned to face her.

Vivian exhaled slowly. She hated hurting him.

"I don't carry this around for nothing, you know," he said. He uncurled his fingers, and in his palm lay the loveliest little sapphire ring. It glinted even in the dim light inside the pagoda.

The breath caught in her throat. "Oh,

Charlie," she said, feeling her insides melt. *Yes,* she wanted to say. *Yes, of course I'll marry you.* She opened her mouth, but her lips seemed incapable of making that one syllable. She swallowed. "You probably shouldn't carry that around with you. What if there's a hole in your shirt pocket and it slips through?"

She'd been joking, of course, to lighten the mood. But the attempt had obviously gone sideways. The vertical line appeared between his brows. He closed his fingers around the ring again and whirled away from her. He charged down the steps and away from her before she could open her mouth to explain. *Yes!* she wanted to call after him. But her throat had constricted. She watched mutely as he strode away, knocking past a gardener in his path. The man dropped his tools to the ground with a clatter.

Vivian stood in the empty pagoda for a few minutes, tapping her fingernails against the railing, and then when that failed to lighten her mood, she went back out to find Charlie. The musicians had set up on the lawn, and a few couples twirled about the makeshift dance floor. She kept her eyes trained for Hap, her stomach tied in knots at the idea of another confrontation.

She climbed the wide steps to the front porch. A few couples lingered there, speaking in hushed tones, holding drinks in relaxed grips over the railings, hovering precariously over the blooming pink rhododendrons below. Where had Charlie gotten to?

It wasn't fair of her to string Charlie along like this. He was old-fashioned, and she knew that going in. If he wanted to get married, then she probably should. Because Vivian was starting to very much fear that it was marry Charlie or lose him. Charlie was an all-or-nothing kind of guy, and she'd much rather have the all than the nothing.

She entered the front hall and glanced perfunctorily through each room as she hurried down the main hall. No one in the parlor or the sitting room. But then she came upon a closed door. The game room. Closed. Echoes of a closed lounge door at WCHI sprang to her mind. What had lain behind that had been a dead woman. Vivian's stomach knotted. She could still see the dead woman's pale face — the eyes open and unseeing, the trickle of blood from her mouth. Vivian hadn't thought of finding Marjorie Fox in months. Why would she think of it now? The quiet, possibly, and the same sense of malignant possibility that hung in the air. Vivian shook the memory away and slid the pocket door open without knocking. It opened noiselessly on well-oiled tracks.

The room was cast in bright sunshine. The curtains of the tall windows on the west side of the house were thrown open. Vivian blinked as her eyes adjusted and she saw the shapes of two men outlined against the blinding light. They were standing between the desk and the billiard table. One of them was Hap, facing her, and the other man stood before him, half turned away. They were struggling. No, not struggling exactly. The man turned away looked to be holding Hap upright. What exactly was she seeing?

Then the other man turned toward her. It was Charlie.

When he spotted Vivian, his eyes went wide. He held both hands up as if he was surrendering, and something shiny flashed from the fingers of his left hand.

Hap and Charlie in here together? Oh no. They could only be fighting. Grappling like two common street thugs in the game room of her aunt and uncle's summer home. She took a step forward, intending to stop whatever nonsense these two had started over her.

57

Then Hap made a strange, strangled sound. Vivian's body went numb as Hap's eyes met hers and he sank slowly to the rug, the front of his white linen shirt stained bright red. Vivian was frozen in place, a faint buzzing in her ears. Her eyes locked with Charlie's.

Charlie looked out of breath and slightly bewildered. Now she noticed the red on his upraised hands, and a bright smear of it across his white suit jacket. The shiny object fell from his fingers and clattered to the floor. She stared at the glinting metal on the rug, unable for a moment to make out what it might be. Scissors, she finally realized, and the blades were wet as well. With blood. Hap's blood.

Oh God.

Oh, Charlie, what have you done?

It was only after she felt the grip of strong fingers on her forearm that she realized she'd spoken aloud. She turned to find Constance beside her, her slender face pale as death.

"He's killed Hap," Constance whispered. "That's what he's done."

Charlie dropped to his knees beside Hap's motionless form, pushing Hap onto his back. He stared at the stain covering Hap's abdomen for a moment, his hands hovering

58

just over the pool of bright red. His blue-green eyes were wild, his breathing harsh and erratic in the hushed silence of the room. He reached up and put two fingers against Hap's carotid artery.

"Someone get a doctor," Charlie said without looking up.

Vivian lurched toward the telephone on the desk, her fingers just about to close over the receiver when Constance fainted, her deadweight dragging Vivian to the floor with her.

CHAPTER FOUR

A small crowd stood on the lawn in silence and watched the ambulance pull away from the house by the unpaved service road. There weren't any clamoring bells. There was no urgency. Vivian had finally wrenched herself from Constance's prostrate form and made it to the telephone to reach the hospital, but Hap had died just after they'd loaded him into the ambulance.

Birds trilled in the trees under the constant whir of the cicadas. Vivian heard a child shout in glee from one of the docks down on the shore, followed by a muted splash. The band had packed up, and everyone except the immediate family had gone home. Charlie was gone as well. Vivian had only told the hospital that there had been an accident when she'd phoned, but the police car had pulled in directly behind the ambulance when it had arrived. They'd made a few inquiries and carted Charlie back to the station for questioning before she could so much as catch his eye, much less speak to him. Vivian had tried to go along, but they'd pushed her away.

She had reached the police, and then Uncle Bernard had burst into the room just as she was putting the telephone receiver back into its cradle. Constance had woken from her faint, and Bernard had shooed all of them, including Charlie, from the room with a terse "You shouldn't see this." Then he'd slid the thick, walnut pocket door closed. Bernard's eyes had been feverish behind his spectacles, darting back and forth between Vivian and Constance. His usually pale cheeks had been flushed with color.

Vivian put her palms against her abdomen and pressed, trying to force down that terrible roiling ball of frustration and helplessness. She had to do something to fix this catastrophe. But what could she possibly do? Hap was dead, and it seemed Charlie had killed him. That's what she'd seen with her own eyes, wasn't it?

Uncle Bernard had climbed into the silent ambulance and gone with Hap's body to the hospital. Or perhaps the morgue? Vivian had no idea where. They'd just gone. Her uncle had been gray, solemn, and unable to speak or meet anyone's eye. Oh God. It was terrible thinking of these things. She sat down heavily on the retaining wall. The rough, uneven stones poked her through her thin dress, and she shifted. But maybe being uncomfortable was precisely what she needed right now. She needed to sharpen her wits. She needed to somehow make sense of this insensible thing.

Hap was a like a son to Uncle Bernard, she thought. She suddenly understood that look of feverish intensity. His surrogate son's life had been pouring onto the thick rug of the game room, and there was nothing he could have done to stop it.

Vivian surveyed the scene around her. Servants were busy wiping away every trace of the party that had been in full swing only an hour before. The family stood in small clusters around the lawn. Lillian was weeping softly into David's shoulder, and Bernard was off with Hap's body. Adaline stood next to Constance as she spoke with the police, near but not touching. Vivian's eyes swept over the scene again. No Gwen, she thought. Where could the girl be? She turned and looked back at the house, but nothing stirred. Vivian felt the adrenaline seep from her body. Her hands were shaking now, and her stomach was queasy.

Charlie had shot one dark, indecipherable look at her as the police led him away — willingly, not in handcuffs at least. Vivian had then placed two phone calls from the telephone in the front hall — one to Cal Haverman, Charlie's detective father, and one to Freddy Endicott, her father's old law partner and family friend. Vivian had no idea how she and Charlie had gotten into this mess, but Charlie would need all the help she could find to get him out.

Vivian watched Constance speak with the police. Constance's eyes were red and puffed from crying, but her tears were gone now. Vivian couldn't hear what she was saying, but her cousin was nodding her head vehemently. Constance had seen Charlie leaning over Hap's prostrate form with blood on his hands, if nothing else. And that was more than enough.

Charlie had been angry. They'd argued over her refusal to marry him, and he'd stormed off. But had he been angry enough to stab Hap with scissors? Vivian tried to imagine a scenario in which that might have been the result. Charlie had left her and run into Hap in the library. Hap had run his mouth — about her. He'd said something truly horrible and crude, something very close to the truth. Charlie's temper was already set to the boiling point, and something Hap said had sent him over the edge.

Vivian shook her head. No. That couldn't have happened. No matter what Hap might have said, Charlie would never have killed him — murdered him in broad daylight in Vivian's family's home. Shoving a scissors into the man's stomach. That was heartless. She shivered. That took cold, murderous rage, and the Charlie she knew just didn't have that in him. Still, all she could think was that she could have stopped all of this if she'd just agreed to marry Charlie when he'd asked.

Someone pressed a glass into her hands. Vivian looked down at the amber liquid inside, likely whiskey. She took a swig without so much as sniffing at it first.

"Vivian, you don't look well." Vivian felt a small, cool hand settle over hers. She looked up and met Gwen's worried eyes.

"I don't feel particularly well."

"I'm so sorry." Gwen swallowed, her dark eyes flitting around and settling anywhere but on Vivian's face.

"Me too."

Gwen sat down beside her. She cleared her throat. "No, I mean . . . I did this. I set this all in motion. I . . . The surprise I

64

mentioned earlier that I had for you. It was Hap."

Vivian's head jerked up, and she narrowed her eyes at her cousin, unable to speak. Hap had been Gwen's big surprise for her? Why?

Gwen's wide eyes searched Vivian's for a moment before she continued in a near whisper. "I ran into him at David's a few weeks ago and told him to come today. I told him you'd want to see him."

An icy ball formed in the pit of Vivian's stomach. "Why would you tell him that?"

Gwen bit her lower lip and looked off at the lake. "It's just that when you told me about him, about you and him, it sounded so romantic. Like you were star-crossed lovers separated by time and forces outside your control. Well, when he came back to the States a few months ago, I started plotting to bring you two together again."

"Oh, Gwen." She was so young and such a hopeless romantic. And Vivian *had* told the story as she'd wanted it to be. Star-crossed lovers. She'd rewritten the past herself until she'd almost believed that's how it had happened. How could she blame the girl for believing that tripe? Vivian shook her head, unable to say anything.

Her young cousin's eyes flooded with tears. "It was so stupid and melodramatic of me. And I didn't tell you of my plans beforehand because I wanted it to be as if fate had finally brought you back together. It would be just like in the pictures. You'd see each other from across a crowded room, and all would be forgiven. Well, I can see now how foolish that idea was. More than foolish . . . dangerous."

Vivian said nothing. What could she say? Her cousin's fool romantic notions had indeed set all of this in motion. But hadn't Vivian really set it all in motion by telling Gwen a version of events that had been so clearly false in retrospect?

"I didn't know about Charlie until you introduced us today," Gwen continued. A single fat tear slipped over her lower lashes and slid down her flushed cheek. "I'm so sorry, Viv. How could you ever forgive me?"

"It's . . ." Vivian wanted to say okay, to allay her cousin's guilt, but it wasn't okay, was it? Charlie might have killed Hap Prescott. And Gwen had been the one to bring those two men into each other's orbits. "Charlie didn't kill him," she said instead.

Vivian stared out across the lake. A sailboat was stalled in the still waters near the middle, the sail limp. A young couple sat helplessly marooned, waiting for a breeze.

"Of course he didn't," Gwen said. She squeezed Vivian's hand, but her voice quavered. She didn't believe it, of course. Vivian wasn't sure she believed it herself.

Hap was short for Happy. He'd been such a smiley toddler that everyone had called him that instead of his given name, Malcolm, and it had stuck. He was the son of Bernard's closest friend, his mother a member of the lesser German nobility. He'd been an only child, doted on and spoiled beyond measure. He'd been twelve when his parents perished in a train accident.

With no immediate family to raise Hap, Uncle Bernard had taken him in as his ward. Hap had attended boarding school most of the year and spent his summers with the family at Oakhaven, where Vivian also resided during the summer months, usually without her parents. And so Hap had always been within Vivian's sphere, if not always in the forefront. He was fourteen years older, and she'd looked on him with a sort of fawning hero worship — even before he'd actually become something of a hero.

He'd trained to be a pilot in the Great War when Vivian was still a toddler, lying about his age to join the service. But by the time he was ready to fly, the war had ended.

Rum luck, he'd always said, to never have gone overseas, never seen action of any kind. He'd gotten a taste of adventure in the air corps and was loath to relinquish it.

So he'd turned to barnstorming like many of those other young men who'd been trained to do a job and then denied the chance to do it. He'd flown shows throughout the Midwest, performing dangerous stunts like barrel rolls and loop-the-loops. He performed aerial maneuvers that made spectators' hair stand on end. Vivian had only seen one of his performances. A young man had walked on the wing and stood there braced against some sort of stand as Hap flew.

Hap had known Charles Lindbergh in passing from the barnstorming circuit and was inspired by his acquaintance's heroics (and newfound fame and worldwide admiration) for his solo flight across the Atlantic in 1927. Hap wanted the same glory for himself. Unfortunately, the target kept moving, the more attainable goals snatched up by those quicker on the draw. By 1931, the only big flying feat left was to fly nonstop across the Pacific, and Hap was preparing to do just that when he crashed while training in the spring of that year. He'd lingered near death for a week afterward. No one was sure he would wake from the coma. But he did, and with his right leg in a cast, he retreated to mend at Oakhaven.

That's where Vivian returned to his orbit and he to hers. For her, seeing Hap again that summer was like setting a lit match to a pile of dry leaves. Vivian's father had just died. She was lonely, vulnerable, and full of longing for things she didn't quite understand. And miracle of miracles, Hap seemed to have finally noticed that she existed.

It had started out harmlessly enough — small flirtations at the dinner table, making eyes when they thought no one was looking, stealing into a corner of the parlor to have hushed discussions about records or movies. Due to his injuries, he spent long idle hours parked in chairs and sofas around the large house with nothing to do but entertain Vivian with tales of his exploits. They chatted, and they did perfectly innocuous things like play cards and backgammon.

Hap treated Vivian like an adult, and as the summer went on, she caught him looking at her with more than friendly interest. She wasn't used to that sort of attention — not from a respectable man, anyway. He was worldly. He was mature. He flew airplanes and got himself hurt in spectacular crashes that made the newspapers. He was dashing and brash and made her laugh. And he made her forget sometimes that her father, the only person who'd ever really understood her, had left her for good.

Vivian had always been half in love with Hap, and that was before she laid eyes on him again that summer. By the Fourth of July, she was a complete goner. Her aunt and uncle had held a party full of polite revels, illegal liquor, and fireworks at midnight. Vivian hadn't had a chance to speak to Hap all evening, and she could feel herself tense all over. Waiting, watching from afar as he flirted with other women, older women, worldly women with knowing eyes. She longed to pull him off into a quiet corner. Jealousy was an unfamiliar feeling. She was used to having him all to herself.

Then she found Hap in the boathouse, sitting up by himself long after everyone had gone to bed, staring morosely out onto the still, moonlit waters of the lake. The dock glowed a muted white in relief against the black water. The rowboat tied below emitted an erratic *thump thump* as it bumped the dock, and the breeze stirred the leaves of the tree just outside. This boathouse was the closest Vivian had ever come to having a tree house. The bottom level was at water's edge, but the top was among the trees, the front open to the air facing the lake.

Her heart leaped at the sight of Hap. Here in the dark, just the two of them. Her heart fluttered madly in her chest. He glanced over his shoulder at her approach with a frown that didn't abate even when he recognized his visitor. He turned back to his view of the lake without speaking.

"What's with the frown, sourpuss?" she said, walking toward him.

Hap glanced at her again and smiled slightly, but said nothing.

"You want to be alone. I'll go," she said.

"No," he said quietly. "Stay."

Vivian's heart hammered in her chest. She stood silently for a moment, afraid to move, afraid he'd change his mind and tell her to leave after all.

"It's just that . . ." He began and then stopped. He hitched in a breath, turned, and cocked a dark brow at her. "Vivian, my dear, I think I've just realized that my life is not going to amount to a hill of beans."

Vivian walked toward him again and stopped behind him to rest her palms on the curved wooden back of the chair. She matched his matter-of-fact tone. "Now what would make you say something foolish like that?"

He exhaled slowly and rubbed the palm of his hand down his uninjured leg. Then he leaned down and picked up a bottle that had been sitting next to the chair. He held it up to her by the neck. She grabbed it and took a swig without bothering to glance at the label. Whiskey. She coughed as it burned its way down her throat and handed the bottle back to him. He took a swig himself and settled back into the chair.

"One wrong move," he said, pointing with the bottle toward the plaster cast on his propped-up right leg. "And I've missed my one and only opportunity for glory."

Vivian made a *pfft* sound through her compressed lips. "Surely, that Pacific jaunt can't be your only opportunity," she said. She looked down at the crown of his head and resisted the urge to run her fingers through that thick, dark hair.

"It can. And some other lucky fellow's going to make that flight and grab the headlines."

"So find some other glory," she said.

He tilted his head back to look up at her, his head resting against the back of the chair. He was dashing even upside down, she thought. A wry smile curled his lips.

"Ah, said with the unwavering confidence of someone young enough to think it's that easy." Hap's tone was light, but Vivian couldn't mistake the bitter edge to the words. His eyes held hers. His wry smile faded, and her fingers trembled on the back of the chair.

Then slowly, ever so slowly, as if he were a wild animal she didn't want to startle, she leaned forward and slid her fingers down the lapels of his dinner jacket. She paused. She felt his heart thump under her left palm, steady and sure. He tensed under her fingertips, but he didn't move, didn't look away from her. She leaned down further, planting her lips close to his ear. "I think you could have whatever you wanted, Hap Prescott," she said breathlessly. She felt his sharp intake of breath in response, felt his warm exhale against her cheek, but still he didn't move. He didn't speak. He smelled exotic — of spice and bay rum and good Cuban cigars.

They remained motionless like that, two statues in the moonlight, for a long moment. Taking shallow, matching breaths. Then his good left hand reached up to rest atop hers over his heart. His thumb stroked her skin lightly. Neither of them spoke as Vivian moved to the front of his chair and slid gracefully into his lap, careful not to jostle his injured leg. She plucked the whiskey bottle from his hand and placed it carefully on the floor beside the chair. Then she hooked one arm over his shoulders and slipped the fingers of her other hand into the slick pomaded hair at his temple.

His good arm stole around her waist, and she pressed her body against his. She ducked her head and nuzzled into his neck. She inhaled deeply of his spicy scent and then impetuously kissed the rough, stubbled skin there. Her lips slid up to his chin, planting warm openmouthed kisses all the way up the length of his neck. She kissed over his roughly stubbled chin. Then she kissed his mouth.

He returned her kiss at first as if it were merely the polite thing to do, his good hand stiffly glued to her lower back. But Vivian didn't want politeness or obligation. She'd seen the way he looked at her. He wanted her too, and she knew it. She pulled slightly away.

Suddenly, it was like some interior spring had uncoiled, and he was kissing with such enthusiasm that she was bent backward. His hand wandered up her back and then down under her skirt, toying with the clasp of her garter. Their breathing grew ragged, their kisses frantic. She pulled the length of his untied bow tie away from his collar and flung it to the side. Her fingers found the buttons at his collar and started to flick them open, one by one. Then he jerked his mouth from hers, turning his head away. He very carefully removed his hand from under her skirt and held it up in something like surrender.

"What is it?" she asked breathlessly.

"We shouldn't," he said. Then he turned and focused his intense green gaze on her. "*I* shouldn't."

She knew what he meant, of course. He shouldn't, because she was young and naive and he didn't want to take advantage of her. She ducked her head again and smothered a laugh in the creamy linen of his half-open shirt. She might have been young, but she was not naive. Nothing could be further from the truth, she wanted to say. Instead, she ran one fingertip up the skin at the base of his throat, along his jawline to his earlobe. She traced the shell of his ear with her fingertip. Then she pulled away from him, cocking her head to the side and leaning back, her fingers laced together at the nape of his neck.

"Are you sure?" she said. "Because I wouldn't mind being seduced."

He blinked, momentarily shocked by her boldness. A tight smile flashed across his face and was gone. "I'm sure," he said.

She didn't know whether he meant that he was sure he shouldn't seduce her or sure that she wouldn't mind it if he did. Maybe both.

She watched his face for a long moment, trying to read the intent there, if he had any. Then slowly, oh so slowly, she extricated herself from the comfort of his lap. She felt his fingertips trailing down her hip as she moved away. She said nothing more, just walked away down the stairs and wandered off toward the house, the crickets chirping in the darkness. She was sure he watched her go. She wasn't embarrassed at her boldness. She knew what she wanted. She knew what he wanted, regardless of what he'd said. That was just her first salvo. Vivian waited an hour before launching her second.

She picked her way through the dark woods to the guesthouse where Hap had taken up residence. And when she knocked on his door, Hap didn't turn her away. He'd said that he *shouldn't,* not that he *wouldn't.* And then she'd crossed that threshold, and they had moved their flirty, forbidden exchanges forward into the land of no return.

Now, of course, she realized that Hap had been playing her like a fiddle. It had all been so carefully orchestrated. He'd gone to the boathouse because he knew she'd show up there, and he'd have her alone. He fed her those sad-sack lines about missing his chance as a way to gain her sympathy, to make her want to soothe his fragile ego. And he knew full well that pulling her in and then putting her off would make her want him all the more. It would seem like all her idea to go after him, and perhaps that soothed his guilt over his seduction of a girl too young to know any better. And it had worked like a charm. She'd thrown herself at him, and he'd caught her with open arms. It had all been a game. And she'd bought it.

But she wasn't as naive as all that even then. She'd known the affair with Hap was wrong, and she'd done it anyway. Hell, maybe that was the only reason she had done it. She knew that it couldn't possibly end well, despite her foolish romantic notions. No, the truth of it was that she'd wanted it, she'd wanted him, and she'd be damned if she'd regret that, especially now that Hap was gone. Gone. He'd been a cad and a bounder, but he'd been her first real love. And despite how things had ended, she'd always liked knowing that he was out there somewhere.

But Hap was no longer in the world, was he? That bold, incorruptible life force had been snuffed out. Quite possibly because of her.

"Miss Witchell?"

Vivian looked up to find a policeman looming over her, notepad in hand. "We'd like to take your statement."

She was numb. Yet she felt herself nod, felt herself rise. Then her knees buckled, and she sat back down again hard. Her teeth rattled. Gwen's hand was on her shoulder.

"Are you all right?" the girl asked.

Vivian shook her head, and as she did, the ice in her mind began to thaw. Oh God. Her statement. The police wanted her statement. She thought again of that terrible night at the radio station when she'd found Marjorie Fox's dead body in the lounge. She'd had to talk to the police then too. Now, like then, Vivian was the only witness. Except with Marjorie Fox, Vivian hadn't seen the murder committed, and the man she loved hadn't been directly involved. She looked down at her trembling hands. She couldn't tell them what she'd seen. But she had to tell the police the truth, didn't she? Hap was dead, and the truth looked so terrible for Charlie.

She stared down at her shoes, which were stained green from the grass. Green like Hap's eyes. She suddenly felt like retching. She placed the back of one hand against her mouth.

"I'm sorry," she said. "I'm not feeling well."

Gwen squeezed her shoulder. "Would you like another drink?"

"No, I-I think I'd like to lie down for a while." What she really wanted was time. Vivian needed time to think, time to phrase her statement in a way that wouldn't be so incriminating for Charlie.

"This has all been a bit much for Vivian," Gwen said, addressing the policeman. "She's probably in shock. She needs medical attention."

"No," Vivian said, more forcefully then she'd intended. "I just need to lie down. That's all."

She looked at Gwen, noting the genuine concern in her cousin's face, and then up at the policemen.

"Just a few minutes," he said. His tone was softer, and Vivian realized she must really look ill. "We're not leaving here until we talk to you."

"There will be no questioning of my client until I've had a chance to speak to her."

Vivian whirled and found Freddy striding up the lawn toward them, his distinguished face set in determination. Vivian exhaled and unclenched her fists. *Thank God for Uncle Freddy,* she thought. She'd never been so happy to see someone in her life.

CHAPTER FIVE

Freddy had coached Vivian on her statement to the police, and she'd given it under his watchful eye at the house. He was adamant that she not tell them exactly what she saw — so she did not tell the police that she saw the scissors in Charlie's hand — only that she saw Hap fall to the floor. It felt wrong to tell a carefully orchestrated version of the truth to the authorities, but what else could she do? The truth would incriminate Charlie.

Freddy had gone ahead to the police station to see Charlie, and Vivian had followed an hour later. The police and fire department shared space in a nondescript brick building on West Main Street that, until very recently, had housed a garage and car storage. She'd worn her sun hat to shield her face from curious townsfolk, but no one so much as glanced in her direction. Vivian walked right through the station's front door.

Freddy was waiting for her in the small lobby. A jowly policeman watched them from behind the front desk.

"How is he?" she asked, breathless with nerves. She imagined Charlie huddled in the corner of a cold, dank cell, his eyes trained out the tiny, barred window at the blue sky of freedom beyond. She had to get him out. She just had to.

"He's holding up well," Freddy said. "As well as can be expected, anyway." He reached out and awkwardly patted her shoulder. He let his hand rest there for an instant, warm and comforting, before he removed it. Vivian wished he'd put it back.

Freddy had known everything her father had done — everything he'd been capable of — and had never said a word until Vivian had uncovered everything herself over the past Christmas holidays. Freddy had been forthcoming when she'd asked him point-blank about what she knew, but it had been too little, too late. How could she trust a man who could keep things like that a secret? Then again, how could she not? She had no one else, and Charlie was in serious trouble.

"Can I see him?" she asked. She glanced

at the policeman, who was not bothering to hide his interest in the proceedings. Frankly, it surprised Vivian that Lake Geneva even had a police station. The only crime likely committed here with any regularity was wearing white after Labor Day.

"You can see him for a few minutes."

"Oh, thank God." She started moving forward toward the doorway that she imagined led to the dank, dreary cells in the back. Freddy put a hand on her arm, stopping her in her tracks.

"Hold on just one moment, Viv. There are a few rules."

She sighed. Of course there were. Hang the rules; she just wanted to see Charlie. If she could just see him and look into those beautifully honest blue-green eyes, she would know he was innocent. Because he *had* to be innocent, and there had to be an explanation for what she saw in that game room. Charlie was the only one who could tell her what it was.

"There will be an officer in the room with you, and for your own good — for Charlie's own good — I advise you not speak of what's just happened."

"Not speak of it? How can we avoid it?"

"I understand it's the elephant in the room, but I don't want either of you saying

83

something that might be used against him. Even in passing. I, of all people, know how innocent words can be twisted in a court of law to imply guilt."

A court of law, Vivian thought. *Please never let it get that far.*

"I need to know what happened, Freddy," she said. She leaned in and whispered, "I need to know that what I saw wasn't the truth."

Freddy locked eyes with her for a moment and then nodded. "I understand. Charlie's told me his side of the story, and after you see him and assure yourself that he isn't being mistreated, we'll have a chat and I'll tell you what he's told me. Will that suffice?"

Freddy's phrasing wasn't terribly comforting. Charlie had told him *his side of the story?* Didn't Freddy believe him?

"Fine," she said. "No mention of the elephant in the room. Scout's honor." She held up two fingers solemnly.

"Okay, then. Chalmers here will escort you back."

The man at the desk jolted to his feet as if he'd been dozing and awoken at the sound of his own name. The sickly lightbulb overhead buzzed and then started to flicker.

"You're not coming with me?"

"I think you two need some time alone.

Just a few minutes, mind." Freddy glanced over his shoulder at the policeman who had started moving toward them. "And watch —"

"What I say. Yes."

Charlie stood when she entered the room. He had discarded his white linen jacket with the smear of Hap's blood across it, Vivian was relieved to see. He locked eyes with her, and one corner of his mouth quirked up as he brushed a lock of errant dark-blond hair out of his eyes.

"Oh, Charlie." She rushed forward, arms outstretched, but the policeman stepped deftly between them.

"No touching," he said gruffly.

Vivian sighed, her fingers still outstretched. Now that it was forbidden, all she wanted to do was touch Charlie. Her fingers itched to slide up his sturdy chest and reassure her that he was real and unharmed and as solid as ever. Charlie slumped into the chair at the battered table in the center of the room. He looked unharmed, if a trifle irritated. Like a man who had been fruitlessly protesting his innocence for hours — which he very likely had.

Finally, she let her arms fall back to her sides. She slid into the chair on the opposite side of the table and leaned forward. "Oh, Charlie," she said. "How did we get here?"

Charlie sighed and placed his palms down on the tabletop between them. His fingertips were so close to hers that she could feel the heat of him on her skin.

"I didn't kill him," he said, his voice pitched low. He fixed his unnerving blue-green gaze directly on her.

Vivian swallowed. He wanted her to say, "I know. Of course you didn't." But how could she say that? She didn't know that for sure. She'd seen what she'd seen.

"I'm not supposed to ask what happened," she said, blinking away the memory of those scissors lying on the rug, the sharp blades coated with blood. "Freddy's orders." She glanced over at the policeman sitting in his own chair in the corner and studiously pretending not to be listening.

"I haven't been charged with anything, Viv. They don't have any proof. And they won't have any proof because I didn't do it."

Vivian stared into Charlie's eyes, looking for a glimmer of reassurance. Her heartbeat slowed as he held her gaze.

"I'll be out of here in an hour or so," Charlie continued in that confident, husky whisper. "You'll see."

"I'll wait for you."

"No, you have to get back to the city. You've got the trip to Hollywood."

"I'll delay."

"I'm not going to stand in the way of your dreams, Viv."

"Oh, posh. Don't be so dramatic. I just mean I'll head out to California on the next train. What's the rush?" She smiled, but it was a lie manufactured to ease his mind. She knew very well that she couldn't miss that train the next evening. The Super Chief left Chicago for LA only twice a week, which meant she'd have to wait until Friday to take the next train to the coast. She'd be days behind the itinerary. She'd miss the screen test at MGM, and she knew how this business worked. If she missed that screen test, she might never get another one.

"I'd feel better if you held to the plan. Go out to California with Yarborough like you're supposed to. Smile pretty for the cameras at Dearborn Station." Vivian looked sharply at him, but despite his words, there was no mocking tone in his voice. "You probably won't believe this, but it makes my day to open the newspaper and find your gorgeous face smiling back at me."

Vivian looked away, embarrassed. Charlie had always pretended to be indifferent to

87

her ambitions in show business, but deep down she knew it meant something to him simply because it meant something to her. But to hear him say it now with that sincerity in his voice made all this real — like he was a dying man who wanted to confess everything he'd kept locked up. Her throat closed up with emotion.

"Really, Viv. I've been in worse scrapes than this. I'll be fine."

She cleared her throat. "Okay," she said finally, if only to make him stop talking like this. It was so somber, so final. "Uncle Freddy will stay with you. I've phoned your father as well. He's on his way."

Charlie's dark-blond brows rose. "That should be an interesting conversation."

"I would think that if there's anyone on earth who would understand something like this, it would be your father." Charlie's father, Charlie Haverman Sr., known as Cal, was a detective as well, retired from the Arlington Heights racetrack. Father and son had worked together for years before Charlie had struck out on his own. Cal had seen his fair share of murders. He'd been acquainted with gangsters, as had Vivian's father. The fathers' paths had crossed long before their children's. Vivian wondered suddenly if there really was such a thing as

fate, wondered if every event in her life —
in all their lives — had been predetermined,
the course plotted from cradle to grave.

Grave. She thought of Hap, of course,
though she didn't want to. She thought of
the way he'd looked at her before he collapsed, as if he'd wanted to say something
— to say everything he'd never had a chance
to say to her. In the end, he'd said nothing.
And that too, she supposed, was an appropriate way to end things. She had come
to expect nothing more from him.

Charlie stared down at his hands on the
table, lost in thoughts of his own. Vivian
cleared her throat.

"And then when I come back from California and you're out of here, we'll talk all
this through," she said. She glanced at the
corner to make sure the guard couldn't see
and then reached out and placed her hand
over Charlie's.

"You'll be coming back?"

"Of course I will. Don't be ridiculous." *I
know you didn't kill him.* She wanted to say
the words, but they stuck in her throat.

He paused for a long moment, fixing her
with one of his disarming blue-green gazes.
"You'll think over what I asked you?" he
said softly.

"Maybe," she said, forcing a teasing lilt

into her voice. She considered telling him yes right now to boost his morale, but she glanced around the utilitarian cinder-block room. Vivian wasn't an old-fashioned girl, but even she knew this wasn't the time or place to accept a proposal of marriage. She didn't want to remember this particular moment forever.

Charlie flipped his hand over and squeezed hers on the tabletop, rubbing his thumb up and down hers lightly, reassuringly. He leaned toward her and lowered his voice. "And maybe then we'll go up to your father's nice, secluded cabin and spend a leisurely week in bed."

A surprised laugh escaped Vivian's mouth as her eyes moved to the policeman in the corner. He wasn't looking in their direction, but no doubt, he'd heard the remark. There was no mistaking the knowing smirk on the man's face.

Charlie leaned closer.

"I've always wanted to take you up to that cabin and have you all to myself," he whispered. He winked at her, and then the policeman cleared his throat.

Vivian glanced down at the table, her cheeks warm. She couldn't think of anything to say. Charlie's oddly amorous turn of conversation had flustered her, and she wasn't one to be easily flustered.

When she lifted her head, Charlie was staring at her, his mouth set in a determined line. "I'm getting out of here, Viv. One way or another. You'll see."

CHAPTER SIX

The sun had set, and the light was softening into a mellow, dusky blue by the time Freddy and Vivian left the station around eight thirty. She had to get back to the city, she thought. It was a full day tomorrow — a recording session for *The Darkness Knows* at the station and then packing for her trip to Los Angeles. The train left at seven fifteen sharp tomorrow evening. But how could she do any of that with Charlie sitting in the police station accused of murder?

Vivian and Freddy walked silently down the street. Vivian worried her lower lip with her teeth and watched a boy skipping toward them with his mother. He pulled a toy wooden dog on a string behind him, while his mother juggled a bag full of beach things. The public beach was only a block away. It was hard for Vivian to imagine families enjoying a leisurely day on the sand when her world was crumbling around her, but they were, weren't they? The world kept right on spinning.

She tried to smile at the boy, but he only stared back at her. When Vivian caught a glimpse of herself in the shiny, black exterior of Freddy's brand-new Cadillac town car, she knew why. She looked bone-tired, as if she'd aged ten years in a day. Freddy opened the passenger-side door for her, and she slid into the car, her fingers trailing over the buttery tan leather of the bench seat.

Freddy got into the driver's seat and paused with his fingers curled around the steering wheel. He looked straight ahead, watching two older women saunter past on the sidewalk in front of the car with half-eaten ice-cream cones.

"You really didn't speak of Mr. Prescott's death?" he finally asked.

It took Vivian a moment to realize he meant Hap. Mr. Prescott, she thought. No, formality still didn't suit him. She shook her head. "Not a peep . . . except for Charlie to insist he didn't do it. And he didn't do it, did he?"

Freddy looked at her for a long moment, his fingers grasping and releasing the steering wheel. "I can tell you as much as he told me, Vivian."

"Which was?"

"That you two had words."

Vivian watched Freddy's expression from the corner of her eye. It hadn't changed. "Did he tell you what about?"

"Not at first, but I insisted, and he finally admitted that you'd fought about Mr. Prescott. Specifically, about involvement of a romantic nature that you'd had with Prescott."

Vivian swallowed and glanced off into the distance. "Well, I don't know how *romantic* it was in retrospect."

"Yes, well." Freddy paused and then charged ahead into the uncomfortable silence. "And Mr. Haverman said he'd proposed marriage to you, and you'd turned him down moments before the incident. Is that true?"

"Yes," she said.

"You may have done well to accept him, my dear. As a matter of fact, I advise you to accept him and marry as soon as possible."

"Why?" Unease unfurled in her like a suffocating wool blanket.

"Because you happen to be a very incriminating witness, and if you are Mr. Haverman's wife, you cannot be forced to testify against him . . . if it comes to that."

Vivian was finding it hard to catch her breath. Testify against Charlie in a murder trial? She knew that might be the endgame, but hearing it from Freddy's lips gave her a shock like plunging her hand into ice water.

"Anyway, Charlie said you two had words and he stormed off toward the main house. He said he was trying to find a quiet place to think things through."

"And he ran into Hap on the way, and they argued."

Freddy shook his head. "He didn't see anyone he recognized and wasn't successful in finding an unoccupied space until he came to the game room. He said the doors of the room were closed. He slid them open, entered the room, and slid the doors shut behind him. He thought he was alone at first. Then he saw Mr. Prescott on the far side of the room."

"And what did Hap say to him?" Vivian asked, tensing. She was afraid it had to be something related to her. Something that had set Charlie's temper off.

"Nothing."

"Nothing?"

"He said Mr. Prescott was on the far side of the room hunched over the desk. At first, it looked like he was just looking at whatever was on the desk — loose papers, clippings of some kind. He looked up at Charlie when he heard him enter. Mr. Prescott had his hands clasped to his stomach. Charlie said Mr. Prescott's eyes widened at the sight of him. They just looked at each other for a moment."

"In silence?"

Freddy nodded. "Then he said Mr. Prescott's eyes rolled up into his head, and he stumbled forward. Out of impulse, Charlie rushed forward to help. He said Prescott looked sick or hurt. When Charlie reached him, he said Prescott put his hands out to him. Charlie grabbed Prescott's hands to keep him upright. Charlie said Prescott had something metal in his hand, and it slipped into Charlie's grasp. There must have been blood all over Prescott's hands." Freddy looked down at his own hands. "Charlie said he didn't even notice the scissors in his hand or the blood until after you came in the door and asked him what he'd done. And then Prescott fell. That's it."

Oh, Charlie, what have you done? That's what she'd said. She'd seen a bleeding Hap with Charlie looming over him. What else would she think?

"So Hap *handed* Charlie the bloody scissors?"

"According to Charlie."

Vivian shook her head. "That doesn't make any sense." If that was the story Charlie was telling the police, no wonder he was still cooling his heels in a holding cell. It was, quite frankly, unbelievable.

"I'm afraid I have to agree with you. It seems an unlikely story."

"Do you think it's the truth?" Vivian asked, and then held up her hand to ward off Freddy's answer. "No, don't tell me what you think. I have to believe he's telling the truth."

Freddy turned the key, and the engine roared to life. He backed the Cadillac away from the curb without further comment.

As unlikely as Charlie's story was, what could she do but believe it? Hap certainly hadn't stabbed himself with those scissors. But if Charlie didn't do it, who did? And where had they gone?

Freddy didn't pull all the way up to Oakhaven, at Vivian's request. He was lodging at a boarding house in town near the police station, and he told her he'd stay there until Charlie was released. Vivian had considered not going back to Oakhaven at all, but she'd left her pocketbook in the parlor when she'd hurried off to see Charlie at the police station.

Vivian nudged the front door open, intending to sneak in and out as quickly as possible. She stepped inside and then paused just inside the door.

"Good evening, Mr. and Mrs. America, from border to border and coast to coast and all the ships at sea. Let's go to press!" The frantic rattle of a telegraph machine followed. She turned toward the sound of the radio in the front parlor. If Walter Winchell was on the air, it must be eight thirty, Vivian thought. And if the radio was on, someone was likely there listening to it.

Vivian edged toward the door, picturing someone in the armchair lit by the warm yellow glow of the radio. Perhaps the entire family, sitting stunned and silent in the wake of Hap's unexpected and startling demise. They'd turn to her, their eyes wide and accusing.

She poked her head around the doorframe, her heart hammering in her chest, but the parlor was empty. She let her breath out in a sigh as her eyes fell on her pocketbook still sitting on the side table. She picked it up and then walked a few steps toward the radio, drawn by the mellow yellow glow of the dial and the soothing flat noise. She should go, she thought. She was tempting fate by staying one second longer than she needed.

Winchell was talking about King George

and Queen Elizabeth's visit to the Roosevelts' summer home in Hyde Park, New York. It had happened just hours earlier. They'd had a picnic with hot dogs and potato salad. Is that what she'd just heard? Before she could comprehend it, the *beep-beep-beep* of the telegraph machine sounded again, and Winchell had launched into yet another story she couldn't quite follow.

"That Roosevelt . . . serving the king of England hot dogs." The male voice was both gruff and amused. "I don't like the man, but I admit that may have been a brilliant move."

Vivian's head jerked up. Uncle Bernard stood in the doorway. Her fingers tightened on her pocketbook. She should have gone when she had the chance.

"Brilliant?" she said aloud. It was a stupid response, but she was suddenly terrified of what Bernard might say next. He'd always terrified her. She couldn't recall ever having had a real conversation with the man. He was big and gruff and had never been around. He'd also never been interested in her as a child. Come to think of it, he hadn't been terribly interested in his own children either.

"Humanizes the king. Makes the average

99

American want to give him and his country aid, by extension."

Vivian nodded, though she didn't understand.

Bernard walked toward her, and the beeping of the telegraph sounded again as Winchell launched into another story.

She wanted to say something, but what? She was sorry, yes. But *sorry* didn't remotely cover it. "About Hap . . ."

Bernard held up one large hand. "It was an accident, Vivian," he said. "A terrible accident."

"An accident," she repeated.

"Hap . . . Charlie . . . What happened in the game room." He waved a hand in front of him. She took in Bernard's flushed face, his half-mast eyes. He was half in the bag, she thought. She couldn't say she blamed him. His surrogate son had just been murdered in his own house. He leaned in toward the radio for another long moment, listening intently.

"I don't understand," she said.

"Hap's death, Vivian. It was an accident."

She shook her head. "How could it be?"

Bernard narrowed his eyes. He spoke slowly, overarticulating every word. "Well, from what I can figure, Hap must have been sitting at the desk alone and leaned forward

100

suddenly into the scissors. Charlie happened along shortly thereafter. An unfortunate circumstance for all concerned."

An unfortunate circumstance?

"Hap stabbed himself with a pair of scissors . . . by accident." Vivian said. The words were so absurd that she almost couldn't force herself to say them.

Bernard looked intently at her. "That's what I'll tell the police first thing tomorrow morning. All of this will be cleared up, Vivian. Don't you worry about your detective."

But she *was* worried about her detective. He was still sitting in jail. Why didn't Bernard go there right now and clear all of this up, if that was his intention? And, actually, it wouldn't really clear anything up, would it? Because it was a lie.

"But Hap is *dead,*" she said, her voice cracking. She fought against the black tide of grief that tried to force its way into her consciousness. She wouldn't let herself think about Hap again. She had no time to grieve Hap with Charlie accused of his murder.

"Yes," Bernard said, frowning, his eyes skittering away from hers. "He's dead. And there's nothing any of us can do about it now."

So Bernard would lie to the police. But

101

not for her benefit and not for Charlie's. For the family's benefit, and for his own. To avoid scandal. The anger and the frustration rose in her. She clenched her fists. Her family and their obsession with scandal. Surely, that couldn't be the only reason. Surely, Bernard didn't want someone to get away with murder. Unless, of course, he knew exactly who'd really killed Hap and was covering up for them. Someone very close to him — a member of his own family, perhaps. Vivian pressed her fingertips to her temples. Her head pounded.

"I'm sorry," she whispered.

"I know," he said. "We all are."

Vivian closed her eyes and tried to shut out the thought that Bernard was covering for the person who had murdered Hap in cold blood. Then another thought occurred to her, a thought so dark and unlike her that she wanted to reject it out of hand. Was it selfish of her to not to care as long as that lie cleared Charlie of all suspicion and brought him back to her?

No, she decided. It wasn't selfish. Bernard was right. Hap was gone, and there was nothing she could do about that now. Despite how things appeared, she didn't believe Charlie had killed him. But someone had. Still, she wouldn't get involved. She'd

let Bernard go to the police, and she would
go to Hollywood as planned.

insistence, go to the police, that she would go to Hollywood as planned.

CHAPTER SEVEN

Vivian stepped off the streetcar on the corner of State and Madison. She took a deep breath and was rewarded with the ripe stench of city in the summer — body odor, sewer gases, and car exhaust. She coughed into her gloved hand, straightened her dress, and adjusted the front pin in her hat. She'd caught the last train out of Lake Geneva the evening before and had expected a night in her own bed to put her to rights, but she hadn't slept a wink.

The city teemed with life around her. It was the middle of a Monday afternoon, and people swarmed the sidewalk, pushing past her with places to go, things to do. She stood for a moment and closed her eyes. The sun beat down on her upturned face. Heat seeped through the thin soles of her shoes from the sidewalk and through her clothes from the swirling eddy of moving bodies around her. It was muggy for so early in June, she thought, the air thick and suffocating. Or perhaps that impression had to do with her general mood.

She didn't want to be here. She wanted to be in Wisconsin, close to Charlie until all this was settled. She wanted to be there when he walked out of that police station a free man. She exhaled, trying to calm her nerves. She couldn't let anyone see the strain the past day had put on her. She'd have to pretend everything was fine. No one at the radio station knew what had happened at Lake Geneva. No one in the world knew — beyond her family, Charlie, Cal, and Uncle Freddy — though she supposed gossip got around a small town like Lake Geneva. Especially when that gossip was about a murder that had happened in their midst.

A car honked irritably, and Vivian's eyes flew open.

So she would pretend. Good thing she was an actress. She smiled — at no one in particular, just as practice — and was rewarded with a double take from a man passing by. So she'd been convincing enough, she thought. She could do this. She would do this. She didn't have a choice.

Vivian made her way toward the Grayson-Cole Building in the middle of the second block west on Madison. She glanced across the street at the Tip Top Café huddled on the lower level of the gargantuan Morrison Hotel and thought of sitting there with Charlie, sipping coffee. If it all went sour in Lake Geneva, he might go to jail or worse, and she'd never get to share a coffee and flirtation with him there again. She shook the thought from her head and glanced at her wristwatch. If she didn't rush up to the studio on the eleventh floor, she'd be late. And God knew she couldn't be late. The ad man would be there, and Mr. Langley would give her a dressing-down.

The national campaign for Sultan's Gold cigarettes that she'd appeared in with Graham had been a success. *You'll be sold on Sultan's Gold,* she thought. It was a catchy slogan. The ad had featured illustrated photos of her and Graham smiling at each other from opposite sides of the page. Speech bubbles came out of each of their mouths. Vivian's said, "Here, Graham, smoke a Sultan's Gold. That mellow flavor and cool menthol taste will assure you of a confident vocal delivery every time." Graham's said, "Thanks, Viv. Harvey Diamond's got to be on top of his game, and with Sultan's Gold, that's assured."

Poppycock, she thought. All of it. Vivian

106

didn't smoke, and Graham wouldn't stoop to smoke the inferior Sultan's Gold brand unless pressed. But the public loved it. Sales of Sultan's Gold had spiked over the past few months, which had entirely to do with Graham and Vivian — specifically Graham and Vivian *together.* She swallowed hard.

Vivian and her costar had been thrown together often over the past several months, at the behest of the station's publicity department. They were seen at all the hot spots around town — the Empire Room, Chez Paree, the Edgewater Beach Hotel, the Blackhawk, the Allerton — and had their photos taken for the gossip pages of the newspapers. It was assumed that they were a couple, and that's exactly what the publicity department wanted.

The truth of the matter was that Vivian was not interested in Graham, and he was most definitely not interested in her. Quite simply, Graham preferred the company of other men, which was a secret only Vivian and the top brass at the station were privy to. Being seen with beautiful women was a means to an end for him. This was show business, and he knew he had to play the game to get where he wanted to go. He was supposed to be a debonair leading man, a man that the females of his audiences felt they had some sort of long-shot chance with. Someone they could daydream about. If they'd heard he wouldn't give any of them a second glance, they'd never believe him as the suave ladies' man Harvey Diamond.

And Vivian knew the common views about homosexuals. If his proclivities got out to the public, his career would be over, along with quite possibly his life. He could never openly be himself. He'd always have to live behind a facade, even if he left show business. And like it or not, Vivian's career was tied to his.

Vivian and Graham had become friends over all the time they'd spent together. So she'd agreed to pretend to be his girl for a bit longer, and then they'd planned to officially "break up" — amicably and without fuss so that Vivian could be with Charlie. They'd just gone through the motions of that breakup, planting discreet notices in the gossip columns. And it had seemed to go over well enough. Show business types were known to be fickle. None of them stayed long in any relationship. And as it turned out, it didn't hurt ratings to have thousands of people hoping they would reconcile and hanging on every mention of them, waiting for just that. It was like a daily melodrama working out in their personal lives.

Despite all of that, interest in *The Darkness Knows* had remained strong. So much so that there was interest in making a feature motion picture — which was why Vivian and Graham were scheduled for a screen test in Hollywood. They were in consideration to play Harvey and Lorna on the big screen. Vivian might be a movie star at last. And if all it took to reach that seemingly unreachable goal was to fib about an imaginary off-and-on love affair and the quality of a certain cigarette brand, then by God, she could do that in her sleep.

But it wasn't quite that easy. Mr. Marshfield, the ad man, was visiting from New York. He was there to oversee a transcribed recording of an episode of *The Darkness Knows.* Transcription was a fairly new technology allowing the engineers to record a live session onto a large vinyl disk. The recording wasn't for broadcast but for the advertisers and anyone else who might help the show along financially. In this case, Mr. Marshfield was going to follow Vivian and Graham out to Hollywood, transcription disk in tow, and share it with movie executives and other advertising big shots.

Vivian pushed her way through the large,

glass front door and entered the huge lobby of the Grayson-Cole Building, nodding to the security guard at the desk. He tipped his hat to her and said, "Miss Witchell." Her heels click-clacked across the floor. The building was busy; it was the first day of the workweek, after all. Everyone was so bright-eyed and bushy-tailed. Vivian headed to the bank of elevators on the far wall and made a beeline for the one with *Express to 11* over it. The elevator was crowded, but Angelo, the elevator operator, saw her coming and held the door for her. She slid inside, grateful for the distracting crush of people. This way, she wouldn't have to make small talk with Angelo. She could do her job today, say her lines, but having to talk about the weather as if nothing else were going on in her life would kill her.

She squeezed in next to him, and Angelo half turned to her as the elevator doors closed. "And how was your weekend, Miss Witchell?"

Vivian's heart thumped in her chest. A perfectly innocuous question. Or was it? She was on edge around Angelo now. He'd sold secrets to a local rag, the *Patriot,* about Marjorie Fox's murder and Vivian's involvement in it. He'd apologized later, practically groveling on the floor for her forgiveness.

But Vivian found she still didn't quite trust him. And had that been a knowing lilt to his voice? Did he know something about what had happened yesterday?

No, she thought. *Impossible.*

"It was fine, Angelo. You?"

"Good. Good. The weather. It was perfect, no?"

"Perfect," she agreed. The weather had indeed been perfect, even if everything else had been a catastrophe.

"You got the big recording today, eh? Ad man in from New York?"

"Yes." She didn't elaborate, even though Angelo arched a heavy brow at her. They rode in silence until the elevator reached the eleventh floor, which housed the operational broadcast studios of WCHI. Angelo pulled the brake lever, and the elevator slid to a stop with the slightest of jolts, the brass needle above the door pointing to eleven. He pulled the door open, and Vivian stepped out.

"Good luck, Miss Witchell," Angelo called as Vivian joined the stream of people walking down the hall. She half turned and raised one hand in salute. Then walked on. She'd accept that luck. She'd need it.

She made her way to Studio C, passing dozens of acquaintances in the hallway but speaking to no one. All she had to do was make it through the next hour. She could do that. She hitched in a deep breath and then opened the door.

A raucous din met her ears. Studio C was already crowded with people. The ad man, Mr. Marshfield, and the station head, Mr. Langley, were chatting in the control room. Mr. Marshfield flicked a long ash into the tray at his elbow as she watched, and the corners of his mouth turned down at whatever Mr. Langley had just said. Vivian glanced around the studio, noting all the usual faces. Dave Chapman, who played assorted heavies and bad guys on the weekly episodes, stood in the far corner, a cigarette pinched between his thumb and forefinger as he read the latest script. The organist was warming up in the corner, sending ominous vibrations throughout the room as she worked through the minor chords used as stingers before the commercial break. The three girl singers that sang the Sultan's Gold jingle were also there, standing in a huddle beside the organ.

This was going to be just like a live performance, Vivian thought, except that no one would hear it outside this studio. It would be contained on a single sixteen-inch vinyl disk. She shook her head in baffled wonder at the idea. The networks didn't allow playback of prerecorded programs over the air, and Vivian wasn't sure they ever would. The excitement of live theater was what the public wanted.

Her eyes landed on Graham at the far side of the studio, leading her to think what she always did when she spotted him from across a crowded room — *Lands, is he ever handsome.* With wavy black hair, dark eyes, and chiseled features, he was the epitome of classically beautiful. He looked the way she imagined Greek gods might have look as they lounged on Mount Olympus. Vivian narrowed her eyes and tried to imagine him in a toga, absently strumming a lyre. She smiled. Graham Yarborough as a Greek god . . . Wouldn't he preen if he ever heard that thought come out of her mouth? She almost laughed, and on a day like today, that was an unexpected blessing.

Graham smiled at her as she approached, and the smile that used to make her weak in the knees only gave her comfort now. He was her friend. He would be gentle with her today if she asked and wouldn't press her about why. She could confide in him, but not here and not now.

"Big day," he said. "Ready to make your mark for posterity?"

"Stop it," she said with a playful tap to his arm. "I'm nervous enough as it is. I've never heard my own voice recorded before. Posterity. Imagine . . . It'll last forever." She said that with a mix of wistfulness and trepidation. What if she was terrible?

"You'll be great, doll," Graham said in his gruff Harvey Diamond voice. He reached out and squeezed her hand gently. "Has Morty shown you how the process works yet? It's surprisingly interesting."

Vivian raised her eyebrows. Morty Nickerson and *surprisingly interesting* were two concepts that didn't usually go together.

She shook her head, and Graham motioned her to follow as he turned wordlessly and started toward the control room.

Morty, one of the station's engineers, had always had a crush on Vivian, a nervous schoolboy-type crush, where he stammered and tripped over himself at her appearance. She'd hoped it would abate with time, but it hadn't seemed to. He was just as nervous around her as he'd always been. But at least he was talking to her again. He'd stopped for months after she'd rebuffed his clumsy advances last fall. She'd felt terrible about hurting his feelings. He'd meant no harm, even if she had suspected him of murder for a short time after Marjorie Fox was killed.

She just wished he would find someone he had more in common with. Someone on whom to fixate all that puppy-dog adoration. Someone who wasn't her.

". . . you see?"

Vivian snapped to attention. Morty was explaining the recording process, and she had been lost in her own world. She nodded, though she didn't see.

"It's expensive to cut one of these disks, and it requires a lot of skill at the lathe to keep the recording even," Morty said solemnly. He frowned down at the large mechanical contraption in front of him. "They sent an engineer from New York City to teach me the ins and outs. Took a whole week." He reached down and pulled a large, red vinyl disk from its paper sleeve. "It's blank, you see, smooth." He flipped it over to show her the other side.

He held it out to Vivian and she took it, holding it gingerly along the outside edge with her fingertips. It was entirely smooth. She'd never seen such a thing before. "It's so much bigger than the records I have at home," she said, handing it carefully back.

"Sixteen inches instead of ten. Recorded at thirty-three and a third RPMs instead of seventy-eight like a regular recording," he said. He was warming to his topic, glancing at her every few moments to make sure she was listening.

"Could I play it back on a regular phonograph once it's recorded?"

"Oh no. You need special equipment." He slipped the blank disk onto the spindle of the recording machine. He pulled the arm of the needle over to the middle of the disk but didn't drop it. He moved the arm slowly outward. "It records backward, as well, from the inside out. It also records what they call 'hill and dale' instead of side to side. Altogether different from the records you're used to."

"It's all so interesting," she said enthusiastically, and was mildly surprised to find she meant it. "And you learned how to do all this for our little show?"

Morty blushed a very slight pink under the spray of freckles high on his cheeks. He nodded. "Part of my job," he said.

"Thank you for showing me how it works," she said. They looked at each other for a long, awkward moment. "How's *Fantasy Ballroom* going?"

Mr. Langley, head of the station, had allowed Morty airtime for this cockamamie idea of playing music records over the air. Morty called it the *Fantasy Ballroom*. Vivian had thought it would fail within weeks, but

Morty was still at it months later, spinning Artie Shaw and Benny Goodman disks into the ether. Morty acted as the master of ceremonies at some posh hotel ballroom, introducing each new song.

He smiled at her. "Well," he said. "Mr. Langley said he might move the show into a more prime-time slot if the ratings keep their steady rise."

"Wow, Morty. That's wonderful."

He ducked his head and started fiddling with the dials on the machine, clearly embarrassed by her praise.

"Viv!" Graham called from the other side of the small room. She turned to see him sidled up to Stuart Marshfield, the New York ad man. Graham waved her over, a lazy, confident smile on his face.

Vivian made her excuses to Morty and walked over to the group. Mr. Marshfield smiled brilliantly at her as she approached. He was a handsome man somewhere in his midforties, the type of man who regularly had three-martini lunches and expensed them to the company tab.

"And how's Lorna Lafferty today? In good voice, I hope," Mr. Marshfield said jovially. He clapped a hand on Graham's back and winked at Vivian.

She smiled in return. "Of course," she

said. "It's a pleasure to see you again, Mr. Marshfield."

"Oh, please, it's Stu." He winked again, and his gaze traveled down the length of her body and back up again. She held her smile and tried not to let any disgust at his presumption show in her expression. Whether she liked it or not, Three-Martini Stu held her future in his hands. His gaze shifted to Graham. "Say, I haven't seen you two in the papers lately. How's my favorite couple doing?"

Graham's eyes flicked nervously to Vivian. He cleared his throat. Panic fluttered in Vivian's chest. Mr. Marshfield knew they were officially no longer an item. Surely, if he hadn't seen the press release, then he'd been informed of the development. Sultan's Gold was his most important client, and Vivian and Graham had just starred in a very successful magazine ad campaign for that client.

"Well, that's because Viv and I are no longer a couple off-air," Graham said, lifting his chin slightly. He looked to Vivian like a Christian about to stare down a lion in the Colosseum.

Mr. Marshfield lifted his cigarette and took a long, thoughtful drag. Then he contemplated both of them through the

118

haze of his exhaled smoke. "I heard that, yes," he said, flicking ash into the tray at his elbow.

"It was amicable," Vivian said. "The split." She looked to Graham and smiled broadly.

"We're still the best of friends," he added. He leaned forward and lowered his voice. "You know how these things are, Stu. Actors are like hothouse flowers. You put two of them together and, well, the egos collide something fierce. Forced to stay together, they both wilt."

Vivian shot Graham a glance that said *Laying it on a bit thick, aren't we?*

But Graham knew his audience. The ad man smiled at the imagery that Graham had invoked. He'd worked with his share of delicate actors and could no doubt relate story upon story about their fragile egos.

"So you're separated at the moment," he said as if he didn't quite believe it. "And that might imply a reconciliation at some point?"

"No," Vivian and Graham said in unison.

But Mr. Marshfield was staring off through the control-room window into the activity in the studio. "We might want to give that a rethink at prime ratings time," he said without looking at them.

Vivian felt her mouth turn down at the

corners. Now that she was out of that sham relationship, there would be no reconciliation. Not even to boost ratings. Not for a thousand national ad campaigns. Charlie would never stand for it, for one thing. Her heart clenched at the thought of Charlie. Had he been released like Bernard promised?

Joe McGreevey, the director, stepped up to the group, nodding his hello at each. A man trailed behind him, and Vivian's stomach sank when he pulled the boxy black camera with the large silver flash disk from behind his back.

"This is Mr. Billings," Joe said, nodding toward the man. "He's going to be taking some candids before rehearsal for the next *Radio Guide.* Langley wants to keep interest in the program up over the hiatus." He leaned in toward Vivian and Graham and pitched his voice lower. "And Langley wants you two to play it up for the cameras. You know, act congenial."

Congenial. Vivian glanced at Graham, and he shrugged unhelpfully in response. After all, what did he care? Being congenial only helped his fictional ladies' man reputation, didn't it?

Then Joe pointed to the large clock over the window. "Time's a-wasting," he said.

"Let's get this show on the road, shall we, folks?"

CHAPTER EIGHT

They were reading a new script of *The Darkness Knows* written especially for this recording. It dealt with dirty dealings at a racetrack. The location was a fictional racetrack, of course, but the idea hit a little too close to home for Vivian's liking. Charlie's father, Cal, had been a track detective at Hawthorne Race Course in the twenties in the near-western suburbs. Not six months ago, he'd told her he'd once seen her father, "Easy Artie" Witchell, at Hawthorne with his pal Al Capone. Vivian couldn't think of a racetrack or anything tangentially related to horse racing without thinking of that moment in Charlie's run-down South Loop office when his father had sat calmly across from her and shattered her memories of her gentle, kindhearted father into a million pieces.

No matter how many times the knowledge tried to lodge itself into her consciousness, it didn't just jibe. The man Cal had known, who had willingly plotted murders with the notorious gangster, would never match the man she'd known as her father. But she couldn't dwell on any of that now.

"How about you two together squeeze together, share a microphone."

The photographer's voice broke into Vivian's thoughts. She sighed and inched toward Graham.

"A little closer now," Mr. Billings said, looking through the viewfinder of his camera.

Vivian leaned over until her shoulder was pressed against Graham's arm. "Hang in there," he whispered. "It'll be over in a minute."

The flashbulb popped.

"Okay, good," the photographer said. "How about you share a script? You know, get cozy."

Vivian dropped her script to the floor, and Graham held his out so they could share.

The flashbulb popped again.

"Good, but how about you shoot old lover boy a loving glance, eh, sweetheart?"

Lover boy? Sweetheart? Who did he think he was, Jimmy Cagney? Vivian opened her mouth to say just that, but then her eyes strayed to the control room. Mr. Marshfield was watching from behind the glass, and Mr. Langley had joined him. So she took a deep breath and then counted to ten. She couldn't afford to let her tongue slip. Not today.

She turned and smiled up at Graham, giving him the daffy, batty-eyelashed girl-in-love look that she imagined Lorna would give Harvey if they were real people.

The flashbulb popped again.

"Good! I got it."

"Thank God," Vivian said under her breath.

Graham retrieved her script from the floor and handed it to her. She smiled her thanks, adding what she hoped was an "I'm annoyed by the situation, not you" look.

He winked back at her and pointed to his script. They had a job to do.

Detective Harvey Diamond had been called to investigate at the behest of local tycoon Aloysius Quint. He'd been threatened, told in no uncertain terms that his prize thoroughbred Kickapoo Lou would lose the sweepstakes — and lose big. Of course, Harvey had brought along his sidekick, Lorna Lafferty. She screamed somewhere in the first two minutes of the program. Lorna screamed at least once in each script. It was her trademark, and Vivian was darn good at it. But Vivian was pleased to see that she also had some substantial dialogue in this script — not just "Oh, Harveys" and near-fainting spells.

They ran through the full script twice before beginning the transcription. Joe nodded to Morty in the control room, and he put the needle to the blank disk to begin the recording. Then Joe pointed to the organist. She pounded the keys with fervor, and as the dramatic minor chords of the intro music faded away, Bill Purdy, the show's announcer, stepped to the microphone, script in hand.

"And now it's time for another episode of that tantalizing tale of detective muscle *The Darkness Knows,*" he said. "Sponsored by Sultan's Gold, the cigarette that's truly mellow. Today, we open at the Blue Valley Racetrack. Detective Harvey Diamond is in the paddock with his right-hand gal, Lorna Lafferty, inspecting a particular bay gelding owned by tycoon Aloysius Quint." Bill nodded to Graham.

"Mr. Quint is sure to lose a fortune on this race, but I just can't figure how," Graham said.

"Well, Kickapoo Lou isn't Kickapoo Lou, for starters," Vivian said.

"What do you mean, doll? This horse has

the same bay coloring, same star-shaped white mark on the forehead . . ."

"Look again."

"Well, I'll say. The star's been painted on."

"The old switcheroo."

There was a pause as Harvey Diamond considered the information. "A look-alike swapped for the thoroughbred," he said thoughtfully.

"That's right. We've been had, Harvey. Someone wants Mr. Quint to lose this sweepstakes . . . and lose big. But who?"

"Gotta be the syndicate. They run the rackets in these parts."

"Oh, Harvey, how can we fight that?"

"Leave it to me, sweetheart. I'll find a way."

There was a dramatic pause before the organ swept in again and the three girl singers started in on the Sultan's Gold jingle.

The episode was recorded without incident, and everyone erupted into spontaneous applause when Joe got the signal from Morty that the transcription was a success. Joe announced into the studio speakers, "That's a wrap, folks." Vivian smiled at everyone in the studio, but she was in no mood to celebrate. She hurried out the door.

"Viv, wait!" she heard Graham call after

her, but she didn't stop. She felt claustrophobic. She needed air.

Vivian's best friend, Imogene Crook, was standing in the hallway just outside, a stack of scripts clutched to her chest. Imogene was the secretary to Mr. Langley, the head of the station. She smiled as she spotted Vivian rush out of the studio.

"*There* you are. How did the recording go?"

"Peachy, Genie." Vivian smiled, using every bit of her acting talent to make the expression seem genuine.

Imogene's dark brows drew together, and she studied Vivian's face. "Oh really?"

"Really."

"I was hoping to make it down there to see it in action, but Langley had me running all over the place delivering memos. You weren't going to come up and see me before you left?"

Vivian started walking toward the elevator, and Imogene automatically kept pace.

"I'm sorry," Vivian said. "I have a lot on my mind. I haven't packed, and the train leaves in three hours."

"Yes, the trip. I'm so jealous! I heard the Super Chief is the tops in luxury. Write me when you make it to Los Angeles and tell

127

me every single detail."

"Of course."

"Speaking of details, how was the big to-do at the lake yesterday?"

Vivian's shoulders slumped. She'd been expecting the question, and yet found she wasn't quite ready for it when it came. It was innocent enough. After all, Vivian had made a big deal about how thrilled she was to be visiting Oakhaven and seeing her cousins after such a long time. Had it really only been two days ago that she'd been discussing that excitement with Imogene?

"It was fine," Vivian said.

"Just fine? You'd made it sound like the most amazing place."

"Not just fine," Vivian said. Her voice sounded mechanical to her own ears. "Oakhaven was magnificent, of course. It was great seeing my family again."

And Hap, she thought. She'd seen Hap again after all this time. It hadn't exactly been great to see him again. What it had done was stir up a lot of long-buried feelings that she was now forced to bury again. And now he was gone. Forever. That knowledge sat in her stomach like a stone. Vivian stopped walking abruptly. Everything had gone still around her. She heard the same faint buzzing in her ears as when Hap had collapsed in front of her and she'd seen the blood on Charlie's hands.

"Viv, what's wrong?" Imogene placed a hand firmly on Vivian's shoulder.

"Everything," Vivian whispered. "He's dead."

"Dead? Who's dead?"

"Hap," she said, her voice a rusty croak.

"Who's Hap?" Imogene looked around and then pulled Vivian forward a few paces into the actors' lounge. Vivian's insides clenched. This was where she'd found Marjorie Fox's lifeless body just before Halloween. She generally tried to avoid coming in here. She shivered, looking down at her shoes and shaking her head.

"An old friend," she said. "I can't explain everything now, Genie. But Charlie didn't kill anyone. He can't have. It's all been a complete misunderstanding."

As she spoke, Graham's dark head poked around the corner, his eyes wide with alarm. Immediately, Vivian knew he'd overheard. He rushed into the room, his voice a hiss. "What's this? Chick's killed someone?"

Oh God. This just got worse and worse.

"Shh!" Imogene hissed at Graham as she pulled Vivian into a wordless hug.

"Charlie didn't kill anyone," Vivian repeated. Her voice cracked, and she knew that she was within a hairbreadth of tears.

Imogene stroked her hair.

"And you're still going to California?" Graham said.

Vivian nodded.

"How?" Graham said. "I don't know any of the details, but I don't know how you can go across the country if Chick's in that kind of trouble."

Yes, how could she?

"If I know Charlie, he probably pushed you out the door and gave you swift kick on the behind for good measure," Imogene said.

Vivian smiled slightly. "You do, and he did." She took a deep breath and exhaled. "I'm fine. Really. Everything's going to be fine. He's going to call the station any minute and tell me so." She had to admit she sounded convincing. She almost believed it herself.

But she looked away from Imogene and Graham. If she admitted her fear to anyone, even her best friend, that would make this absurd situation real. Someone was dead, and Charlie might have killed him.

CHAPTER NINE

Vivian hurried down the length of Track Five. Engines thrummed, and compressed air hissed out of the trains lined up for departure. The porter in his crisp, dark uniform hurried along beside her, taking one long stride for every two of hers. He carried her matching valise, hatbox, and toiletry case. She glanced up at the large clock at the end of Dearborn Station and found she wasn't running as late as she'd feared. The Super Chief left at precisely seven fifteen. She had a full ten minutes to spare. Still, she did not slow her pace. Her nerves refused to be soothed. Her gloved hands were clenched into fists at her sides. She was wound like a spring. And it was no secret why.

Vivian had had no news of Charlie all day. She had hurried home after the transcription session at the station but hadn't been able to reach anyone by telephone. She'd left messages with Freddy, Cal, and several at Oakhaven, but none had been returned by the time she had to leave for the train station. Vivian had thrown items into her open suitcases in a haze as unease settled over her like a suffocating blanket. Uncle Bernard had promised to go to the police this morning and sort everything out, hadn't he? But the morning had ended hours ago. She'd expected to hear from someone by now about any developments. In fact, she'd expected to hear from Charlie himself that he'd been freed of all suspicion and was coming home to her.

She reminded herself of the old adage "No news is good news." But still, she couldn't help but think that something was wrong. In fact, she could feel it in her bones. The unease prickled over her skin like a thousand tiny pins.

The train stretched down the length of Track Five like a sleek, stainless-steel serpent. The lights of the station flickered off its polished metal surface. Vivian and the porter approached the rounded tail of the observation car, the circular glass Super Chief logo lit up in purple under the rear window. A goatskin-shaded lamp glowed warmly in the window above them, and as they passed, Vivian could see several men milling about inside with drinks already in hand.

It was an impressive machine, she thought. All fluted, smooth steel and rounded corners. The very height of stylishness. Despite everything, she still felt a little thrill that she would be boarding this famous train in a few minutes.

The Train of the Stars would soon be speeding her across quiet, green Illinois prairies toward Hollywood. Stars of stage and screen and radio making the circuit from New York to Los Angeles were forced to endure an almost ten-hour layover in Chicago at the halfway point to change trains. That made Dearborn Station prime hunting grounds for the entertainment reporters of the major newspapers. Every major star had had their photo taken with the Super Chief at Dearborn Station at some point: Bing Crosby, Carole Lombard, Eddie Cantor, and of course Jack Benny. So Vivian wasn't surprised to see a huddle of reporters and photographers halfway up the platform. And she had no problem spotting Graham holding court among them. Graham and a dark-haired woman. *Oh no,* she thought. It was Frances Barrow.

Frances had been Vivian's rival at the station from the first. She was beautiful, with luscious raven hair and blue eyes. Vivian would also concede that Frances was moderately talented. They had fought for the same parts, especially when they were both starting out, and Frances had almost turned that competition into open warfare when Vivian had won the plum role of Lorna Lafferty on *The Darkness Knows* about nine months ago. Since then, Frances had taken the opportunity to undermine Vivian at every turn.

It was obvious what Frances was doing here. She was angling to become Graham's next public smoke screen — even if Frances didn't quite understand that a smoke screen was all she would be to him. Vivian watched Frances fawn over Graham for the cameras, her delicate kid-gloved fingers sliding down Graham's cheek as she leaned in to whisper something in his ear. Vivian decided that no, Frances didn't fully understand what taking on someone like Graham Yarborough meant.

She unceremoniously pulled her suitcase from the surprised porter's grip and marched forward, pushing her way through the pack of reporters and sliding smoothly between Graham and Frances. Releasing her grip on the handle of her suitcase, Vivian let it fall heavily on Frances's toe.

Frances gasped and stepped away, and Vivian didn't bother to hide the pleased smile that sprang to her lips.

"Hello, darling," Vivian said, turning to Graham and giving him a kiss on the cheek.

"Viv, you made it," he said. He smiled and returned her kiss, but his dark eyes were concerned. "Is everything all right?" he whispered into her ear.

"I'm fine, Graham. Really." He squeezed her hand — once, quickly — and then let go.

"Any word from Chick?" he said out of the side of his mouth.

She shook her head.

"A photo with the stars of *The Darkness Knows*?" someone shouted.

"Of course," Vivian said with a smile. *Time to perform,* she thought. Frances had sidled back up to them at the mention of photos, and Vivian deftly bumped her out of frame with her hip. Then she looped her arm around Graham's trim waist and turned toward the cameras, smiling brightly. Flashbulbs popped, blindingly white in the dimness of the platform. Vivian strained to keep her eyes open, her smile relaxed.

"I hear this is your first trip on the Super Chief," someone yelled from the back.

"That's right," Vivian said. "I'm very

135

much looking forward to it. I've heard so many marvelous things about its amenities."

"What's the first thing you're going to do onboard?"

"Have a nice, big drink," she said. The gaggle of reporters erupted into guffaws.

"How about a picture with the engine, Mr. Yarborough?" The engine of the Super Chief was done up in the red-and-yellow warbonnet style of the Plains Indians. Quite striking. Too bad the photos wouldn't be printed in color.

Graham raised his eyebrows at her in a silent question.

"You go on," Vivian said. She was suddenly bone weary.

Frances made to follow Graham, but Vivian grabbed her arm and held her back. Frances turned to her with a sigh, pulling her arm irritably from Vivian's grasp. Vivian smiled sweetly back at her.

"Frances, darling, what a surprise to see you here. I expect your agent's lurking around somewhere?" Vivian made a show of glancing around the platform, scanning for the pudgy, balding figure that had been Frances's constant companion for the past six months.

"Oh, him," Frances snorted. "I dropped him a few weeks ago." She pulled a compact out of her handbag, opened it, and studied her lipstick. She wiped away a smudge with the tip of her pinkie in a perfect show of studied nonchalance.

Vivian's hand flew to her chest in feigned shock. She'd known this already, of course. Gossip swirled at the station about everything and everyone, but she just couldn't miss the opportunity at a dig — especially when Frances had been so condescending over acquiring said agent in the first place. "But I thought he was doing wonders for your career. Wasn't he going to get you a screen test for Scarlett O'Hara?"

Frances frowned at her reflection and smoothed her luxuriously shiny black waves of hair behind her ears. Then she snapped the compact shut with a sigh. "Arnie was a loafer," she said dismissively. She looked off toward Graham and the reporters at the front of the train. "I'll get another agent. A better one."

One that isn't just a con trying to make time with her, Vivian thought. She wondered if that sweaty, bald man *had* made time with Frances through the force of a couple of insincere promises about getting her a contract with a movie studio. The thought made Vivian's skin crawl.

"What are you doing here, Frances? Don't

tell me you were just in the neighborhood."

Frances turned slightly away from Vivian with a brilliant smile. A flashbulb popped. Frances was like a bloodhound for cameras, Vivian thought. Then the photographer moved off toward Graham, and the smile disappeared as Frances leaned toward Vivian. "Now that you and Graham are kaput, you don't mind if I give him a go, do you?"

Vivian almost laughed. Frances was as transparent as a pane of glass. "Why would you even bother to ask, Frances? Isn't your MO to just take what you want?"

Frances cocked her head to the side and narrowed her eyes. "I could snatch him away from you in my sleep, my dear, if I had to. But I thought we were playing nice of late. Perhaps I've misread the situation?"

Playing nice? That was a laugh. *Take him,* Vivian thought. Frances could take Graham anywhere she wanted. She wouldn't get far. She wondered how long someone like Frances would put up with nothing more than polite dinner conversation and pecks on the cheek. Vivian glanced over at Graham holding court with a gaggle of reporters beside the engine and bit down a smile. Vivian suspected that Frances wanted quite a bit more from Graham than he was willing to give. She'd be in for a struggle. Would Graham take her into confidence? He'd have to eventually.

"You have my blessing," Vivian said. "He's no bowl of cherries, you know."

Frances's sapphire eyes rolled heavenward. "What man is? I'll suffer a few pits for a leg up."

A leg up, Vivian thought, containing a smile. *Well, she certainly won't get* that.

Graham had returned, the reporters following closely behind him. The group laughed at something Graham said. He could be so charming when he wanted to be.

The conductor followed behind. *"All aboooard!"* he shouted.

The train whistle blew, and the big diesel engine thrummed. Graham hopped up the first three steps of the unfolded staircase before turning around, holding a hand out to Vivian. She took it and paused halfway up the steps. "Turn back and smile," she told Graham. They both turned back from their position on the stairs, their hands raised in farewell. Flashbulbs popped. *That* was the shot that would be in the papers tomorrow, she thought with satisfaction. And Frances had been nowhere in sight.

CHAPTER TEN

The Super Chief was a marvel of modern engineering. Vivian had never been on a mode of transportation so luxurious, including the ocean liner on which her family had crossed the Atlantic when she was twelve. She'd freshened up in her own compartment, a luxurious double berth with its own sitting room and powder room, and now she sat in the observation car, the Navajo, next to Graham, who was puffing away on a Cuban cigar.

She took in the sand-colored carpeting, the copper walls, and the turquoise ceiling. Vivian had never been among the Navajo, had never been anywhere near the desert Southwest, but she'd heard that the train's decor had been taken directly from those ancient motifs. The porter had told her that the upholstery on the chairs and sofas was based on the design of an authentic bayeta blanket that the interior designer had found in New Mexico. Vivian smoothed her hand over the cushion absently. She wished she were of a mind to enjoy it more.

A copy of *Along the Way* sat splayed on her lap, a brightly colored photo of the Super Chief's engine with its red-and-yellow warbonnet displayed on the cover. She'd been fruitlessly trying to read about the locations the train would speed past. It would only take about forty hours to cover the two thousand miles from Chicago to Los Angeles. The Super Chief was a marvel of speed and efficiency all right, but that speed and efficiency also made Vivian claustrophobic.

The train wouldn't stop at any platform for more than a minute or so until they reached Kansas City sometime in the early hours of tomorrow morning. She couldn't get off this train before then if she wanted to, no matter what happened. She glanced at Graham. He sat back in his armchair and tapped a long ash into the freestanding tray at the edge of his armrest. He caught her eye and stubbed the cigar out.

"Tops in luxury, I'd say," he said, easing back into his seat again. She'd say so too. It cost the average American a month's salary for a lesser berth on the train, and it was even more for her splendid double bedroom.

141

She followed Graham's gaze out the windows at the night-shaded countryside streaming past. The train's horn blasted faintly and consistently as they passed through the small towns that dotted the landscape. But this room was a warm, yellow cocoon where the outside world was of no consequence. At least it was to everyone else. She looked around at the other well-heeled passengers, who seemed to be mostly businessmen and their exquisitely coiffed wives. Vivian recognized no one. No other celebrities were onboard this trip. She closed her eyes and tried to imagine that everything in her outside world was fine as well. She opened them again almost immediately. How could she be expected to sit on this train for the next forty hours without any sort of contact? She'd go crazy. She gripped the arms of her chair.

Graham leaned down to a bag at his feet. He pulled a script out and held it up. CARLTON COFFEE HOUR, it said on the title page. She and Graham were going to guest star on next Sunday's show. The show had originated in Chicago at WCHI. Graham and Vivian had worked with nearly every actor on that show before it moved to Hollywood late the previous year. Marjorie Fox's old costar on *The Golden Years*, Little

142

Sammy Evans, had jumped ship to warmer climes with *The Carlton Coffee Hour* shortly after Marjorie's demise and had gone on to great success.

"Do you want to run lines with me?" Graham asked.

Vivian didn't, but she nodded anyway. Anything to distract herself. It was rather a clever script, a parody of *The Darkness Knows* with the lead characters flipped on their heads. Vivian played the gumshoe and Graham her sidekick. It would get laughs, she had no doubt. If she could hit her lines, that was. She didn't have much experience with comedy.

Graham leaned to his right, resting the open script between them on the arms of their chairs so they could both see it. He pointed at her to start.

"Say, doll," she said gruffly. "What's with the long face?"

There was a note under that: *Pause for laughter. The Carlton Coffee Hour* was broadcast in front of a live studio audience. That was something else Vivian had no practical experience with. This entire trip to California was uncharted territory for her.

"Oh, Lorna," Graham said, his voice high and breathy. "It's this rope the kidnapper has left on my wrists. It's got me tangled up in knots."

Vivian sighed. That was a terrible joke. Would anyone really laugh at that?

"Viv."

"Hmm?" She looked up. Graham was pointing to something in the script.

"Your line."

"I'm sorry, Graham. I'm afraid I can't concentrate. Maybe we can try it later?"

"Of course." He pulled the script away and reached down to put it back in his bag. He rummaged for a few seconds. "Would you like something to read? Take your mind off things?"

He pulled out a book and handed it to her. It was bound in a colorful dust jacket with a moss-green cover that showed a man shoveling coal into the blazing engine of a steam locomotive.

"Well, don't you have a morbid sense of humor," she said.

"Morbid?"

"Or do you find it soothing to read about grisly murder on a train while . . . on a train?" Vivian smoothed her fingertips over the raised type: *Agatha Christie — Poirot Solves a . . . Murder on the Orient Express.* Graham's dark brows drew together in distress.

"Ah, hmm. You see, the . . . coincidence

144

hadn't occurred to me." He gave her an embarrassed half smile. "Does it bother you? I mean, with Chick . . ."

She pinched her lips together and looked over her shoulder out the window behind her seat. "No," she said. She had only been making a joke, and it had backfired on her. She turned back to him and lowered her voice to scarcely above a whisper. "Charlie didn't murder anyone. Besides, I'm sure he's out of jail by now." Her voice was light, but her stomach constricted. She'd half expected Charlie to show up at the station to see her off, rumpled and whiskered, that beautiful lopsided grin lighting his face. But he hadn't, of course.

Graham just nodded. He regarded her thoughtfully for a moment, his usually smoldering dark eyes now brimming with concern.

"Say, how's he getting on?"

Fine. The lie was on the tip of her tongue. She didn't want to discuss any of this. If she didn't discuss it, she might be able to pretend it wasn't happening. "I don't know," she said instead, swallowing the lump in her throat.

"I thought you said it was a misunderstanding and that it would all be smoothed over."

"I know I did. It's just . . . Well, the situation's more complicated than I thought."

Graham leaned forward and said in a barely audible whisper, "Who's he supposed to have killed . . . If you don't mind me asking?"

Vivian found she didn't mind the asking as much as searching for an appropriate response. How should she describe Hap to someone who didn't know him or her history with him? An old flame? Her first love?

"A family friend," she said, picking at the paper dust jacket of the book in her lap.

"He killed a friend of the family . . . of *your* family?"

"He didn't *kill* anyone," Vivian hissed.

Graham held up both hands in surrender. "Sorry," he said.

"I'd just prefer not to discuss it . . . not right now." She felt her cheeks grow warm, and she glanced around, but no one in the smoking car seemed to take any notice of their whispered conversation. Then she looked down at the book, the orange-and-yellow tongues of fire leaping from the coal furnace on the cover. She passed her fingertips over the image. "Why this book?" she asked, desperate to change the subject.

Graham blinked. He looked down at the cover again. "Frances gave it to me. She thinks I should adapt it for radio."

"Adapt it?"

"Yes, for the *Sultan's Gold Paragons of Literature* program," he said.

Besides being a mouthful to say, it was a monthly program on which Graham and a team of writers adapted a famous work of literature for a radio audience. It had all started with Graham's adaptation of *The Scarlet Pimpernel,* which had aired locally in the Chicago area this past New Year's Day. Sultan's Gold had liked it so much that they decided to sponsor further forays into paragons of literature.

"And it would give me a fine platform to practice my French accent."

"French." Vivian heard herself mindlessly repeating everything Graham said, but she couldn't seem to help herself. Her brain was operating as if stuck in low gear.

Graham's brows drew together as he regarded her. "The detective is an eccentric Belgian chap named Hercule Poirot, you see," he said. "Ever read any Christie?"

She shook her head.

"She ees quite good, *n'est-ce pas*?"

Vivian smiled. "It needs a bit of work," she said, meaning his accent, not the book.

He smiled affably in return. "Keep it, if

you like. It might help take your mind off things."

"Maybe."

"Say, where's Banks? He's aboard, isn't he?"

"He's supposed to be, but I haven't seen him." She hoped the station's head of publicity had missed the train, actually. He was not among her favorite people, and she just wanted to be able to stew in peace until they reached Los Angeles rather than be forced into strategy sessions about making their mark in Hollywood.

"Where do you think we are right now?" Graham asked.

She lifted *Along the Way.* "Would you like to see if we can puzzle it out?"

"Sure. Give me a little of the local color."

"Well, we've only been moving for an hour, so I suspect we're scarcely outside the Chicago suburbs." She turned the page and moved her finger down to the entry in the middle of the page and began reading. " 'Lemont, Illinois. The name means "Little Mountain." Elevation 594. Two aluminum production plants; view of drainage canal. Oil refinery three miles west.' "

"Drainage canal, eh?"

Vivian laughed and tapped the book with her finger. "Right. On second thought, I think I actually prefer the grisly murder on a train."

Dinner was a formal affair in the Cochiti car. White-gloved waiters served them fresh lobster cocktail and Romanoff caviar. The menu included such delicacies as calf's sweetbreads and filet mignon, though Vivian and Graham had both opted for the chicken à la king for their main course. Vivian ate little and spoke even less. She occasionally managed to smile when Graham cracked a corny joke in an effort to lighten the mood. He hadn't asked her once about Charlie, though she could see the desire to written all over his movie-star face.

The main course had just been served when Graham looked up and locked eyes with someone behind her. He smiled, his fake Graham Yarborough dazzler, and leaned back in his chair.

"There you are, Banks," Graham said. "Viv and I were afraid you'd missed the train."

Vivian turned to find Mr. Banks walking up the aisle toward them. He stopped beside their table, an uncharacteristic smile on his round face.

"Glad I ran into you two," he said. "I have some brilliant news. Brilliant."

Vivian took a sip of her wine and waited. Mr. Banks had the tendency to overstate things. She'd judge for herself if the news merited the "brilliant" rating or not. Mr. Banks paused for dramatic effect. He leaned forward slightly and lowered his voice to a conspiratorial whisper.

"I received word just before boarding that Mr. Mayer is very interested in meeting personally with both of you," he said.

"Mr. Mayer . . ." Vivian said. She looked to Graham and then back to Mr. Banks. She must have misheard. Or perhaps he was referring to another Mr. Mayer in Holly-wood? Surely, he couldn't be serious, but Mr. Bank's face was the picture of delighted reserve. In fact, he looked proud enough to burst.

Graham completed Vivian's sentence for her. "As in Louis B. Of Metro-Goldwyn-*Mayer*? *That* Mr. Mayer?" he said. Vivian turned to him as a dazzling smile unfurled across his face.

"The very same."

Vivian swallowed, a lump of the delicious chicken à la king wedged in her throat. She took a long sip of her wine, but it didn't help. She'd assumed she and Graham were small potatoes, minor radio stars who would be passed off to underlings to handle at the

150

movie studio. But somehow, this little publicity man had stolen a meeting for the two of them with the most powerful man in Hollywood. She looked at Mr. Banks in shock. He was good at his job after all.

This is really it, she thought. *The chance of a lifetime.* When else would she get the opportunity to meet someone with as much influence on the film world as Louis B. Mayer? Never, that's when. What would she do? What would she say to him? Her palms had already gone clammy at the thought.

"That's amazing," she croaked. "How did you manage that?"

Mr. Banks straightened again, hands clasped over his ample stomach in satisfaction. "I have connections," he said vaguely.

"Would you like to join us for dinner?" Graham asked.

"Oh, no, no," Banks said, already turning to go. "I promised Mrs. Banks I wouldn't talk business on the way out to Los Angeles. This train trip's got romance on her mind." He shot them a dubious look.

"Enjoy it," Graham said jovially. He looked fit to burst himself. And why wouldn't he? Vivian thought. In a few days, they could be signed to Hollywood contracts. It didn't seem real. She glanced around. None of this seemed real.

"Well, well. This turn in our combined luck calls for dessert, I think," Graham said. He glanced down at the menu. "They have vanilla ice cream . . . fresh strawberries and cream . . ."

Vivian shook her head. The food she had managed to get down sat like a rock in her stomach. "I think I'll turn in early. It's been a trying day."

Graham quirked a dark brow at her.

"I'll walk you to your berth," he said.

"You don't have to."

"I want to."

They were silent on the way there. It wasn't a long walk — perhaps fifty feet or so. Vivian felt the claustrophobia settling in around her like a blanket. She hadn't traveled much by train, and everything about it was starting to unnerve her. They were hurtling at breakneck speed down a track in the darkness inside a metal cylinder. Even the gentle, rhythmic rocking of the train unsettled her. She doubted she'd sleep at all tonight.

They reached her door, and she turned before opening it. "Thank you, Graham."

"For what?"

"For being so understanding. For not pressing me to talk about it."

Graham's jaw tensed. "Well, I have to

admit that I'm not really that understanding. I'm dying for the details." He laughed lightly. Then his expression turned serious. "I'm concerned for Charlie too, you know. And you." He squeezed her shoulder gently and lowered his voice to a whisper. "If you want to talk about it, you know where to find me."

"Thank you. I'll tell you all about it when everything's cleared up. I promise." She pulled him into a hug. He patted her back awkwardly before releasing her. She turned and put her hand on the knob and then half turned back toward him. "Hey," she said. "You called him Charlie. Not Chick."

Graham smiled. "I thought it was time I dropped that silly affectation. I've tried to make that nickname stick for months, and it just won't. I know when I've been beat." He shrugged good-naturedly and turned to make his way back down the corridor to his own berth. She smiled at his retreating form with the *click-clack* of the wheels in the background.

But her smile faded as she unlocked the door.

CHAPTER ELEVEN

Vivian woke to a short, businesslike rap on her door and sat bolt upright in bed. She'd left Graham's copy of *Murder on the Orient Express* splayed open on her chest, and it fell to the floor with a thump. The train was stopped but the engine still thrummed, and a feeble light filtered in through cracks along the sides of the drawn window shade. She picked her watch up from the berth side table. It was 2:12 a.m. The rap sounded again at the door. She jumped from bed, heart hammering, and threw on her chenille robe before she opened the door a crack to find the porter staring gravely down at her.

"Telegram, miss." He held a paper out to her.

She took it, heart thumping even harder now, and held up one finger for the porter to wait. She turned back into the room and rifled blindly through her handbag. She fished a handful of coins from the bottom and returned to the door, dropping them into his palm.

"Thank you, miss," he said. He turned to go.

"Wait," she said, her fingertips sliding over the smooth surface of the telegram. "Where are we?"

"Just arrived in Kansas City, miss."

Kansas City. Who would be sending her a telegram via Kansas City at 2:12 a.m.? Vivian stepped back into her room and shut the door with the click. She turned on the bedside table lamp and sat on her open berth, ripping the telegram open with trembling fingers.

MISS VIVIAN WITCHELL ABOARD
SANTA FE SUPER CHIEF
C CHARGED — ON LAM — PHONE ME
FREDDY

Charged. Charged with murder? How could that be? And what did Freddy mean by "on lam"? He couldn't mean that Charlie had run. Vivian shook her head and read the telegram all over again. But there wasn't much to read. Just the same confusing, heartrending line. Charlie had been charged with murder, and he'd somehow escaped police custody. Oh God. Why? He was go-

155

ing to get himself killed.

What had he said to her at the police station? *I'm getting out of here one way or another. You'll see.* She shivered.

Vivian rang immediately for the porter and began throwing items into her suitcase. She knew enough about the Super Chief's schedule to know that if she didn't get off now, here in Kansas City, she'd have to wait hours for the next stop — every *click-clack* of the wheels taking her further and further west and further and further away from any way to help Charlie. How could she sit helplessly on a train knowing that Charlie was out there somewhere, possibly running for his life? Why had he run? Did that mean he'd killed Hap after all? No, she wouldn't even entertain that possibility.

The porter returned, and she thrust her half-latched suitcase at him as she slipped into her shoes. She was still wearing her peignoir, having slipped the jacket of the traveling suit she'd worn earlier over it. She just hoped that at 2:12 a.m., there was no one around the Kansas City station to take much notice of her.

"I'm disembarking," she said, plucking her hat from the table and giving the berth a once-over for anything important she might have forgotten.

"Beg pardon, miss?" The porter's eyes were wide as the suitcase slipped from his grasp. He bent at the knees and caught it before it could fall to the floor and spill the contents.

"Getting off the train here. Now." She had her handbag, money, a change of clothes. That's all she needed. She moved past him and marched down the corridor, listening for his sharp footsteps to follow her.

She hopped down the steps onto the platform and turned to retrieve her suitcase. "Can you do me a favor?"

He nodded, eyes still wide.

"Please tell Mr. Yarborough that I had to leave. If he can delay in LA, please do so. Otherwise, go ahead without me. Can you remember that?"

He nodded. "Mr. Yarborough. Miss Witchell had to go. If he can delay in LA, do so. Otherwise, go on without you."

"That's right," she said. She rummaged in her handbag and then pressed a ten-dollar bill into his hand. "Please go tell him this instant. Wake him if you have to."

"Of course, miss," he said.

The train's engine began to rumble, setting the platform vibrating under the thin soles of her shoes. The whistle blew, and the train started its infinitesimal movement forward. The shiny silver wheels whispered on the tracks and picked up speed.

"I hope everything's okay, miss," the porter said, raising his voice to be heard above the noise of the engine.

I hope so too, she thought.

Vivian rushed across the empty lobby toward the bank of pay phones on the far wall, her heels clacking madly on the marble floor. She realized she'd given all her change to the porter for his tip, leaving her without even the nickel for a local call. She whirled on her heel toward the newsstand opposite. She'd assumed it would be closed at this time of the morning, but a solitary light burned inside, and she saw the soles of a pair of shoes propped up on the counter. The man was dozing at his post. She walked up and slapped her hand on the counter. The man jolted awake with a snort, his shoes slipping to land on the floor with a discordant double thump. His eyes widened as if he wasn't quite sure that this lady in a feathered peignoir and tweed jacket before him was not part of a particularly titillating dream. He opened his mouth and then shut it again.

"Would it be possible to get some change for the pay phone?" Vivian said impatiently. She pulled the edges of her jacket together.

The man's eyebrows went up in sleepy surprise. "Of course." He paused for such a long time that Vivian thought he'd fallen asleep again with his eyes open. "But you'd have to buy something. I'm not allowed to just give out change, you see."

She sighed. She selected a pack of Wrigley's Spearmint and slapped it on the counter, along with a twenty-dollar bill. Then her eyes snagged on her own face staring back at her from the newsstand display.

It was the latest edition of *Radio Stars*. There she was, her smiling face in three-quarter profile next to a beaming Graham. The headline underneath read RADIO'S "DARK" STARS SHINE. Vivian exhaled slowly. Being on the cover of this magazine had once been her wildest dream come true, but she felt nothing.

"Miss, your change?"

Vivian pulled her eyes from the cover of the magazine.

"Would you like to buy that too?" he asked. He obviously didn't recognize her. She pulled her hat down over her eyes anyway.

"No, thank you." She took her change and walked off toward the bank of pay phones on the far wall.

Vivian installed herself in the little wooden

cubicle. There were no doors, but a quick glance told her there was no one around to overhear. She dumped the pile of change on the shelf next to the telephone with shaking fingers, then fished out the card where she'd written all of the important telephone numbers she might need on her trip west. She placed a fingernail under Uncle Freddy's name. Then she plucked the horn-like receiver from its cradle on the left side and slid a nickel into the vertical slot at the top of the telephone, dialing zero when she heard the tone.

"Number, please," came a singsong female voice at the other end of the line.

"I'd like to place a call long distance to Mr. Frederick Endicott in Lake Forest, Illinois, please. The number is CEDar-3455."

"Would you like to hold the line or receive a call back when the party answers?"

"I'll wait."

"One moment, please."

There was a series of clicks. After an interminable amount of time, the operator came back on the line.

"Your party is on the line. Please deposit one dollar seventy-five cents for the first three minutes."

Vivian plucked coins at random from the pile on the counter and jammed them in.

They made a satisfying metallic *clank-clunk* as they fell into the metal receptacle of the pay phone.

"Proceed with your call," the operator said.

There was another click, and then Freddy's voice came over the line — low and insistent.

"Vivian?"

"Yes, it's me. I got your telegram. What's going on?"

"Charlie's left."

"Left? I don't understand."

"He's wanted, and he's disappeared."

"Wanted? Why?" That couldn't be true. That could only mean the police had something against him — enough evidence to charge him with murder.

"We can't talk about it over the telephone."

Frustration welled in her chest. They couldn't be sure that the operator had disconnected. She could be listening out there somewhere. The police could be listening, for that matter.

"Vivian, now this is important. Do you have any idea where Charlie might be?"

She swallowed. "No," she said automatically. Why would she? But something niggled at the back of her mind. Where would she go if she were wanted by the police? Where would no one know to look for her?

"Okay," Freddy said, sounding unconvinced. "Where are you now?"

"I'm calling from a pay phone at the Kansas City station."

"I'm sorry I don't have any more information, Viv, but I had to let you know. Get back on the train. Go to California. There's nothing you can do. And if you hear from Charlie, let me know as soon as possible."

"I will. You do the same."

"Of course. Goodbye."

She replaced the receiver and stood, staring at the telephone. Her mind worked, her foot tapping on the checkered linoleum. Then she collected her things and headed off toward the quiet ticket booth. She hadn't technically lied to Freddy, she reasoned. She didn't know where Charlie *might* be. She knew *exactly* where he was, and she was going to him.

CHAPTER TWELVE

Vivian remembered Louis B. Mayer twenty minutes east of Eau Claire, Wisconsin. The thought flitted across her mind as if it were something happening to someone else. She was going to miss her meeting with Louis B. Mayer. The loss of it registered only in the cerebral sense. She felt no panic, had no sweaty palms about losing her one chance to impress the most influential man in Hollywood. Getting to Charlie was the only thing on her mind. She supposed it might bother her once she'd found Charlie and squeezed him tightly and knew he was safe. But first, she had to find him.

She tightened her grip on the steering wheel, her fingers aching. She had sweaty palms all right, but it had nothing to do with Mr. Mayer. It had to do with Charlie running from the law and the fact that she was driving a 1928 Ford Model A in the deepening dusk of rural Wisconsin without a driver's license. That, and she had only the vaguest notion of how to get where she needed to go. A rumpled map lay spread out in the passenger seat. She'd studied it before setting off, but she was doubting her memory already, and she might have to pull over soon to verify the route.

Vivian had reversed her route, catching a train to Minneapolis, then another to Eau Claire, where she'd arrived three hours earlier. She couldn't get any farther into the north woods by train — and in any case, driving would be faster. There weren't any cars for hire in Eau Claire — none that would take her into the north woods — but the man at the ticket counter at the train station had told her his brother Irv was selling a 1928 Model A in great shape.

She had bought the Ford for fifty dollars cash without so much as kicking the tires. When she'd turned on the waterworks and laid it on thick with a story about a sick mother in Minocqua, Irv had thrown in a full tank of gas. But it was becoming apparent that she'd been the one taken for a ride. The tires were bald. She'd learned that the hard way by skidding around the curve of the dirt road, her heart in her throat as she nearly sank the rear of the car into a ditch. She'd fishtailed for a heart-stopping five seconds or so before she got the car under control.

The interior reeked of stale cigarettes, so she'd been forced to drive with the window rolled down and the chill air numbing the left side of her face. It had taken her the full first hour to learn the nuances of the finicky clutch. And a high-pitched clicking noise had started from somewhere near the right side of the engine. It would seem kind-hearted Irv from Eau Claire had lied to her. The cad had sold a grieving woman a jalopy.

She was just glad that she knew how to drive. If this had happened six months ago, she'd have been up the veritable creek without a paddle. Charlie had been teaching her to drive for the past couple of months. Off and on — whenever his nerves could take it. She had enthusiasm to spare, but her attention wasn't always up to par. As with most things she attempted, she thought ruefully. Charlie liked to clutch his hat to his chest and then fan himself like an old lady with the vapors when Vivian failed to yield or popped the clutch going out of first gear. It made her laugh, and that's precisely why he did it. Her heart thumped hard with love for him.

Dusk was rapidly turning to night. She just hoped the Model A would refrain from breaking down until she reached her father's cabin on Cranberry Lake. Each pothole jangled her nerves as well as her bones. Charlie had to be there. Where else would he go? He'd never been to the cabin, but she'd told him all about it, including how to find the nearly hidden turnoff. A sign appeared out of the darkness. This was her turnoff. She had to get off the relative safety and comfort of the state highway and onto the side roads now. The unpaved roads. The potholed roads. The roads thick with dark woods on either side — the dark woods frequented by black bears.

Her entire body tensed as she made the left turn onto the dirt road. She didn't know how far she was from the cabin, and she wished she'd paid more attention the few times she'd been up here with her father. The headlights sent two columns of weak yellow light into the darkness — just two feeble pinpoints of light against the dark that closed in on both sides. Her eyes darted from left to right, right to left, hunting for any sign of an animal in the underbrush about to burst onto the roadway in front of her. She was so intent on her mission that she almost missed the turnoff to the cabin. But there it was. A tiny, rutted track, hidden among a wild tangle of bushes and saplings. She hitched in a breath and turned, hoping to God this was the right place because there would be nowhere to turn around until she reached the end of this track — wherever that might be.

Just as Vivian was about to give up, there stood the little cabin. It was completely dark, locked up tight. There weren't any cars out front. The shutters were closed and latched over every window. Charlie wasn't here.

She sat in the car for a long moment, the engine idling. Her mind skittered over the possibilities. She'd been so certain. Vivian thought again of his oddly amorous talk in the jail. Charlie had specifically mentioned this cabin. Where else could he possibly be? Surely he hadn't gone back to Chicago, where the law could find him in an instant. And surely he wouldn't ask his father for help. He'd want to keep his old man out of any trouble. She stared at the cabin. An owl hooted somewhere nearby, and Vivian flinched. Finally, she pried her sore fingers from the steering wheel and shut the car off, grabbing the flashlight from the passenger seat. She might as well have a look around.

The heavy metal cylinder was a comforting weight in her hands, the beam of light bright and strong against the darkness. It was so quiet here — only the subtle rustling of the leaves and the occasional hoot of an owl. Something swooped out of the darkness, gliding just over the top of her head. She ducked instinctively, the hairs on her arms standing on end.

She'd have to spend the night. She certainly wasn't going to drive any farther in the woods in the pitch-darkness. She couldn't see the lake from here, but she knew it was there behind the cabin — black and fathomless, with all kinds of creatures slithering and sliding and swimming in its depths. The thought made her shiver.

It was chilly this far north. She pulled her jacket more tightly around her. She'd finally had a chance to change out of her nightgown after securing passage northeast from Kansas City, but she'd been wearing these clothes all day. She wanted nothing more than to change, light a fire if she could manage it, and crawl into bed.

She approached the front door, climbing up the thick wooden steps. Nothing would be turned on inside, of course — the electricity, the water. No one had been up here yet this season. But at least it would be shelter from the elements. *And the bears,* her mind added helpfully. She opened the screen door and was careful to not let it slam behind her. The screened-in front porch was still set for winter — the wicker furniture stacked in the corner, draped in sheets. It smelled of dust and damp.

Vivian moved forward and grasped the knob of the interior door, realizing only when it didn't turn that she didn't have the key. She pushed against it with a fruitless grunt and glanced down at her feet, which rested on a woven doormat. She bent and flipped the mat over. Nothing. She felt around the top of the doorframe. Nothing. She glanced around the porch, but she had no idea whether the last person to have stayed — likely Everett last fall — had left a key somewhere.

There was nothing for it. She'd have to break in. Her mother would kill her. Well, that would be among the smallest of Vivian's transgressions before this was all over, she supposed.

She picked up a rock from the ground at her feet and hefted it in her hand, bouncing it in her palm a few times, working up the courage to vandalize her own family's property. *It's for a good cause,* she thought. She hitched in a breath and tossed the rock. It smashed through the pane of glass. The noise was unbearably loud in the stillness of the nighttime forest. A bird squawked in protest and flew off from the top of a nearby pine. Vivian flinched and held still for a long moment. Nothing happened. She pulled her sleeve down over her fist and gingerly pushed her hand through the hole in the glass, reaching around inside and unlocking the door with a click.

Vivian entered the cabin, careful to step over the pile of broken glass just inside the door. She closed the door behind her and sighed. The moon was only about a quarter full, and the trees looming over the cabin blocked any feeble moonlight there was. She'd need to find a lantern and matches. She stepped forward, glass crunching under her heel.

She almost couldn't bear to think about what she would do in the morning.

From somewhere in the darkness, Vivian heard a metallic *click-click,* followed by a man's calm, measured voice. "Don't move."

Vivian stopped walking, stopped breathing. Adrenaline coursed through her veins. She held her hands up, the lit flashlight pointed at the ceiling. She could see nothing of the interior of the cabin now, could hear nothing but her own sporadic breathing. *A squatter,* she thought. Yes, she'd surprised someone who was lurking in her father's cabin. Someone with a gun.

"Who are you?" the gruff voice called out again.

Vivian's heart stuttered, half in residual fear, half in joy. She knew that voice.

"Charlie?" she whispered.

There was a pause, then a sigh. "Jesus, Viv."

CHAPTER THIRTEEN

Vivian rushed forward blindly, arms outstretched. Charlie caught her and pulled her to him. They didn't speak. He breathed into her hair, and she buried her face in his chest. She could feel the cold weight of his handgun against her shoulder blades. She squeezed him tighter and tighter until she could feel that he was real. He squeezed her back hard, and then pulled away. He moved toward the other room. She heard him fumbling, uttering muffled curses. Then there was the sound of a match, the sizzle of a flame, the faint *whoomp* of a gas lantern being lit.

He came back to her, holding the lantern at waist level, the light throwing shadows up under his chin. She could clearly see blood-shot eyes, a scowl. He was not pleased to see her.

"What the hell are you doing here?" he hissed.

"I came to find you," Vivian said. She fought to keep her voice steady. She clenched her hands at her sides. She wanted to run to him again, hug him, feel the solidness of him.

"You're supposed to be on your way to California."

"Freddy sent me a telegram, so I got off the train."

"Did he tell you to get off the train?" Charlie held up his free hand to stop her explanations before they started. "No. No, of course he didn't."

"Not in so many words," she said.

"Did you tell him you were coming here?"

"Of course not."

Charlie sat down heavily at the small kitchen table. There was a day's growth of stubble on his cheeks, and a lock of greasy hair fell over his forehead. Vivian had never seen him looking so rough. He placed the lamp and gun carefully on the table in front of him and let his head fall into his hands. He spoke without looking up. "You've done a lot of stupid things in the time I've known you, Vivian Witchell. But this takes the cake."

Vivian felt her face flame. *Stupid?* It wasn't remotely stupid. "You as much as told me you'd be here, Charlie. Why did

173

you do that if you didn't want my help?"

"I most certainly *do not* want your help. I only told you so that you'd have an idea of where I was if I got the chance to run. I didn't want you to worry. I suppose it's my own fault, isn't it? I should've known you'd worry *and* come straight here." He lowered his chin and fixed his glare on her. "You *drove* here, didn't you?"

She nodded.

"By yourself? In the dark?"

She nodded. "Just from Eau Claire." She forced her tone to be light, but there was no "just" about it. That drive had terrified her. She'd white-knuckled it all the way, but there was no reason Charlie needed to know that.

He shook his head. "You're lucky you didn't get yourself killed."

"I'm not that bad of a driver."

Charlie looked at her and cocked one eyebrow. "Are you sure you weren't followed?"

"Followed?" She glanced toward the shuttered front window, her stomach in knots all over again. The thought hadn't even occurred to her. What if this was all an elaborate scheme by the police to use her to flush Charlie out of his hiding spot? But that was ridiculous. No one knew she'd gotten off that train, and no one knew where she'd gone. "No, I don't think so. I'm pretty sure I've been the only idiot out driving on these roads in the pitch-black tonight. I think I would have noticed headlights behind me . . . or anywhere."

Charlie considered that for a moment, his head cocked to the side. Outrage and admiration fought for control over his sharp features. "Where did you get the car?"

"I bought it from the brother of the train station attendant in Eau Claire. I told him I needed to get to my sick mother in Minocqua as quickly as possible." She stuck her lower lip out in an exaggerated show of sadness and lowered her voice to a choked whisper. "She likely won't make it through the night."

"And he bought that load of manure?"

Vivian shrugged. "It helps if you can cry on cue."

Charlie shook his head. "I can't decide if you're brave or thoughtless."

"Neither," she said. "Both." She looked down at her hands and slowly unclenched the fingers. It was going to be fine, she told herself. She'd found him. He was okay. He was alive. "I just couldn't stay away, Charlie. Not after I spoke with Freddy, and he told me you were in trouble. How could I go on to Hollywood knowing that? I had to do something." She reached across the table and squeezed his hand. She smiled. "I'm just so glad you're all right. I've been going out of my mind the past two days with worry. Bernard was supposed to get you out of jail, and I hadn't heard anything. I called, and I couldn't get ahold of anyone." She stopped speaking suddenly, afraid that all the pent-up emotion would come out as a sob.

Charlie leaned forward. His voice was low and deadly quiet. "Bernard was supposed to what?"

"Get you out of jail. He told me on Sunday evening that he was going to talk to the police first thing Monday morning and explain that it was all a tragic accident."

"A tragic accident?"

"Yes, he was going to tell them that Hap leaned into those scissors and accidentally stabbed himself."

Charlie's eyebrows rose.

"I know. It doesn't make any sense."

"No, it doesn't." Charlie looked at her, frowning. "And your uncle never told the police anything, Viv."

"Of course he did. He told me he was going to fix everything."

Charlie shook his head.

"Why would he tell me that and not follow through?"

Charlie sat back in his chair. "To appease you."

"Appease me?" Vivian's stomach turned over.

"To get you to stop asking questions. To get you on that train to California and far away from here."

"But why?"

Charlie spread his hands on the table. He stared down at them for a moment. "He's covering for someone, and it was convenient for all of the suspicion to fall on me. It was convenient for him to let me rot in jail."

Vivian's mouth opened, but she could think of nothing to say. She'd had the same thought that evening in front of the radio. Bernard was covering for someone, the real murderer. And in order to do that, he'd lied to her. He had always intended for Charlie to take the fall.

"But Freddy said they had nothing on you. He said he'd have you out in no time. So what happened? Why did you run?"

Charlie stared at her for a long time — so long that Vivian's stomach clenched and she had time to regret the liverwurst sandwich she'd forced down on the drive. She had the sudden, terrifying realization that he was going to tell her that he'd done it after all, that he'd stabbed Hap in a fit of jealous rage. She stared back at him, willing it not to be true.

"They have evidence," he said.

"What evidence?" she whispered.

"Well, what they think is evidence, I suppose. Someone heard me telling you earlier in the day that I was going to kill Hap Prescott."

Vivian blinked. "What?" But even as she was questioning it, she had a glimmer of memory. He had said something like that, but he hadn't been serious. Had he?

"Who?"

"One of your aunts, I believe."

Oh no. "Not Great-Aunt Wilhelmina? She's deaf as a post."

"Apparently she's not. And your cousin, that whey-faced one, backed her up. She says she heard me threaten him too."

"Constance? But you didn't say that, did you? That you'd kill him?"

"I said something close enough."

Vivian let out a shaky breath. *I'll shut him up for good.* Isn't that what Charlie had said? But he hadn't meant it. Certainly, he hadn't meant it.

"That's premeditation, Viv. Murder 101. My fingerprints and Hap's are the only ones on those scissors."

"But you didn't do it."

Charlie stared at her, her unasked question hovering in the air between them: *Did you?*

"Of course I didn't do it. But I couldn't just sit there in that jail while I was framed for a murder I didn't commit."

Vivian stared at him for a moment, her heart pounding with relief. *He didn't do it. Of course he didn't do it.*

"But how did you manage it . . . the escape?"

Charlie leaned back in his chair. "It was surprisingly easy, actually. Once I was officially charged with murder, they decided to transfer me to the county jail. I'd made friends with the men escorting me. Not a bad lot, those two. I managed to convince them that I'd behave, so they agreed not to cuff me. About ten minutes in, I told them I had to go to the john something terrible. So they let me, pulled over at some lonely country service station. I hopped out the back window of the restroom and took a car parked out behind the service station and just drove away. I don't know how long it was before they realized they'd been had. Long enough for me to get a good head start, I suppose."

Vivian shook her head. "Took a car . . . You stole it?"

Charlie shrugged with one shoulder.

"Where is it?"

"I dumped that one not far away and picked up another. *That* car is a quarter of a mile further down the road, hidden under some brush. You passed right by it on your way in. You didn't see it?"

Vivian shook her head.

Charlie went on. "Baby Face Nelson spent time up at Lake Como. That was before the feds got him in, what, '34? Even the police had a sort of hero worship for the guy, and I think they lumped me in with that kind. The glamorous gangster type. Actually, I think they wanted to believe that I'm like a detective from the pictures."

Vivian could barely hear him through her swirling thoughts. How could he be so casual? What a mess. What a completely unmitigated mess. Suddenly, the dam burst. Every bit of frustration and terror and fear she'd been feeling for the past two days came out at once. This was insanity, and there was no way that any of it could end well. Charlie was wanted for murder. He was on the run. She had to prove he didn't do it. She had to, but how? She slumped and buried her face in her hands, sobbing.

Charlie pushed his chair back abruptly, and Vivian glanced up. He grabbed the gun and slid it toward himself over the tabletop. Charlie put a finger to his lips. There was a moment of silence, and then a metallic rattling came from just outside the door. Vivian's blood ran cold. She'd been followed.

Charlie stood, gun held at his side. Vivian started to get up, but he pushed her back down into the chair as he slunk to the back door. Glass crunched under his heel as he opened the door and slipped outside.

She didn't know what to do. She was frozen to the chair, afraid to think, to move, to speak. What if the police had followed her here? She'd signed Charlie's death warrant. She watched the open back door, her ears trained for any noise. A loud, rattling bang exploded outside. The breath stopped in her throat.

A man's shape appeared in the open doorway.

"It's me," Charlie said.

Vivian let her breath out in a *whoosh,* but she couldn't reply. She just stared at him in silence, waiting for him to tell her the cops had the place surrounded. The jig was up.

"Raccoon," he said, putting the gun on the counter with a sigh. "Rooting in the garbage cans, hoping some morsel was left behind by whoever had been here last."

Vivian jumped up and launched herself into his arms. He caught her ungainly mass of limbs and swept her up off her feet. He held her so tightly that she thought her ribs would crack. She latched her arms around his neck and lifted her face to his. He kissed her hard. It hurt, mashed her upper lip to her teeth, but she was glad for the pain. That pain meant they were alive; it meant they were here together.

"I'm glad you found me," he whispered into her hair. "I thought I might never see you again."

She leaned forward and kissed his neck . . . and took in the sharp smell of fear. Charlie was afraid. She rested her forehead against his chest and matched her breathing to his. He was alive, and she was here with him. That's all she would allow herself to think. Nothing else mattered at this moment. Then he carried her to the bed in the other room.

Vivian stared at the rustic cabin ceiling, one arm thrown over her forehead. She couldn't sleep, and she could tell by Charlie's shallow breathing next to her that he couldn't either. She spoke before she could second-guess herself.

"Let's get married," she said. "Now. Tonight."

The bedsprings squeaked as Charlie turned on his side to face her. She could feel his warm breath on her shoulder, but he didn't answer. She couldn't read his expression in the dim moonlight. Then the bed springs squeaked again as he rolled back onto his back and sighed with exasperation.

Her face grew warm with indignation and embarrassment. "You don't want to marry me?"

"You know I do."

"Then what's the problem?"

He reached up and touched her cheek with the tips of his fingers. "You and I both know what this is. An offer to save my hide . . . if it comes to that."

That's not the only reason, she thought but didn't say out loud. Charlie would never believe it. She'd spent the better part of the past two months rebuffing his proposals. Why would he believe she'd changed her mind so suddenly about something so important?

"I'm marrying you," she said in a tone that brooked no arguments. "I'll go out right now and find a justice of the peace."

"Wake him up and bring him groggy in

his nightshirt and tasseled cap to marry us in the middle of the night?"

Vivian nodded. She sat up and began trying to untangle herself from the sheets.

"This isn't a Laurel and Hardy short," he said.

Vivian stopped and glared at him, unwilling to admit she knew what he was getting at.

"It just doesn't work that way in reality, Viv. We'd have to get a license. There are residency requirements, blood tests, a waiting period . . . Even if I agreed to such a harebrained scheme, it's not possible tonight. Not even in the next week."

Vivian stuck her lower lip out and exhaled in exasperation. He was right. She did watch too many movies. She knew nothing of Wisconsin's marriage laws — or any state's marriage laws, really. Besides, she had no idea where to find a justice of the peace in the middle of the north woods. What would she do, go skulking about the countryside knocking on cottage doors? No, that wouldn't be suspicious at all. Not to mention all the bears lying in wait out there.

"Well, we have to do something," she said.

"Look, Freddy spoke to me too. He said that it was in our best interest to lock ourselves into wedded bliss as soon as possible, and I told him I've been trying to do that for months." Charlie smiled slightly. Even he could see the dark humor in the situation.

"What did he say to that?" Vivian asked quietly.

"Nothing. He just shook his head. The man knows you almost as well as I do, Viv."

"But now I'm offering to marry you," she said. "Quite willingly."

"And I'm very gently turning you down."

"Even if I'm forced to testify against you in a court of law? Even if I'm the one to send you to the electric chair?" She'd meant to sound firm, but her voice cracked, ruining the illusion.

"It won't come to that." He sounded like he believed that as he folded her into his strong arms. "And just know I'm not turning you down permanently. I have every intention of making good on your offer when all of this is settled. If I had the engagement ring with me, I'd put it on your finger myself."

He lowered his head and kissed her throat softly, his lips roving over the sensitive skin just beneath her earlobe. "Don't worry. I'll make an honest woman of you yet," he said. She nuzzled into him.

"And vice versa," she said. "You're prone

to finding trouble, Mr. Haverman. Once we're married, I plan to tie you down and keep you at home where you belong."

He laughed, his breath hot against her cheek. "Promise?"

CHAPTER FOURTEEN

Vivian left the cabin the following morning with Charlie's solemn vow that he would leave shortly after and not tell her where he'd gone. She worried someone had seen them, but people in the north woods had a long history of keeping their mouths shut. There had certainly been dubious activities taking place at that cabin during her father's heyday with Capone, and no one had ever said a word to the authorities.

That code of silence didn't hold true everywhere in Wisconsin though. She thought of John Dillinger's gang's shoot-out at the Little Bohemia Lodge and the murder of gangster Jake Zuta at the roadhouse outside Milwaukee while he picked out songs on the jukebox. People *had* talked there, and people *had* gotten killed. She shook her head. This train of thought wasn't helping.

Vivian didn't know where Charlie would

go, or how he would contact her again. For her own safety, he'd refused to give her any way to get in touch with him. Once she cleared everything up with the police, he'd find her. She just hoped she *could* clear everything up.

She made the five-hour drive to Oakhaven in four and a half. The answer to everything was there, after all. If she couldn't solve the mystery around Hap's death in the next day or so, she might never see Charlie again. What if the police found him before she could figure out what had really happened? No, she wouldn't let herself think of that possibility. Her nerves jangled and her lower back ached, but the old jalopy made it to Lake Geneva. She unfolded herself from the driver's side and stretched.

The sky was clear, and the late-morning sun was warm on her skin. The cicadas were already in good voice, their song a low hum among the trees.

The bushes along the path in front of her rustled and then Gwen emerged, dressed in her bathing suit, a towel slung over her arm. Gwen stopped short. She blinked, her eyes narrowed as if she couldn't believe what she was seeing. "Vivian?"

"In the flesh."

Gwen's eyes widened. "What are you doing here? What about California and your screen test?"

Vivian shrugged. "Postponed."

Gwen frowned and glanced over her shoulder at the house. "But what are you doing *here*?"

"Well, I'm going to find out who killed Hap and clear Charlie's name for starters."

Gwen's eyebrows rose. The towel slipped from her grasp, and she bent to retrieve it. When she straightened back up, her mouth was set in a grim line. "I don't think Father's going to like that."

"Why ever not? He doesn't want to know who killed Hap?" Vivian asked innocently.

Gwen glanced over her shoulder again at the house. Cicadas whirred in the trees from all directions. "You should probably go," she said.

"Go? I just got here."

"I . . ." Gwen's eyes darted again to the woods behind Vivian. Then she sighed and started over. "I'm sorry, Viv. This has been a terrible few days for all of us," she said.

Vivian eyed Gwen's bathing attire. So terrible that the girl was going out for a leisurely morning swim?

"I know it has. It's been terrible for me as well, Gwen. After all, my fiancé is on the run for a murder he didn't commit."

Gwen eyed her, the frown still curving her mouth downward. There was a shout from the dock.

"Gwen, come on. Shake a leg! I don't have all day!"

Vivian turned. A young man stood with his toes curled over the edge of the dock, his bronzed torso bared and his shoulders hunched toward the water. He pressed his hands together in front of him and mimed diving into the lake.

"Strapping boy," Vivian said.

"Marshall Wentworth," Gwen said, every exposed portion of her skin going pink under her early-summer tan. "He's . . . the neighbor. We swim together in the morning sometimes." She glanced over her shoulder again at Marshall.

"By all means, run along. Don't let me keep you," Vivian said.

Gwen looked at her for another long moment, brow furrowed, as if she was struggling to decide whether she should say something else. "See you later" was all she said before turning and heading toward the dock and Marshall Wentworth.

There had been perhaps a hundred people at that garden party, and Vivian had only known a handful personally. That meant she needed to whittle down the suspect list. Who had Hap known? Did he have any enemies? Was there someone who had wanted him dead? She knew virtually nothing about Hap's life in the eight years prior to his death.

Vivian gazed up at the house. It was splendid. A beautiful piece of Victorian gingerbread, frosted at the edge with intricate wooden lacework. Several of its ilk had burned to the ground in recent years — victims of bad wiring or lightning strikes. But Oakhaven was still standing, a testament to a family that would not quit, she thought, despite whether it should or not.

She opened the front door and stepped inside, pausing for a moment in the cool silence of the front hall. Both the parlor and the sitting room were empty. Someone stepped down into her line of vision from the stairway halfway up the hall. Aunt Adaline.

Adaline's mouth fell open. She snapped it shut and glided down the hallway. "Vivian. This is a surprise."

"Yes, the trip to California's been postponed."

"You haven't brought that man here, have you?" She looked over Vivian's shoulder as if she expected Charlie to burst through the door behind her.

That man? Vivian took a breath. She could not let Adaline get her ire up. "You mean Charlie? No, unfortunately, I have no idea where he is."

"He's run from the law, you know."

"Of course I know."

"But what are you doing here of all places?" Adaline's eyes darted around the hall as if she might find the answer somewhere in the pastoral scene of the wallpaper.

"I'm going to find out who really killed Hap."

Adaline blinked, but her face betrayed no emotion. "That's a job for the police," she said.

"And the police have the wrong man."

Adaline didn't answer.

"Charlie didn't kill anyone."

Adaline narrowed her eyes at Vivian and then glanced into the empty parlor, her mouth pressed into a thin, white line. "Constance heard him threaten Hap's life," she said. "I was standing next to her on the lawn when she gave her statement to the police."

"That simply isn't true."

"Are you calling Constance a liar?" Adaline glared at Vivian, her dark eyes narrowed in suspicion.

192

"No, I just think that Constance may be under a misapprehension about Charlie's intent." Vivian chose her words carefully.

Adaline looked down the hall toward the kitchen before turning slowly back toward Vivian. Adaline looked so much like Vivian's mother. The same brown eyes, same strawberry-blond hair turning to gray. But unlike her mother, Aunt Adaline was all razor-sharp edges. Julia Witchell had her moments of genuine motherly affection. There were no soft spots to Aunt Adaline — figuratively or literally. No warmth for anyone, not even her own children. Vivian had never seen Adaline offer the slightest scrap of affection to any of them.

Vivian thought of the first time she'd stayed overnight here as a child. It was the first time she'd slept anywhere other than her own home, and she'd been homesick. She'd gone up to her aunt, intending to give her the good-night peck on the cheek she gave her own mother and perhaps get a little comfort in the exchange. Aunt Adaline had given her the same stony look of contempt she'd given Vivian and then turned her face sharply away. "Little girls should be in bed at this hour," she'd said.

"I think you're the one who's under a misapprehension, Vivian."

"Meaning?"

Adaline leaned forward, her voice low. "Meaning just how well do you know that *friend* of yours? I think you might want to look a little deeper into his people, his background, where he comes from . . ."

Vivian felt the sting of the words as if she'd been slapped. So all of that at the garden party had been an act of exaggerated politeness. They'd tolerated Charlie's intrusion into their lives for a few hours in order not to cause a scene. They hadn't accepted him, and they never would. To them, Charlie was a lowlife. The kind of scum that would walk into a garden party and stab the first man that looked at him sideways — or threatened to take what belonged to him. Vivian clenched her hands at her sides to stop them from wrapping around her aunt's neck.

The thump of footfalls on the stairs caused both of them to look up. David and Lillian were coming down, David struggling with a large suitcase.

David set the suitcase on the floor at his feet. When he lifted his head, he spotted Vivian and his eyes widened. "I thought you'd gone to California."

"Change of plan," she said.

David nodded, but his forehead creased

in confusion. He was opening his mouth to ask another question when Adaline interrupted.

"Who's leaving?"

"Lillian," he said. "She's going back to the city. Her nerves can't take it."

"Her nerves?" There was the slightest tinge of disgust in Adaline's voice.

"Yes, Lillian's a gentle creature. Aren't you, dear?" He turned to his fiancée as she made her way down the last few steps. Her fingers were pressed to her temples.

"I'm afraid I have the worst headache."

"Prone to headaches," David said. "In times of stress."

Lillian's eyes snagged on Vivian before she moved toward the front of the house.

"I'm sorry to hear that," Adaline said. "You're driving her back to the city?"

"David offered, but I told him it's not necessary," Lillian said from the front door. "I'll take the train."

"I don't mind driving you," David said.

"That's ridiculous. A two-hour trip into the city and then a two-hour back here? I can't ask that of you. I'll be fine."

"We can get a driver," Adaline said.

"No, no, really. Stop fussing." Lillian winced and put a hand to her temple again.

"David, it's not right. You'll drive her."

"Mother, will you listen for once? She said it's not necessary."

Adaline blinked. Vivian saw her aunt's jaw clench. It was the same reaction her mother would have had to such insolence in mixed company.

"Goodbye," David said to Vivian. "I'll return shortly."

"Goodbye, Lillian. It was lovely to have met you. I hope we get a chance to catch up soon." Vivian said.

Lillian nodded and forced a faint smile before leading David out the door.

Vivian stood next to a silent Adaline. They both looked at the closed front door for a moment in silence. Vivian could feel the anger coming from Adaline like heat waves radiating from a radiator.

"Lillian seems like a nice girl," Vivian said.

"I only just met the girl," Adaline said, her voice measured and impersonal. "She seems to be of good stock . . . went to boarding school in France. I've heard of the Dacres, of course, but have never met any of the family."

The perfect nonanswer, Vivian thought.

"Her family isn't from Chicago?"

"New York and Paris, I believe."

Well, la-di-da, Vivian thought. Lillian was perfect. If Adaline had made a list of credentials for a potential daughter-in-law, Lillian would check every box. So why was animosity rising off Aunt Adaline in waves?

"And she and David are marrying after only three weeks?"

"It's not as unusual as you might think," Adaline said, pursing her lips. Then she lowered her voice. "Does your mother know what's happened?"

Mother, Vivian thought. So Adaline had pulled out the dagger she knew would strike home. Vivian knew the next thing out of Adaline's mouth would be a threat to track Julia Witchell down in Washington and inform her of Hap's murder and Charlie's arrest. As if Vivian were still a naive seventeen-year-old and would be cowed by such threats.

Before she could respond, the front door opened again and David came striding back in. "Mother, a word?"

Vivian held Adaline's icy gaze for another moment, then turned to David with a smile. "Excuse me," Vivian said, stepping politely down the hallway as David and Adaline moved into the parlor. She heard the whispered beginnings of an apology before she walked out of earshot. *Poor David,* she thought. He wasn't known for his even keel, and today he seemed very much off-kilter.

You'd have to be to rail at someone as formidable as Aunt Adaline.

CHAPTER FIFTEEN

There was nothing for it. Much as she never wanted to step into the game room again, Vivian would have to go back to where Hap had been stabbed. She glanced over her shoulder to make sure she was alone in the hall, then hitched in a breath and pushed the pocket doors apart. The drapes were closed and only let in one bright slit of sunshine. Vivian took one small step forward and waited for her eyes to adjust before entering all the way. She turned and locked the doors behind her. It wouldn't do to be surprised poking around a crime scene.

She surveyed the room. The rug where Hap had fallen had been taken away, exposing the polished hardwood floor underneath, but that was the only change as far as she could tell. Nothing about this quiet room made it seem like the place where a man had lost his life. Balls were scattered over the green felt surface of the billiard table, as if play had just stopped in the middle of a game. She reached out and touched her fingertips to the cue ball, rolling it back and forth under her palm, cool and smooth.

The clippings that Charlie had mentioned were still on the desk, little rectangles of newsprint scattered over the blotter. She bent down to survey them and sucked in her breath. Her own face smiled back at her. Vivian's eyes skittered about the dozens of photos and articles clipped from newspapers and magazines. She brushed her fingertips over the papers, separating them. That was her at the Blackhawk with her blue velvet backless number. There was the one of her and Graham from Chez Paree just after Marjorie Fox's murder, the picture where she looked out of sorts and Graham had his hand out to shield them from the photographer's lens — but with his fingers deftly splayed so that their faces could still be seen. Charlie said that Hap had been looking at these just before his death. Had he clipped them himself?

She glanced about her, but the scissors, of course, were gone. The police would have taken them, since the scissors seemed to be the murder weapon. The thought sent a chill up her spine. She'd have to call Freddy and ask him about what the police knew — if anything at all.

The game room didn't feel especially melancholy or tinged with something foul, like the actors' lounge at WCHI had felt after Marjorie Fox's murder. There had been a heaviness to the air in that room, a certain charge that rang in her bones. Here, Vivian felt nothing. She knew she needed time to process all of this — to think everything through. But there just wasn't any time. Each minute wasted was another minute the police had to catch up with Charlie. She didn't want to think about what would happen if they found him.

Vivian turned in a slow circle, surveying the room, and her eyes fell on the deer head mounted on the wall behind the desk — the majestic eight-point buck stared down at her with glassy eyes. Then her eyes slid down to the wooden case underneath the buck. A gun case, she presumed. She pulled the latch up, but the case was locked.

Then she walked slowly back the way she'd come, her fingertips trailing along the floor-to-ceiling bookcase that ran the entire length. Then she stopped. She turned. *The hidden door.* How could she forget? She scanned the shelves, finally spotting that vertical line running down all of the shelves, making it so the two halves of each shelf didn't quite line up. There was a door hidden here — a door camouflaged to look like part of the built-in bookcase, not for any nefarious reason but for the decorative purpose of not breaking up the wall of bookshelves with a doorway. She ran her fingertips down that vertical stripe and found the latch. She and David had pretended this door led to a magical fairyland when they were children. She pushed the latch, and the door opened upon the less-than-magical back stairs.

The police had not been back because they thought they had their man. There were eyewitnesses to the crime, and people who had heard Charlie's threat of violence. It seemed to be an open-and-shut case.

But what if someone had stabbed Hap and disappeared within seconds by taking this hidden door to the stairs? That someone would have needed to know this secret door existed. That likely meant a member of either the family or the house staff. It was plausible, she thought. Not likely. But plausible.

Then she heard voices. Male voices, coming from Bernard's study next door.

Vivian backtracked down the hallway, listening for David and Adaline in the parlor, but she heard nothing. *Apology accepted,* she thought. She turned and pressed her ear to Bernard's study door, but the voices she had heard were now silent. She knocked. There was no response for a full five seconds before Bernard answered in his self-assured voice.

"Who is it?"

"It's Vivian."

She pressed her ear to the door again and heard the sound of a chair sliding back on a rug.

"May I come in?" she said, placing her hand on the knob.

"Just a —"

She turned the doorknob and found it unlocked. When she stuck her head through the door, she spied Bernard half standing at his desk. He was holding a sheaf of papers, which he dropped as he caught sight of her.

"Am I interrupting something?" She glanced around the room. The door between the office and the sitting room was open. She hadn't heard footfalls on the parquet floor of someone scurrying off. Her eyes fell on the small cathedral-style radio perched on the edge of Bernard's desk. Perhaps the voices she had heard had been the radio. Perhaps he'd snapped it off when she

203

knocked. Perhaps her nerves were playing tricks on her.

"No, of course not." Bernard leaned forward on his hands and lowered his head briefly. He was breathing heavily, as if he'd done more than just stand from his chair as she entered. Then he looked up at her, concerned. "What are you doing here? Is something wrong?"

Vivian almost laughed at the inanity of the question. *Is something wrong?*

"Nothing at all," she said. "Except that my fiancé is accused of a murder he didn't commit."

Bernard stared at her for a long moment. Vivian had spent nine summers here as a child, but she knew Uncle Bernard even less than she knew Aunt Adaline. He'd only come up to Oakhaven on the weekends, and even then had little to do with Vivian or his own children. He hadn't had much to do with Adaline either, as Vivian could recall. It wasn't an unhappy marriage; rather, Vivian got the sense that they tolerated each other. They had their own interests, and their orbits rarely crossed even when they were under the same roof.

Vivian knew her mother had sent her to Oakhaven those summers because she saw her sister's family as a civilizing influence.

Vivian's father spoiled her, her mother thought. He doted on Vivian, gave her too much attention, let her run wild. Spending time among the stilted dynamics of the Lang family had taught young Vivian civility, yes, and also the delicate skill of swallowing any and all feelings as they occurred lest she cause an uncomfortable scene. Vivian soon learned that crying after scraping her knee got her nothing but a disapproving stare. Stiff upper lips were the order of the day around Oakhaven.

She didn't know how to read the man before her. She stared into gray-blue eyes slightly magnified behind the lenses of his spectacles. His color was high — perhaps from the surprise of finding her at his door? Or perhaps he'd just spent too much time in the warm June sun. Bernard picked up the sheaf of papers again and tidied them. Then he sat down and motioned for her to do the same. "Fiancé? You didn't tell me you were marrying the fellow."

"Would that have made any difference?" She sat. The seat was warm. From someone that had just been sitting there, or from the morning sunlight streaming through the open window?

Bernard pushed the papers aside and leaned forward, resting his elbows on the desk in front of him. "What happened to your trip to California?"

"Uncle Freddy, Charlie's lawyer, sent me a telegram while I was on the train."

"So you know that your . . . fiancé . . . has escaped police custody."

She nodded. "I came back to help."

Bernard scowled at her. "How can you help?"

Vivian swallowed. She'd come this far; she had to press on. "Why didn't you go to the police like you said you would?"

"I did go to the police," he said, looking down at his hands. "I told them Hap's death was a terrible accident."

"And?"

"And they thought I was trying to cover for family."

"They didn't believe you?"

He shook his head and glanced toward the closed hall door behind her. He lowered his voice. "They said they had evidence. Several people heard Charlie threaten to kill Hap, Vivian."

She swallowed. *Aunt Wilhelmina. Constance.* "But that's not evidence."

He shrugged. "It's premeditated intent . . . enough to start building a case. They called in the district attorney. He filed charges. And then Charlie ran. It's as good as stamping 'guilty' on his forehead, isn't it?" He pulled something from under the stack of papers on his desk and slid it toward Vivian. It was the front page of a newspaper, with Charlie's picture under a headline that read MANHUNT!

Vivian stared down at Charlie's mug shot, rendered in cheap black-and-white newsprint. Charlie looked hunted, haunted, with dark circles under his eyes. He looked like a criminal. And if all she knew of him was this photograph in the newspaper, that's exactly what she'd think he was. Everyone in the county had seen this mug shot by now.

"No one saw Charlie stab Hap," she said, sliding the newspaper back across the desk.

"Except you."

Vivian shook her head, unable to speak for a moment. Anger welled up in her. She clenched her hands in her lap. "I didn't see anything," she finally said. "I jumped to conclusions."

"By the evidence presented. You told the police what you saw, Vivian."

She felt sick.

"He says he didn't do it, and I believe him."

Bernard stood and walked off toward the window on the far side of the room. It

207

looked onto the side yard and ran all the way to the floor. Vivian watched a robin busily yank an earthworm from the thick turf, stretching its long, lanky body until it snapped.

"I understand that you want to believe that. But if Charlie didn't kill Hap, who did?" he asked, glancing over his shoulder at her.

Vivian opened her mouth and closed it again. She swallowed. "I was going to ask you the same question, quite frankly." *Are you covering for someone? Family, as the police suspected?*

"I'm sorry all this has happened," Bernard said. "Truly I am, but he's only hurting his case by running, you know. And I worry about you getting yourself mixed up with someone who's capable of running from the police. Capable of doing God knows what."

Vivian gripped the sides of the chair and squeezed. *God knows what?* Someone who's capable of murder — that's what Bernard meant. Someone of a lower class, someone of the criminal element.

"You don't know where Charlie is, do you?" Bernard asked, turning back to her.

She shook her head. That was the truth as of this moment.

Perhaps Cal would be able to get Charlie a message, she thought. And perhaps that's exactly what Bernard was after. Perhaps he was angling to get Vivian to lead him and the police right back to Charlie so that they could pin a murder on him. Clearly, Bernard felt the same way about Charlie as Adaline did. People like Charlie didn't belong at places like Oakhaven, with people like the Langs. It wasn't beyond the realm of possibility that Bernard would offer Charlie as the sacrificial lamb to make this whole nasty business go away. Charlie wasn't family — and he could never hope to be, according to what Adaline had said in the hallway. Vivian didn't know what to do. Who to trust.

She swallowed and stared at the swirling vine pattern of the rug. Her eyes fell on a little brown shell lying on the floor. Someone had tracked a cicada in from the woods. Those shells clung to everything. She thought of running into Hap on the path in the woods, the cicadas whirring around them. He'd been so alive. That had only been three days ago, and it already seemed like a lifetime ago.

"Where is Hap?" she asked, her voice raspy with emotion. When Bernard didn't answer, she looked up at him. His eyebrows drew together over the bridge of his nose in concern. She realized the phrasing of her question had been odd. Perhaps he was worried the stress of everything had unhinged her somehow. She pictured Hap's body on a slab at a mortuary somewhere, pale blue with death. A shiver crawled up her spine. She shook her head and tried again.

"There's going to be some sort of service, I presume. His death was so . . . abrupt. We parted on bad terms, and I regret that. I'd like to pay my respects."

Bernard nodded. "There will be a service, of course, but arrangements have not been made as of yet with the pending . . . situation." He reached out and patted her hand, then cleared his throat. "I think Hap knew how you felt about him, Vivian," he said. "I don't think he bore you any ill will."

Vivian sighed. A meaningless platitude. Uncle Bernard knew nothing of what she and Hap had shared. He had no idea how Hap had felt about her. The problem was, neither had she. Not really. And now she'd never know.

CHAPTER SIXTEEN

Bernard and Adaline wanted her to leave, and there had to be a reason for that. Something was going on here. Vivian snuck up the back stairs, unsure of how much time she had. Adaline was probably composing the telegram to her mother right at this moment. Adaline and Bernard wouldn't remove her from the house with force, but they'd certainly ice her out — make it so uncomfortable that she'd leave of her own accord. In fact, she was already so uncomfortable that she wanted to do that right now. But first, she'd poke around.

The bedroom Hap had used the evening before the party had been thoroughly cleaned. Vivian wandered around for a few minutes, picking up objects: hairbrushes, mirrors, the pad of writing paper on the desk by the window. No personal items of his remained. Where had they gone? Had the police taken them? Had Adaline had the staff pack them up and put them in storage? Vivian pulled back the curtains, shook them out. She lifted every corner of the mattress, looked under the bed, in the corners of the closet. There was nothing to find.

She sat on the edge of the bed for a minute and closed her eyes, trying to find some sense of Hap's presence in the room, but detected nothing other than the scents of furniture polish and clean sheets. She stood with a sigh and smoothed the counterpane. After giving the room one last lingering look, she closed the door quietly behind her. She started down the hall toward her own room but then paused at the next door down the hall.

Vivian rested her hand on the cut-glass doorknob and wiggled. It was unlocked. She opened the door and peeked in. Her eyes searched the cluttered room, but she was unable to assign an occupant until she spotted the bureau near the window. Every available surface was taken up with bottles and pillboxes. This bedroom was occupied by someone in alarmingly failing health, or someone who wanted it to appear they were. *Constance.*

Her cousin's lack of vigor had always intrigued Vivian, but it seemed less a physical malady than a mental one. Constance had been active and sun-bronzed like the rest of her cousins in Vivian's earliest memories at Oakhaven. She'd had tennis lessons, jumped off the dock with the lot of them, and won swimming contests to the floating raft. She'd been healthy enough to get married and give birth to two children. Vivian had never discussed her cousin's health with anyone who knew, but she surmised that somewhere along the way Constance had gotten ill and realized that it garnered her more attention than she'd ever received in good health. There was always the outside chance that Constance truly was wasting away, Vivian thought, but her odds were on it all being manufactured.

Vivian glanced down the empty hallway and stepped lightly into the room, heading straight for the bureau. The blue Bromo-Seltzer bottle stood out among the clutter — an aid for the pleasant relief of stomach upset, nervous tension, headache. She had her own bottle in her toiletry bag. The radio jingle ran through her mind: *Bromo-Seltzer, Bromo-Seltzer, Bromo-Seltzer* chanted like a train picking up speed.

She picked up a small package lying next to the distinctive blue bottle. Dr. Shoop's Restorative Nerve Pills — relief of acute constipation, nervousness, biliousness, sleeplessness, trembling, hysteria, spasms, conditions of the brain and nervous system. Chase's Tonic Tablets — a tonic for the sick, convalescent, overworked. *Overworked?* Constance had never worked a day in her life. *Snake oil,* Vivian thought with the shake of her head.

Vivian passed her fingertips over the brown glass bottle with the yellow label. Ironized Yeast — builds strength fast. There were a dozen more bottles like this. Vivian's eyes skimmed over them and then snagged on a small, clear glass bottle almost hidden in the back. She reached over and plucked it from the bureau. The white paper label said VERONAL in rusty red print, with flowers blooming from the end of the *V* and the *L*. Vivian squinted at the long scientific name underneath, followed by *Descriptive name: Barbital.*

Barbital? Barbiturates?

"It helps me sleep."

Vivian whirled around. The glass bottle slipped from her hand and fell to the floor, landing on the rug with a muffled thump.

"It hasn't helped much in the past few days." Constance glanced down at the bottle and back up at Vivian. She stood for a moment just inside the doorway as if she wasn't entirely convinced she should enter her own

214

room. Then she stepped forward, her legs moving jerkily. She walked to the edge of the bed and sat, staring down at her hands in her lap.

She looked terrible. Wan, fragile, and her skin — pale even in the best circumstances — seemed translucent. Vivian could clearly see the delicate tangle of blue veins in her cousin's temple.

"Are you feeling well, Constance?" Vivian stooped and picked up the bottle and replaced it on the bureau.

Constance shook her head. She raised a hand to her brow and shaded her eyes as if she were outside on a bright, sunlit day instead of in a dim bedroom with the drapes drawn. She squinted at Vivian.

"It's really you, isn't it, Vivian?" Her voice was a whisper. She held her fingers out as if she wanted to touch Vivian to verify her existence.

Vivian nodded. "Yes, it's me."

"Oh, thank God." Constance's body went limp with relief.

"Is something wrong?"

"Everything's wrong," she said. She closed her eyes. Vivian thought perhaps Constance had fallen asleep sitting up, but then her eyelids fluttered open again. "I thought I was seeing things again."

"Seeing things?"

Constance waved her hand dismissively.

"Are you all right?"

"No," Constance said. For a moment, it seemed as if she might say more, but she didn't speak. Seeing the state her cousin was in, Vivian suddenly wasn't so sure of her assessment of Constance's nerves being a product of her own imagination.

"Would you like to talk about it?"

Constance shook her head. "I'd like to sleep." Her voice was plaintive, full of desperation, as if it were a wish she desperately wanted and knew she could not fulfill. She looked longingly at the bottle of Veronal that Vivian had replaced on the bureau. "Sleep, and then I need to pack. I'm heading to Europe on the first boat I can get."

"Oh?" Panic fluttered in Vivian's chest like a butterfly trapped against her breastbone.

"Yes, I've decided to meet Gil in Paris."

"But aren't you a witness? There'll be an inquest."

"I'm not well. The police said I could go," Constance said defensively. "They have my statement. I promised to come back if I'm needed."

Yes, her statement. That damning statement about Charlie. Vivian eyed her cousin.

216

But would the police trust the word of someone so obviously unstable? Constance had just said she'd been seeing things, hadn't she? Would it be so far off to assume she could also have imagined arguments that hadn't happened? Threats that hadn't been made in earnest?

"Constance, about that —"

Constance shook her head. "I can't. I can't speak of it."

"But . . ."

"Sleep. Just let me sleep, at least for a few minutes."

Vivian nodded. Constance was not in her right mind. That much was clear. Vivian looked long and hard into her cousin's face, but saw only fatigue, both of the physical and the mental variety. Vivian stood and walked to the door.

"Wait," Constance said. "Are you staying the night?"

"I'm not sure."

"Would you . . ." Her dark eyes were focused on the door that connected her room with the next bedroom — where Hap had slept. "Would you mind switching rooms with me?"

"Switching rooms?"

"Only for the night. I can't sleep here with the constant reminder that Hap's never coming back to that room. Please?" Constance looked so miserable, Vivian thought. What would it hurt to give her a little peace of mind?

"Of course," Vivian said.

"Good. I'll have the housekeeper switch everything as soon as possible. Thank you."

As Vivian turned to go, Constance rose from the bed and stood at the bureau, speaking again softly.

"What was that, Constance?"

Constance looked up, startled. "What?"

"Did you say something?"

"Oh. No. Nothing, Vivian. Thank you."

Vivian nodded, taking a last look around the room. Constance *had* spoken. It had sounded like she'd said *There aren't any ghosts in Paris.* Vivian shivered. Yes, there were certainly ghosts here. Not the literal ghosts of the dearly departed, and certainly not the ghost of the recently murdered Hap. But the air fairly prickled with unresolved feelings and emotions: resentment, longing, hatred, fear. She could feel them in all corners, could feel them closing in and constricting the air.

Vivian wished she could just run off to Paris. Avoid the ghosts — her own and everyone else's. But they were all around her, and she had to sort her way through them to get to the truth.

Over the course of the afternoon, it became clear that the entire family was stonewalling her. They were all content to believe that Charlie had murdered Hap in cold blood. She wasn't any closer to solving anything, and now Charlie was being hunted. Everyone in Wisconsin would know his face, as soon as they opened their newspapers.

She walked down the hall to the next bedroom. It was the one she'd always stayed in as a child. She opened the door and peered inside. It had been redecorated since she'd been here last — brightened, a new floral wallpaper installed. The window was open slightly, the breeze rustling the gauzy white curtains. She made her way to that window and gazed out upon the deep-blue expanse of lake. A sailboat floated past, and closer to shore, two figures lounged on the wooden raft, their bare, tanned legs intertwined. Gwen and Marshall.

Gwen, Vivian thought. Gwen had said she felt responsible for bringing Hap to the party. She was further responsible for the animosity that had cropped up among family members, and for getting Charlie accused of murder. She really had set everything in motion, hadn't she? Vivian could use that kernel of guilt to ask Gwen to help her. Gwen might be able to get the guest list for the garden party. It wasn't much to go on, but it was a start.

In order to do any of this, Vivian needed to get Gwen alone, and what better place than out in the middle of the lake where no one could interrupt or overhear? Vivian had left her bags in the car, but maybe she'd left something here from that summer eight years ago that would do the trick. Her eyes fell on the trunk at the foot of the bed. Everything else had changed, but this trunk remained the same. She lifted the lid and began rifling through it. After a few moments, she triumphantly held up a shapeless piece of faded red-and-white wool. It was saggy and belted and hopelessly out of fashion, but there was no time to waste.

She dressed in record time and snuck back downstairs. But by the time she reached the dock, there was no sign of either Gwen or Marshall. The raft where she'd spied them not ten minutes ago was now an empty square of white in the distance. She held a hand up to her eyes and scanned the water. There were no heads bobbing, no splashing. Vivian sighed. She'd missed her chance — for the moment anyway.

She looked down at the faded suit she

wore. It was a little tight around the hips. She'd changed a bit in the past eight years, but not much. It would probably hold up to a swim, and maybe a swim could help her think. She glanced back at the silent house and then dove in.

The water was just as Vivian remembered, slightly chill and faintly earthy tasting. She swam hard for the wooden dock about one hundred yards out. It took longer than she expected. When she got there, she pulled herself onto the sun-warmed boards and sat panting. She was out of shape. She stretched her arms overhead and looked off toward the shore.

This raft was anchored halfway between Oakhaven and the neighboring estate, which was now owned by the Wentworths. They hadn't lived here during the summers of Vivian's childhood. At that time, the sprawling property had been owned by a man named Mills, flush with railroad money. He was an older unmarried man, if she recalled correctly, with no children Vivian's age — and certainly no virile young men with which to share morning ablutions.

Vivian doubted morning swims was all Gwen shared with Marshall, and she didn't blame her. *Oh, to be seventeen and carefree again,* she thought, lying back on the warm, wooden boards of the raft. Though at seventeen, Vivian had been far from care-free. She closed her eyes and bathed in the summer sunshine for a moment. The drone of the cicadas was soothing white noise that lulled her into drowsiness. She had almost drifted off when the skin on her arms prickled. She was being watched.

Opening her eyes, Vivian sat up, resting her weight on one elbow. She scanned the shoreline as nonchalantly as she could. A few mallards floated on the water nearby. One dove, flipping neatly upside down, and she watched his tail feathers waving in the open air, his webbed feet kicking.

Vivian squinted to see further down the shore. The lakeshore path wound its way along the edge of the water just beyond a grove of trees. There was a flash of white among the dark tree trunks. Yes, it was a person. But perhaps just a passerby. The lakeshore path was open to the public, after all.

But the sense of being watched didn't abate. The hairs stood up on the back of her arms. The flash of white grew larger. Someone was coming toward her out of the trees. Charlie?

No, it was a smaller figure. A woman, perhaps, but the face was in shadow.

Then there was a shout from down the shore. "Vivian! Vivian!"

Vivian turned away from the figure, shielding her eyes with her hand.

Gwen stood on the dock, waving her arms over her head to get Vivian's attention. When Vivian turned back to the spot in the trees, the woman had disappeared. She sighed.

"Yes?" she called back to Gwen.

"Telephone! Long distance!"

Vivian gave an exaggerated shrug, lifting her shoulders high. She was one hundred yards from shore. Surely Gwen didn't expect her to swim back at this moment to take a phone call. She cupped her hands on either side of her mouth and yelled, "Take a message, I'll call them back!"

Gwen shook her head and waved her arms frantically. "Swim back!"

Vivian pushed herself to her feet and dove into the water, staggering onto the shore a few minutes later. Gwen held a towel open for her.

"Surely, whoever it is hasn't held on the line this whole time," Vivian said.

"They have. It sounds serious."

"Who is it?"

"A friend of yours. Imogene, I think she said her name was."

Imogene? Vivian wrapped the towel around her shoulders and hurried to the house, dripping. The receiver lay on the hall table.

Vivian's heart thumped painfully in her chest. She took a deep breath and picked up the receiver. Before she could even say hello, Imogene had already started talking. Her voice was a whisper. "I need to warn you. Mr. Langley is extremely upset with you."

"Mr. Langley is upset," Vivian repeated. It took a moment for the words to register. Mr. Langley. The station. The trip to California. Vivian's stomach dropped. She'd never called anyone at the station. She'd never explained anything to anyone, not even Graham. She'd been too preoccupied with Charlie since getting that telegram.

"Yes, about your aborting the trip to California without telling him. He's been fuming in his office for fifteen minutes. Then he finally calmed down long enough to tell me to get you on the line. So I did. You have to tell me all about this as soon as you can. Oh no, here he comes . . ." Imogene switched to her professional, nasally secretary voice. "Hold for Mr. Langley please."

"Vivian." Mr. Langley's voice was gruff

224

and tremulous with barely controlled anger.

"Yes, Mr. Langley, let me explain. There's been a family emergency."

"That's what Graham told me. Said it was serious enough that you rushed off the train at Kansas City."

Thank heaven for Graham, she thought. He had at least deflected some of the fallout. "My mother . . ." she heard herself say. She had no idea what tripe was about to come out of her mouth, but thankfully Langley interrupted.

"I'm not interested in the details, but I'm not happy with you not calling and explaining the situation yourself, young lady."

Vivian cringed. *Young lady.* So it would be the disapproving-father routine.

"Yes, I'm terribly sorry about that. Things have been a whirlwind, and I guess it slipped my mind."

"I don't know what's really happening in your life, but be sure you're on that train Friday evening," he said. "If you aren't, well, I don't think I'll be able to keep Mr. Marshfield interested in your sponsorship of his company's products. And you can kiss any ideas about having anything to do with any movie version of *The Darkness Knows* goodbye."

"Yes, I'll be on the Friday train. I promise," she said automatically, and before she could qualify that statement, Mr. Langley had hung up. She replaced the receiver and stood staring down at the telephone. Today was Wednesday. She'd just promised to be on the train Friday evening. There was almost no way this would turn out the way she wanted. She was sure of that.

Her hands shook as she pulled the towel tighter around her. She heard the click of the radio in the den, the static noise of someone moving the dial between stations. Gwen? She hurried down the hall and peered around the open doorway. Not Gwen, but a man with his back to her. The man straightened as he found a radio program he could tolerate, and the sun glinted off his coppery-blond hair. David. She was in no mood to speak with anyone right now. She stepped backward out of sight, but not in time.

"Viv? Is that you?"

She stepped back into the doorway. David held a pipe in one hand, stuffing tobacco into it with the other.

"Everything all right?" he said. "I couldn't help but overhear your telephone conversation."

"It's fine," Vivian said, watching as David folded the cover of a matchbook back and pulled a match from the pack. He pulled it across, but the match glanced off without lighting. He frowned and repeated the process with a new match. "Since when have you smoked a pipe?"

David glanced up and touched the match to the tobacco, inhaling several times until it lit. Then he exhaled and stared at her through the cloud of smoke.

"Since Father said it would improve my image in the boardroom," he said with a shrug of one shoulder. He shook the match out, and then it slipped from his fingers and tumbled to the rug. "Damn," he said, snatching it up quickly and rubbing at the sooty mark it left.

Vivian pulled the towel tighter around her. The parlor was bathed in sunshine, but the air felt dour. The whole house felt like it was under a pall. A newsman chattered from the radio about impressions from the king and queen's visit. Vivian listened for a moment, thinking of her mother. Julia Witchell was in Washington now but would be returning soon. Adaline's threat to contact her must have been just that, because if she had, Vivian would have heard from her mother by now. *Thank God for small favors,* she thought.

"You've delivered Lillian to the station?"

"Yes," he said, frowning. "I tried to get her to change her mind, but she was set on going back."

"Do you know where Gwen's gone?" Vivian asked.

"Off with that neighbor boy somewhere, I assume." David sat in the armchair closest to the radio.

"And Aunt Adaline? Uncle Bernard?"

"Off somewhere as well. Everyone seems in a big hurry to get away today. Except me and you." David leaned back in the chair, stretched his legs out in front of him, and crossed them at the ankles. "Why *are* you here, Viv?"

He sounded offhand, but Vivian knew it wasn't a casual question. She weighed the pros and cons of telling the truth. She'd already told Adaline and Bernard what she was after. Why bother lying to David?

"I'm going to find out who killed Hap," she said.

David lowered his chin and studied her. "I'm sorry to say that most everyone in this house — hell, everyone in Lake Geneva — believes Charlie killed Hap."

"Do you believe that?"

David puffed on the pipe without answering.

Vivian felt her face grow warm with

indignation. "Well, I don't believe it," she said. "And I'm going to prove it."

"*You* are? Little old you?" He pointed the pipe at her and then smiled slightly. "Still full of piss and vinegar, aren't you? I always liked that about you. You were always willing to fight — literally — even as a little tyke."

Vivian said nothing.

"I can't imagine my parents are too pleased about what you're up to."

"They aren't," she said. "They've told me as much. Charlie's guilty, and I'm wasting my time coming to the defense of someone like him."

David's smile faded. "I'm inclined to agree," he said, then held his hands up in a placating gesture when he saw her bristle. "I just mean that you shouldn't have come back here." He paused and removed the pipe from his lips as if he wanted to say something else, but then changed his mind.

"Then you'll be happy to know that I'm not staying."

Vivian turned on her heel to go, but David's quiet voice stopped her in her tracks.

"I don't hold anything against you for what Charlie may have done, you know," he said. "I don't think any of us do, despite what my parents may have told you. I don't want to run you off, Viv. This is my home too, and I say you can at least stay the night. I think Gwen would back me up on that."

"But Adaline . . . and everyone else?"

"I'll handle everyone else," he said gravely. Then a smile curved the corners of his mouth. "And if I were the guilty party in this affair, Viv, I'd sure as hell want someone like you in my corner."

CHAPTER SEVENTEEN

Vivian went looking for Freddy, but he wasn't at the boarding house in town. The landlady said he'd gone into the city for the day and that he may not be back until morning. Vivian was loath to return to the strained atmosphere at Oakhaven, so she had a hamburger and sat on the beach for hours, throwing rocks into the water and thinking things through. There had to be something she was missing.

The only suspects at this point were members of her own family, and it was ludicrous to think that any of them could have run Hap through with a pair of scissors in the middle of a garden party. Poison or shooting a person from a distance was one thing, but stabbing? That kind of visceral killing took an abundance of passion, and none of her relatives seemed to have a passionate bone in their bodies — barring Gwen and Adaline. But surely neither of them was strong enough or foolish enough to stab a man with a pair of scissors. Maybe if that man had been a stranger and had threatened them bodily in some way, but Hap? A man Gwen had grown up with and Adaline had known over half his life?

The one person with a clear motive was Charlie, of course, but the jealousy angle just didn't ring true for Vivian. He'd shown jealousy in the past, but never like this. He may have knocked Hap's lights out with a right cross, but he would never have stabbed him in the stomach.

Beyond all of that, the thought Vivian's mind kept returning to was how odd everyone was acting since she'd returned. None of them behaved like people who'd just had a death in the family. No, not just a death, she amended. A *murder.* A murder of a family member under their own roof, no less. There were no signs of mourning, and not so much as a sniffle or a somber turn of phrase from any of them — not even Gwen, and she was the softest of the lot. Why? The only answer was one that Vivian couldn't accept. They were all implicated somehow, and if they all hung together, she'd never get to the bottom of things and clear Charlie.

Vivian drove back to the house after dark and snuck in through the back door. There was light in the front parlor and music from the radio. She'd agreed to stay the night, mostly to spite Adaline and Bernard, but now, tiptoeing up the creaky back stairs, she wasn't so sure she'd made the right choice. She knew that no one in the family would confront her directly. No, they would give her the infamous Lang cold shoulder, icy politeness until she couldn't stand it anymore and left of her own accord. They were all hiding something and using Charlie as a smoke screen. She knew she was only allowed to stay because it would seem suspicious if they put her out.

She paused at the hidden door to the game room. A faint yellow light shone through the cracks in the door, but she didn't hear any movement from inside.

Vivian opened the door to her bedroom and realized only after she did that it was no longer her room, since she had agreed to switch with Constance. The curtains were open in the darkened room, and Vivian could clearly see Constance's form outlined on the bed in the moonlight. Her brow was smoothed in sleep. Vivian paused long enough to hear the wheezing of a deep, drugged snore.

As Vivian closed the door again, her eyes fell on the dinner tray on the side table. It had not been touched. God willing, Constance would sleep through to tomorrow morning and regain some of her coherence in the process.

Vivian went to the room next door and entered. Her blue suitcase and matching hatbox sat near the bureau. She sat down at the vanity and removed her earrings. Constance's bottles and potions were gone, the vanity top bare. Vivian placed the earrings on the eyelet covering and sighed. She looked at herself in the mirror for a long moment. She wasn't any closer to clearing Charlie's name, and things weren't looking good. Her thoughts drifted to Mr. Langley. If she didn't fix this and get back to her duties at WCHI, she'd lose her job too.

Vivian didn't need her job to support herself, of course. With the inheritance from her father, she had more money than she knew what to do with. Still, panic welled in her at the thought. If she didn't have her career, what did she have? She'd marry Charlie and learn how to make pork chops, she supposed. Or hire someone to make pork chops for her — and then she'd have even less to do. She sighed. Regardless, she had to make sure she was on the Friday evening train to Los Angeles. Time was running out to put things right.

She slipped off her shoes and bent down to rub her feet. Then she saw it. There was a folded square of paper lying on the rug next to the bureau. She bent down and picked it up.

Boathouse 9:00.

It was handwritten and unsigned. She flipped the note over, but it was blank on the other side. Boathouse? Someone wanted to meet her at the boathouse? Why? Perhaps someone wanted to offer her an explanation about Hap and Charlie, but who could it possibly be? The skeleton staff had gone home for the evening, and assuming Adaline and Bernard had not returned, there were only three other people in the house — Constance, David, and Gwen. Maybe the family wasn't quite the united front she'd assumed them to be. Maybe there was a crack. Gwen was the most likely, Vivian thought, and there was only one explanation she wanted. Who had killed Hap, and why had Charlie been allowed to take the blame?

There was only one way to find out. She glanced at the bedside clock. It was ten to nine now.

She slipped out into the hall and tiptoed to Constance's room, pressing her ear against the closed door. She heard her cousin's rattling snore at once, steady and regular. Then she crept down the back stairs.

Vivian paused at the bottom of the stairs and rested her palm on the panel of the hidden game-room door. Could someone have stabbed Hap and then disappeared through this door without Charlie or anyone else seeing them? She moved forward a few steps and stood at the end of the main hall, looking toward the parlor at the front of the house. She couldn't hear anything, but someone had turned a light on. She moved forward again and noticed there was a slight gap in the pocket doors of Bernard's study letting out a golden sliver of light. Voices came from within. Men's voices. She approached cautiously and looked into the crack. She could see the back of a reddish-gold head of hair. David was talking to Bernard. She paused to listen, but couldn't make out what they were saying.

Adaline and Bernard were back from their afternoon excursion, and Vivian definitely didn't want to run into either of them right now. She turned and moved quickly toward the back door. Too quickly. Her foot caught on the upturned edge of the hall runner, and she stumbled against the hall table. The legs screeched against the wooden floor, and Vivian clenched her teeth, waiting to see if she'd been heard. A moment passed. Then two. Vivian sighed with relief, but then a voice rang out from the hall behind her.

"Vivian, is that you?"

Vivian turned slowly back to the open parlor doorway. Aunt Adaline stood in the doorway, her hands on her hips. "What in the devil are you doing?"

"I'm . . . I . . ."

"You decided to stay the night, I see," she said. "Well, don't just stand there like a booby. Fix that runner before someone hurts themselves."

Adaline stood, unmoving, and watched as Vivian bent and smoothed the floor runner. She couldn't very well scuttle out the back door with Adaline watching. Damn it all. She'd have to pretend she wasn't up to anything. She glanced at her watch and then walked toward the parlor. There wasn't much time to spare.

Adaline had returned to a seat at the card table. She sat across from Gwen and strapping young Marshall from the dock this morning. Adaline picked up the deck of cards and began shuffling.

"Wonderful timing. We're in need of a fourth for bridge."

The radio mumbled softly from the corner of the room, playing dance music from some live broadcast in the city.

"I'm sorry," Vivian said. "I was just on my way out."

She glanced at Gwen, and the younger woman rolled her eyes. Adaline was playing eagle-eyed chaperone, and from the looks of it, Gwen wasn't in any hurry to meet anyone in the boathouse. If Gwen hadn't left her that note, who had? Constance was sawing logs, David and Bernard were talking in the study, and Adaline was right here keeping a watchful eye on her youngest daughter and her suitor. Who did that leave?

"Out? Out to where?" Adaline looked at her incredulously.

"To take a walk," Vivian said. "Clear my head."

"In the dark?" Adaline said.

"I . . . Well, I was hoping to find a flashlight," Vivian said lamely.

"There's one on the top shelf of the hall closet," Gwen said.

Vivian flashed a quick smile of gratitude at Gwen. "Thank you." She stood awkwardly in the doorway for a moment more before turning back to the front door. "I won't be long." She hurried through the door and down the steps before Adaline could delay her any longer.

Halfway across the lawn, she realized she'd forgotten the flashlight. She stopped and glanced around the clearing. There was only a sliver of moon tonight, and everything was delineated in shades of gray and black. She had that feeling again — of being watched. She scanned the black copse of trees off to the right. A tiny pinprick of orange-red glowed among the yellow-green of the winking fireflies and then disappeared. A cigarette. Someone was standing there watching her as she walked across the lawn. She started moving toward that orange glow. Something small and black raced in front of her, and she jumped backward. A squirrel had scampered through the tangle of vegetation and up the huge elm in front of her. She paused, catching her breath, her hand over her heart.

She heard a muted pop, like someone springing cork from a bottle of champagne. Vivian looked in all directions, but she failed to locate the source of the noise. Perhaps it had actually been a champagne bottle. Sometimes on calm evenings, sounds traveled all the way from the estates on the other side of the lake.

Vivian started walking again, the ginger-bread boathouse coming into view as a dark shape against the slightly lighter shape of the moonlit lake. There were no lights inside — no lantern, no flashlight.

She opened the outside door, which screeched on its hinges. People didn't come up here very often anymore. Her heart fluttered erratically in her chest as she started to climb the stairs. There was a growing tension in the air — a thickness; it fairly crackled with electricity.

It was dark above. The three sides open to the air emitted the welcome breeze from the lake. It could have been that night eight years ago, Vivian thought, when she'd come up here and found Hap. She had the same giddy sense of anticipation thrumming through her veins. For a moment she saw him sitting there, looking out onto the lake with his broken leg propped up on the railing, and her heart skipped a beat. But it wasn't Hap, of course — just a rolled-up tarp and her mind playing tricks on her.

"Hello?" she whispered. "It's Viv."

Nothing. No sound. No movement. She checked her watch. It was 9:06 p.m. Maybe she'd missed the note writer. Then she heard a noise — a sort of strangled gurgle from the shadows. Then the shuffle of feet.

240

Someone was coming toward her.

It's Charlie, she thought. *Charlie! He's here. He's fine.* Relief flooded through her. She took a step forward, her arms already rising to embrace him. But then the man moved into a shaft of moonlight, and though she still couldn't make out his face, it was clear that this man was shorter than Charlie, his shoulders narrower. His hair was dark instead of blond. It almost looked like . . . No, it couldn't be. That was impossible.

A ghost, she thought then, her mind spinning to make some sense of what she was seeing. But she could not see through him, and his shoes made a scuffling sound against the floorboards as he moved out of the shadows.

No, it was Hap in the flesh, and he was very much alive. He moved toward Vivian slowly, shuffling forward toward her across the shadowed boathouse. *Hap is alive. Alive.* She opened her mouth to speak, but couldn't think of anything to say. Or rather, she could think of so many things to say that they all jammed up in her throat, allowing none of them through her lips. How was this possible? Had he faked his death? Why would he do such a thing? She stared at him openmouthed as he crossed the distance between them, her pulse pounding

241

in her ears.

Charlie hadn't killed Hap. He would not go to the electric chair. None of it made any sense, but the details didn't matter to her at the moment. Everything was fixed. Everything would be fine. Despite what Hap had put her through, she felt a dizzying smile spring to her lips as she watched him advance out of the shadows.

"You have a lot of explaining to do," she said.

Hap's dark brows knit together over his nose. He stretched one hand out to her. His mouth fell open. He paused a few feet away from her, and a fine trickle of dark liquid spilled from the right side of his open mouth. Then his knees gave way as if he'd been felled from behind, and he tumbled inelegantly to the floor at her feet, the odd angles of his limp body thumping against the boards of the boathouse, the fingertips of his outstretched hand coming to rest on the top of her left shoe. His forehead hit the floor last between her pumps, landing with a meaty thump.

She didn't move for one long moment. Then she wiggled just her foot, attempting to dislodge his fingers. They were like individual lead weights. Deadweights, she thought. The alarm bells started in her head

— shrill and piercing. Still, when she spoke she found her voice calm, if slightly exasperated.

"Hap, this really isn't the time for a tasteless joke."

There was no response.

"Hap?" He didn't move. "Hap?" His hand was heavy and unmoving on her foot. She stood motionless and watched his back. It was not rising and falling with his breath. She crouched beside him, poked his ribs with a finger. He didn't acknowledge her. This was taking it too far, she thought numbly. "Hap, come on."

She pushed his shoulder with the heels of her hands and grunted as she heaved him over onto his side. The metallic coppery tang hit her in the face immediately. Blood. A lot of blood, judging from the sheer force of the smell. Her hand came away wet. In the dim light of the moon streaming through the row of windows facing the lake, she could see the still-growing stain on his chest. She sat back on her heels. That pop she'd heard crossing the lawn hadn't been a champagne bottle. *Shot,* she thought numbly. *He must have been shot.*

"Oh Jesus," she whispered. Her fingers ran down his stubbled cheek, down his jawline to his throat. She pressed her fingers there, not sure what she was looking for. Something. Anything. She felt nothing. No blood pumped through Hap's veins. She placed her hand on the wet spot on his chest where his heartbeat should be — thumping strong and solid. There was nothing. She shook him and smacked his face, then leaned down and shouted nonsense into his ear. No response.

Then she just sat back and stared silently into his grass-green eyes. They were already vacant.

Hap was dead. Again. Somehow, absurdly, he had died in front of her twice now. As Vivian stared down at her bloodstained hands, an insensible ditty to the tune of the Sultan's Gold cigarette jingle started to run through her mind:

Murder's so nice, they did it twice.
A most killable fellow.

Vivian stared at the blood on her palms and fought the hysteria rising in her chest. She took in a hitching breath, intending to scream, to cry, to do something. Nothing came out, save a dry wheeze. This was a nightmare. *Hap,* she thought. *Oh, Hap, wake up. Please don't be dead. Please. Not when you could explain everything. Not when you could save Charlie.* She pressed her fingers to her throbbing temples. What now? What

244

would she do?

Something rustled outside and Vivian froze, the breath ragged in her throat. The door to the boathouse opened.

CHAPTER EIGHTEEN

Vivian looked up into Aunt Adaline's shocked face, the older woman's mouth open in surprise. Adaline gasped as her eyes fell on Hap's lifeless form. Vivian lost her balance and fell heavily onto her backside. She grunted in pain, and Adaline finally rushed forward. She paused a moment over Hap's body, her hands held out in front of her, elbows locked as if pushing the very idea of him away. Then she seemed to steel herself. She crouched near his torso and leaned forward to feel for his pulse.

"He's dead," Vivian whispered.

Adaline's hand fell away, and she sat back on her heels. She looked around the boathouse, over the railing and out toward the lake and the star-dusted sky above, and then back to Hap's prone form. She stared down into his face, reaching down to close his eyes with a delicate swipe of her fingers. She clenched her jaw and nodded once. And then she stood, skirting Hap's body, leaned down, and grasped Vivian by the shoulders. She squeezed, and when Vivian didn't respond, Adaline shoved both hands under Vivian's armpits and began pulling her upright. Vivian got sluggishly to her feet.

The air around them was heavy, stagnant. It would storm soon, Vivian thought. She heard a rhythmic thumping from somewhere below. Her first thought was that it sounded like someone chopping wood. But how could that be? How could any of this be? She stared numbly into Adaline's pale face.

Adaline's eyes flitted over Vivian's face, her chest.

"You're not hurt, are you?" she said.

"He's dead. Again," Vivian said. She swayed toward Adaline, staring down at the blood on her hands, a black smear in the dimness of the boathouse. "How? How is —"

"Vivian," Adaline said sternly, placing her hands on either shoulder to steady her. "Have you been hurt?"

"Hurt? No. But Hap . . ."

"Come on." Adaline pulled on Vivian's arms as she walked backward, maneuvering them both toward the door.

"Yes, we have to call the police," Vivian

murmured. "I think someone shot him."

Adaline didn't answer. She shoved Vivian through the open doorway, but did not follow, slamming the door in Vivian's face.

Vivian stood on the stairway landing just outside the closed door and bit her tongue in an attempt to come to the surface of her haze. This was important. She had to pay attention. She pushed the door open again, stepped back over the threshold, and glanced around the near-empty room. Adaline's body blocked most of her view. Adaline whirled, grasped Vivian's arm, and pushed her back out the open doorway. Vivian felt oddly detached from her own body. Her feet moved, but she felt nothing. Every bit of her was numb with shock. Adaline pulled Vivian, without speaking, down the steps and across the darkened lawn.

Vivian glanced over at the copse of trees where she'd seen the orange glow of a cigarette prior to entering the boathouse. There it was again. The tiny orange pinprick of light glowing and dimming and then disappearing. She lurched toward the light, but Adaline held her fast by the arm. Vivian lost her balance and stumbled, coming down hard on one knee. The grass was sparse in that area of the yard, and the skin on her knee was scraped raw.

She grunted in pain as she pitched forward and caught herself with her hands. She stayed motionless on all fours, stunned.

Adaline had dropped Vivian's arm as she fell, but took it up again. She said nothing, but simply yanked Vivian to her feet once again and began walking.

"Adaline," Vivian said. But Adaline didn't seem to hear.

The world was a blur of motion and sound for the next few minutes. Vivian was hustled into the house. She couldn't stop shaking. Smears of rusty blood covered her fingers. Hap was dead. Well and truly dead. He had not died in the game room, stabbed by Charlie with a scissors. No, he'd been alive until a few moments ago when someone had shot him in the boathouse. Hap had wanted everyone to think him dead the first time. Why? None of this made any sense.

"Adaline, I —"

"Hush now. You've had quite a shock."

"But Hap." She couldn't manage to say any more.

"Everything will be taken care of, Vivian. I think what you need to do right now is rest."

Vivian shook her head but allowed Adaline to lead her toward the stairway. Two faces watched from the parlor as they passed, silent, wide-eyed. But Vivian could not register who they were. They were round, white orbs without definition. A man? Two women? Two men? Gwen and the boy next door? Perhaps no one at all. Vivian shook her head, but the haze would not clear.

They climbed the stairs slowly, Vivian grasping the banister as if it held the secret to life itself. *The police,* she wanted to say. *We must call the police.* But her tongue felt too thick in her mouth. Her hands were cold, and when she glanced down, she saw her skin was tinged blue under the smears of Hap's blood.

Vivian blinked as they reached her bedroom, and found that her eyelids wanted to stay closed. *Sleep,* she thought. Yes, perhaps Adaline was right. Sleep would be a blissful release, and perhaps when she awoke, all of this would have been just a terrible dream.

Adaline settled her into bed. Vivian's eyes drooped. She was unbearably, unaccountably exhausted. *Likely in shock,* she thought vaguely. Something warm touched her hands. Vivian felt Adaline's hand wrap around hers. She looked down at a mug, the sides warmly soothing against the palms of her hands.

"Drink this, dear, and try to sleep," Adaline said, hovering somewhere in the darkness.

"What is it?"

"Warm milk and brandy. It'll settle your nerves."

Vivian stared down into the mug. Thin wisps of steam escaped and hovered in the air. "Thank you," she murmured. She took one tiny sip. It was indeed warm milk, heavily laced with brandy. The liquor burned pleasantly. Warming her from the inside, setting light to kindling in her belly. She took another sip and smiled up at Adaline.

"I feel better already," Vivian said.

"I'll be back to check on you in a few minutes," Adaline said. "Be sure to drink that whole thing."

Vivian nodded as her eyes drifted shut. She heard the door of the bedroom click and Adaline's muffled footfalls on the hall rug as she hurried away.

Dear.

Vivian's eyes snapped open. She stared up at the elaborate curlicue molding in the center of the ceiling where the gas lamp used to be, before electricity was installed in the cottage. The leaves on the tree outside her window whispered softly, shadows from the branches drifting over her bedroom walls. What had woken her? A dream. No, not a dream exactly. Something else. Something had happened, but what?

Dear. The word spun around in her mind like a top. *Dear,* spoken in her Aunt Adaline's softly nasal voice. Her aunt never called her dear. Adaline never called *anyone* dear — not even her own children. Vivian sat up in bed, heart hammering in her chest.

Hap. She sucked in her breath.

Hap was dead again. He'd died right in front of her. His blood was on her hands. She lifted them in front of her face and stared at them. But they were clean — no traces of blood at all. Adaline had found them in the boathouse and brought her straight to bed. Vivian pressed her hand to her chest.

How long had she dozed? She looked at the clock on the bedside table. It was ten fifteen now. She'd gone to meet Hap just after nine, so she'd been out for less than an hour. She leaned over the side of the bed and saw the mug Adaline had handed her, lying on the rug. The contents had spilled, leaving an ominous stain.

Warm milk and brandy, and perhaps something else? She plucked the mug from the carpet and drew it under her nose. She didn't know what she hoped to smell.

Something bitter, perhaps? The brandy was sharp and overpowering, and she could detect nothing else. Still, she'd only had the two sips, and that was a lucky thing. No doubt she'd have slept through the entire next day if she'd ingested the full contents of the mug.

Adaline wanted her out of the way. Perhaps they'd all try to convince her that everything she remembered from the evening before had been a bad dream. She looked down into the empty mug. Suddenly, she was certain of it. Her mind cleared.

That note *had* been for her. Hap had wanted to explain things to her. Explain why he'd left her like that eight years ago. Explain why he'd faked his own death and let Charlie take the blame. And someone else hadn't wanted him to explain.

Vivian jumped from the bed, pausing as soon as her feet hit the floor. Adaline had said she'd be back to check on her, hadn't she? Vivian shoved the bed pillows under the sheets, arranging them to look like a sleeping form, and drew the quilt up high. She thanked her lucky stars for all of those nights in her irreparable youth when such subterfuge had been necessary. Still, Vivian would be sunk if Adaline took more than two steps into the room.

She paused for a moment to slow her breathing and reached for the doorknob. It wouldn't turn. She jiggled it as quietly as she could. She was locked in. The ire rose in her. Now there was no doubt. She was meant to be kept in this room until morning, and everything she'd seen tonight would be swept under the rug. She crossed the room to the window, sliding up the sash as silently as she could. She leaned out the window and spotted exactly what she was looking for, just a foot away — a trellis.

There was one other skill from her disreputable youth that would come in handy in this situation, she thought as she hooked one leg over the sill. She reached over and gave the vine-covered trellis a hearty yank. It wasn't a drainpipe, but it would do.

Vivian picked her way across the lawn, hugging the shadows. She glanced back at the main house and noted that every light facing her on the ground floor was still ablaze. She paused to watch two shadows pass before the shaded window in the front parlor, but she couldn't say who they might be. Perhaps Adaline and Bernard, cooking up a story to cover what had really happened here tonight. Vivian clenched her fists at her side and then continued on. She glanced off to the right at the dark copse of trees, where she'd seen the flow of a cigarette before, but it was completely dark now. Still, she felt the small hairs on her forearms bristle. Someone could still be there, watching.

The boathouse loomed ahead in the darkness, quiet and still. The late-summer evening atmosphere was heavy and pregnant with humidity. Vivian glanced up at the sky. The stars were still visible, a thick dusting of white. The clouds had not rolled in yet. *Later,* she thought. The storm would come later.

She removed her shoes and climbed the boathouse steps on tiptoe. If the murderer had come back, she certainly didn't want to give them advance notice of her arrival. That went for anyone else too, she thought. For some reason, she imagined Adaline here sitting vigil over Hap's body in the dark, and shivered. But when she inched open the door at the top of the stairs with a creak and a moan of the old hinges, there was no one there.

Vivian stood still for a moment until her eyes adjusted to the darkness of the interior. Hap's body was gone. She moved silently, still on tiptoe, to the center of the room and crouched down to examine the spot where he had fallen dead at her feet. She hissed as sharp pain exploded from her right knee. She'd fallen at some point, hadn't she? Everything was a blur.

The blood had been cleaned up. All that remained was a slightly discolored patch on the wooden floor where Hap had lain. Vivian stayed rooted to her spot, blinking in the dim light. She held her hand out, hesitated, then brushed her fingertips over the floorboards. Her fingers came away dry. Perhaps it wasn't blood after all.

She should have brought a flashlight. The sliver of moon reflected scant light, and she could barely see her hand in front of her face, much less make out whether a dark spot on wooden floorboards had once been human blood.

Vivian's gaze swept the dark corners of the boathouse. How could things have been cleared away so fast? Had she imagined all of it? Hap stumbling, falling at her feet, dying before her eyes? Dying twice in front of her in the span of a few days? She stood, and her knee shrieked again with that sharp, stinging pain. She gasped and pressed her fingertips to it. The freshly formed scab had torn open, and a trickle of blood slid down her shin. She *had* fallen on the lawn earlier when Adaline had dragged her from the boathouse. The scrape was real; the pain was real.

She thought of the cigarette glowing in the trees not far away, the person who held it lurking and watching. But Vivian had heard the shot as she'd approached the boathouse — after she'd seen the cigarette glow. She'd been perhaps thirty feet away when she'd heard the shot that she'd assumed was a champagne bottle being uncorked. It was dark, but surely she would have seen someone running down the wooden steps of the boathouse. She would have heard them, at the very least, and she'd heard nothing.

She crossed to the other side of the boathouse. Here, the second floor was open on three sides to the waters of the lake. Perhaps the shooter jumped over the railing? She judged the distance to be about fifteen feet straight down into a weedy thicket near the water's edge. A tricky prospect even in broad daylight. Could someone have accomplished it in the darkness? Possibly, she thought, but not without hurting themselves. She considered the suspects available — all of them her family and half of those women. That's not something she could see any of the female members of the family doing. Bernard and Adaline weren't exactly sporty. The only one who might have been able to do it without breaking his ankle was David. But why would David have killed Hap?

She started out toward the copse of trees where she'd seen the light of the burning cigarette. Then heard something. She paused, held her breath. There it was again, the *click-clack* of heeled shoes. Someone in a hurry. Someone rushing out to the end of the dock.

Without time to think it over, Vivian ran the opposite way, around the corner of the boathouse and down the length of the dock, glowing white against the night-black water of the lake. A woman stood in the rowboat at the far end of the dock, struggling with the bowline. As the boat drifted away from the dock, Vivian leaped the foot or so from the dock to the drifting boat. She banged her knee hard against the plank bench seat, and something small and heavy slid from the bench and fell to the bottom of the boat with a thump.

The woman jerked and looked up. Gwen's face was a pale oval in the moonlight. Stern and stony as she stared at Vivian. Her big eyes were wide.

"Viv, what are you doing?"

"What am I doing? What are *you* doing,

Gwen? And don't tell me you felt like a late-night constitutional."

Gwen sat silently for a moment, one hand splayed over her heart as she caught her breath.

"Hap is dead," she whispered. "Shot." She lowered her chin and locked eyes with Vivian.

Vivian nodded.

"Did you do it?"

"No," Vivian said.

"But someone *did* shoot him about an hour ago. And he's dead." Gwen sounded as if she was trying to convince herself of that fact.

"Yes," Vivian said. "How do you know all of this? *You* didn't . . ."

Gwen's eyes met Vivian's again, the whites glowing in the near-total darkness of the lake. "No," Gwen said. Vivian wondered if she was the only one in the house who didn't know that Hap had faked his death at the garden party. Was she the only one who wasn't in on it?

Gwen seemed to consider Vivian for a moment. Her brows drew together and then smoothed. She nodded and leaned forward, pulling something from the floor. She placed it gingerly on the bench seat before her and stared at it as if it might jump up and bite her. It was a gun. Vivian's stomach twisted. If Gwen didn't shoot Hap, then why did she have a gun?

"I found it," Gwen said.

"Found it?"

She nodded. Vivian looked past Gwen toward the shore. They were drifting away from Oakhaven.

"In some bushes beside the summer kitchen. I was still in the parlor with Marshall when Mother came back with you. I heard enough to understand that something had happened to Hap in the boathouse. Mother told me to send Marshall home, so I did. Then I stopped to have a smoke. I smoke there, by the far corner of the summer kitchen, because you can't be seen from the house." Vivian nodded. That was precisely where Vivian had smoked her smuggled cigarettes when she was Gwen's age. "I dropped my cigarette on the ground, and when I bent to retrieve it, I saw something sticking out from underneath the bushes. It was this."

They both stared down at the gun. Vivian had only seen the starter guns used as sound props at the radio station. She had no idea how to use a real gun — or even how to differentiate between them. This one was small and old, with a curiously thin barrel and hatch-marked butt. It was flat, without the round chamber for bullets like the prop guns used at the station. So it was not a revolver. A pistol? Whatever it was, it radiated menace.

"Do you recognize it? Is it your father's?" she asked.

Gwen stared down at it. "It could be. I never paid much attention to his guns."

"You said you just found it in the bushes?"

"Yes."

Vivian looked over her own shoulder at the water, lying still as glass. "And your first thought was to throw it in the lake?"

Gwen shrugged. "It wasn't my first thought, no. My first thought was that I couldn't believe that whoever had shot Hap hadn't thrown it in the lake themselves." She nodded toward the boathouse receding into the distance behind them and mimed a lazy overhand throw. The killer could have easily thrown the gun over the side into the lake.

"And because of that, my second thought was that whoever had shot Hap had panicked. They panicked and ran, and by the time they realized they were still carrying the gun, they were near the summer kitchen, and they wanted to get rid of it as soon as possible. So they tossed it in the bushes and kept running."

Vivian nodded. Yes, that made sense. If this story of Gwen's was true, that is.

"And your third thought?"

Gwen didn't answer right away. Vivian heard her sigh, hitching in a breath as if she were gathering courage.

"My third thought was that I could see David doing exactly that. Shooting in anger and panicking afterward. You know David. He has such a quick temper."

"But why would David . . . ?"

Gwen looked up at her. Her face was pale, her mouth set into a grim line. "Jealousy," she said. "Hap and Lillian were having an affair."

Vivian exhaled. "How do you know that?"

"I *don't* know, I suppose. They were acting strangely around each other during the garden party — like that wasn't the first time they'd met but they were both pretending like it was. Then Constance told me she saw them together."

"When?"

"The Saturday evening before the party, at the guesthouse."

"I don't understand." Vivian massaged her temples.

Gwen sighed and slumped forward, her elbows on her knees. She sat with her head in her hands for a moment. "This is all my fault, Vivian. All of it. I brought Hap here because I wanted to get you two back together. I was so convinced that it all would work out in the end that I tried even after Constance told me her suspicions about Hap and Lillian." She looked up at Vivian, tears rimming her big, brown eyes. "I figured love conquers all . . . right?"

Vivian's mouth fell open, but she didn't know where to begin. Love didn't conquer all, and had there really been that much love between her and Hap in the first place? It must have seemed so to her starry-eyed cousin.

"Gwen, I . . ."

Gwen looked over Vivian's shoulder, and her eyes widened with alarm. She put her fingers to her lips. Vivian turned to look back at the shore but saw no movement among the shadows.

"What is it?" Vivian said.

"I thought I saw someone on the shore. But it's nothing." Gwen picked up the oars and started rowing with one oar to turn the boat toward the middle of the lake.

Vivian opened her mouth again to try to explain, to try to soothe Gwen's guilt, but nothing came out. She *did* blame Gwen, especially now that she'd heard all this.

Gwen had interfered in her life, and she might have gotten Hap killed because of it. She'd stuck her nose into things that she didn't understand. But it was also just the sort of thing Vivian would have done at Gwen's age, she thought. She would probably still do it, if faced with the same situation. Vivian leaned back against the stern of the boat and the large metal box wedged there and sighed. This was a Grade-A mess.

It was plausible that Hap and Lillian had been having an affair, knowing Hap. If Constance had seen them together in the guesthouse, that could really be the only explanation, couldn't it?

"Did Constance tell David about what she saw?" Vivian said.

Gwen stopped rowing. The boat continued to drift. "I don't think she needed to tell him. I think David already knew."

"But David was with your father in the study just before it happened. I saw him when I passed the study door."

"That's the thing, Viv. I saw David walking past the parlor room window while Mother was trying to talk you into a game of bridge. He was headed toward the front of the house — toward the lake, toward the boathouse. And I . . . Well, I didn't see him come back." She frowned, and then she continued with her original train of thought. "So I thought if I got rid of this gun that no one could ever prove David had done anything. The lake's more than a hundred feet deep in the middle. No one will ever find it."

Vivian's pulse quickened, and she sat up. Without a murder weapon or a body, it would be very hard for anyone to prove that Charlie *hadn't* murdered Hap on Sunday. Especially if Bernard couldn't or wouldn't help persuade the police.

"But you can't do that," she said quickly.

"Why can't I? As far as the police know, Hap has been dead for days. Now he's dead for real."

"And Charlie's been wrongfully accused."

Gwen bit her lip. "Yes, there's that. We'll just have to get Constance to recant her statement," she said. "Tell them she didn't hear Charlie say he wanted to kill Hap. Without that, they don't have much of a case. Frankly, I don't know why they'd ever believe a word she says. She's been hitting that nerve tonic pretty hard lately, if you hadn't noticed."

Yes, what had Constance said this morning? That she'd been seeing ghosts? Vivian had assumed she meant in the metaphorical sense — the ghost of what had been, what

265

might have been. But maybe she was being literal. Maybe she'd seen Hap after his supposed death on Sunday and assumed that she was seeing things. Maybe that's why she'd been hitting the nerve tonic. She thought she was losing her mind.

Vivian felt each rocking of the boat in her gut now. None of this made any sense.

"But Hap is dead, Gwen. And someone here killed him. Doesn't that matter to you?"

Gwen continued rowing again with a grunt. Her expression didn't change. "Of course I care. But he's dead. I can't change that. What I *can* change is someone I love going to prison over a horrible mistake."

What about the someone I love? Vivian thought.

Gwen stopped rowing again. She leaned forward, forearms resting on the pulled-in oars, and considered Vivian for a moment. Then she tilted her head back and looked up at the sky. Vivian followed her gaze, her eyes sweeping over the dots in the sky — the Milky Way clearly visible as a white arc across the darkness. Before Vivian could register what she was doing, Gwen had picked up the pistol and held her arm straight out to the side so that her hand dangled over the water.

"No, Gwen —"

Vivian lunged forward, but she knew even as she reached for Gwen that she was too late. A small splash echoed across the still water.

The gun was gone.

CHAPTER NINETEEN

Everyone at the house except Vivian had known that Hap had not died on Sunday. That much was becoming clear. There had been a plan in place, and things had been going according to that plan until Vivian had shown back up at Oakhaven and thrown a wrench into the works. Why the subterfuge? Why would Hap fake his death — and need the collusion of the entire Lang family to do it? She'd asked Gwen all of these questions but had gotten no answers. The girl had simply shut down after tossing the gun.

She'd rowed them back to shore in complete silence and had spoken again only after she'd stepped out of the boat. She'd begged Vivian to forget what she'd told her, and what she'd seen with her own eyes. Since the adrenaline fueled by her sense of purpose in getting rid of the gun had worn off, Gwen had seemed terrified. Her hands were shaking, and Vivian had to help her cinch the knot in the rope to moor the boat. Vivian told Gwen to go to bed and stay out of it from now on. The girl had already made enough of a hash of things.

And it certainly was a hash, Vivian thought. She went over the jumble of the night's events as she made her way slowly across the lawn toward the forest path in the back of the house. Hap was dead. She'd seen him die, but if she hadn't, she may not have believed it herself. His body had disappeared, and the apparent murder weapon was now lying at the bottom of Geneva Lake, thanks to Gwen jumping to conclusions.

And what about those conclusions? Gwen suspected David because she thought Hap and Lillian were having an affair. But had those two even known each other prior to the garden party? Gwen had said Constance told her she'd seen them together at the guesthouse the evening before, but Constance had been seeing a lot of things lately, hadn't she? She'd admitted that to Vivian herself.

Once again, Vivian cursed the fact she hadn't thought to bring a flashlight. It was dark in the forest, and she could barely see the path before her. Crickets chirped from the underbrush as she picked her way awkwardly in the darkness. Mosquitoes buzzed maddeningly close to her ears, and she slapped ineffectually at them. Something small scurried across the path in front of her, and she stumbled over her own feet in surprise. She stopped and pressed an open palm to her thumping heart. What was she doing? She should just leave. Go now while the getting was good.

But there was Charlie to think of. She had to clear all of this up to save him — wherever he might be. *He may already be dead. Shot by police in a standoff.* The thought sprang to her mind unbidden, and she pushed it away. He couldn't be dead, not on her watch. She would fix this. So she swallowed her fear and her doubts and kept walking, eyes trained on the dark path in front of her for small, scuttling creatures.

Eventually, the path opened up into a small clearing. The guesthouse stood in the middle. It was a tiny, half-timbered storybook cottage with a thatched roof and a fieldstone chimney dominating the facade. Ivy snaked up artfully around the mullioned windows to the roofline. Vivian's grandfather had had it built as a playhouse for his daughters. Julia, Vivian's mother, had been the youngest by a decade and the only one actually young enough at the time of its completion to play in it. Vivian had never been able to picture that: her mother as a child playing damsel in distress among the ivy — or playing anything at all.

When Hap was orphaned and taken into the Lang family, the playhouse had been renovated and electricity wired in to allow him some privacy when he stayed during the summers. That had never struck Vivian as odd until this moment. From the first, Hap was a member of the Lang family, yet not. He'd been both included and set apart. Then Hap had joined up when the Great War broke out, and the playhouse had been vacant for ten years or so while Hap gallivanted about the country barnstorming. She and David had taken over, and the cottage had served as Cinderella's castle, Hansel and Gretel's cottage, and Grandma's house in "Little Red Riding Hood." Yet the cottage had always been considered Hap's, and they all knew he would come back someday.

Then Hap *had* come back that summer when Vivian was seventeen. That summer when she'd left childish things behind with that late-night visit to Hap in this same cottage, and all the trouble had started.

Vivian cocked her head to the side, narrowing her eyes. She'd expected to feel something more at the sight of it than distant, cobwebby nostalgia, but she didn't. The cottage hadn't changed. She had. The cottage was smaller than she remembered, and now it was dark, shut tight against the night. The curtains were drawn. The diamond-shaped panes of the lancet windows reflected only glints of sparse moonlight. Tiny and hollow, she thought. Still, it was best to take a look around. Maybe Hap had left something behind that might help explain all of this. Vivian tried the front door. The metal latch depressed under her thumb, and the wooden slatted door swung inward under the tentative pressure of her fingertips. She held her breath.

The inside of the cottage was simple, made up of one large room. The fireplace took up the entirety of the front wall. A small secretary and phonograph stood against the wall directly in front of her. A brass daybed occupied the opposite wall, with the door to the tiny water closet next to it. But Vivian had been mistaken — the cottage was not empty.

A lamp burned in the corner next to the daybed, casting a feeble yellow glow over the small room. Papers covered the floor; the drawers of the small secretary had been pulled out and overturned. And in the middle of it all sat a hunched figure — a man. His head was in his hands, his shoulders racked with mute sobs.

"Uncle Bernard?" she said.

He lifted his head. Bernard's eyes were swollen from crying, and tears had left moist tracks down his cheeks. Vivian sucked in her breath at the sight of him. She'd never seen him such a wreck. He sat back on his heels with a grunt.

"You shouldn't be here," he said, his voice a rasp. He wiped a hand across his cheek. He reached into his back pocket and took out an immaculate white handkerchief, blowing his nose with a fantastic racket. *You shouldn't be here,* she thought. An echo of what he'd said on Sunday: *You shouldn't see this.*

He'd said that after they'd all been led to believe that Charlie had stabbed Hap. At the time, she'd thought Bernard was trying to shield her delicate female sensibilities from the sight of gore and impending death. But now she realized *You shouldn't see this* had simply meant that Vivian shouldn't see that Hap wasn't dead. What had Bernard and Hap been playing at? And how dare her uncle think he could put her off now, with all that had happened tonight! She'd had quite enough of Bernard telling her what she should and should not see, what she should and should not think.

"I think I deserve the truth," Vivian said, stepping into the room and letting the door close with a dramatic bang.

She waited for Bernard to respond, but he said nothing. Vivian skirted her uncle and the papers on the floor and walked over toward the daybed. A small valise lay open upon it, and items were scattered over the bedspread — clothing, a pair of brown leather dress shoes, a gaudy green silk tie. The paltry remains of a man's life, she thought. She slid her fingertips down the cover of a book lying facedown, then flipped it over to read the title — *Homage to Catalonia* by George Orwell. She flipped through the pages, pausing only briefly to survey those that Hap had dog-eared. She replaced the book as she'd found it. Her eyes snagged on an unopened package of cigarettes. She picked them up and turned the small rectangular package wrapped in brown paper around in her hands. They were Gauloises, a French brand. She stared down at the winged helmet illustrated on the front, then brought the pack to her nose and inhaled. The strong, unfiltered tobacco stung the back of her throat.

"Hap didn't die on Sunday," Vivian said. Bernard was facing away from her, and he didn't turn at her statement of fact.

"It's a long story," he said softly.

"No better time to tell it, in my opinion." She turned and sat on the edge of the daybed, training all of her attention on Bernard's back. Sweat had soaked through his shirt, leaving semicircular stains under the armpits. The fabric clung to his back. It was stifling inside the guesthouse, and she realized all of the windows were shut tight.

Bernard turned slowly to face her, but he did not stand. It was strange seeing a man like Bernard sitting on the floor like a child. She'd always known him to be powerful, demanding, in control.

"Hap had gambling debts," Bernard said.

"Gambling debts," Vivian repeated. She picked up the pack of cigarettes again, suddenly wishing for nothing more than a smoke to calm her nerves. She felt a bead of sweat forming along her hairline and wiped it away with her free hand.

"Yes, a lot of debts. He'd run through his family fortune quite quickly in Europe. He made enemies of some powerful people there. He escaped it for a time with the Spanish war, but those people he was indebted to have long memories."

"You're saying Hap faked his death to escape some money he owed?" she said.

"Yes."

Vivian dropped the pack of cigarettes onto the bed before standing and walking slowly toward the window. She lifted the roman shade with her index finger and looked outside. Blackness greeted her. She unlatched the lock and lifted the sash, but the air outside was only slightly less stifling and provided almost no relief.

She glanced over her shoulder at Bernard and let the shade fall back into place. "I don't buy it."

Bernard's eyebrows were raised so that they were visible over the metal frames of his spectacles.

"I mean, that's the type of problem that's easily remedied in a family like this," she continued. "That's a problem you can truly throw money at. Why wouldn't you have just given Hap the money to repay his debts? Why would he need to go through the considerable trouble of faking his death over something so simple?"

She paused to give Bernard a chance to chew on that and to decide whether to think up another lie or to give in and tell her the truth. She glanced around the room. Her eyes came to rest on the phonograph near the secretary — an old Victrola, the kind you had to crank to get going. The song "Stardust" flitted into her mind in the tinny, far-off way Bing's voice had come through the metal trumpet speaker that night eight years ago.

Hap had put that record on and then played it again and again. The anger and sadness inside her grew into an impotent lump in the pit of her stomach, and she pressed her fingertips to it. *Hap did that,* she thought, *a living, breathing man.* And now that man had been killed in front of her — twice.

"What's the real story?" she said softly.

Bernard sighed. Then he struggled to his feet inelegantly and trained his eyes on her. He wiped his brow with the handkerchief and stuffed it in his trouser pocket. "Hap was a spy," he said.

Vivian blinked. She felt one of her eyebrows rise of its own accord. Was Bernard having a laugh at her expense? Had she taken a huge gulp of Constance's nerve tonic?

"A spy," she repeated with a snort of disbelief.

"I knew you wouldn't believe me."

"I don't, but I'm listening." She sat back down on the daybed and settled in. "Begin at the beginning, please."

Bernard turned on his heel and took a few measured steps toward the small fireplace at the opposite side of the room. There wasn't much room to pace in here, but he was going to give it a go. He turned back toward her and jingled the coins in his pocket before he spoke again.

"Hap had been in Spain, you know."

"Yes," she said. "Flying supplies to the rebels."

"It started out that way, but he quickly became a squadron leader. The Republicans were short on supplies, short on manpower, short on everything. It was a losing battle from the first, I'm afraid." Bernard fell silent. He looked up at the low ceiling as if he would find the way to proceed stamped on it.

"It started out that way . . ." Vivian prodded.

"Yes, well, eventually he was shot down, you see. Captured and put in a Nationalist prison."

Vivian gasped. "I never knew that," she said.

"No one did. We'd lost all contact with Hap after he'd gone to Spain. I knew nothing of what had happened to him there until he came back to the States a few months ago."

"And what had happened to him?" Images of Hap sprang into her mind: filthy, shivering, shackled, and sharing a dank, dark cell with rats and lice.

"He was kept there for a month or so. Tortured." Bernard waved his hand to indicate that he wouldn't go into detail about that and resumed his pacing. "But eventually, Franco's men realized what they had in Hap. He wasn't just an enemy pilot. He was a rich American with connections. And eventually, they realized he was more useful to them alive than dead. In short, they offered him his life in return for turning on everything he stood for. Hap became a member of Franco's fifth column."

Vivian didn't recognize that name.

"What's that?"

"Franco's Nationalist sleeper agents in Madrid," Bernard said. "Hap was outwardly Republican, a member of the International Brigades. But he was really an agent for Franco and the Nationalists, out to undermine the rebel's cause and make the city ready for Franco when the time came to take Madrid."

Vivian leaned forward, elbows on her knees.

"Hap was fighting *with* Franco . . ."
Vivian's mind struggled to latch on to that
information. If he was fighting with Franco,
then he was also fighting with Hitler and
Mussolini by extension. Germany and Italy
had heavily supplied the Nationalists with
provisions and troops. The Germans sent
bombers specifically, and airplanes were
what Hap knew best. She felt her stomach
sink.

"Yes, and I think he actually started to
believe in the Nationalist way of thinking.
Believing in the cause of a united nationalist Spain, a Catholic Spain. He was raised
Catholic, you know. Well, until his parents . . ." Bernard waved his hand again.
"But then he started to see what was really
going on there. He saw a lot of horrible
things. Priests murdered. Priests *murdering.*
He was exposed to horrible ideas from the
Germans and Italians. He could see what
was coming . . . what *is* coming."

"War," Vivian said.

"Spain was a sort of practice ground for
the Germans and Italians," Bernard said.
"They aided Franco with supplies and men
and planes in order to test out strategies
and fight a practice war, so to speak. So
when Hap saw that the Spanish war was
coming to an end and that Franco would

280

triumph, he also saw the writing on the wall. He had German associates . . . high-ranking members of the German Luftwaffe. He knew he was valuable to them as an American pilot. Hap knew important people like Lindbergh. The Germans would send Hap back to the States and ask him to spy for them."

Vivian sat up straight. "Lindbergh?"

"He has been in Europe the past couple of years, touring German airplane factories and reporting on the strength of the German Luftwaffe for the American government."

"Is he . . . is he working for the Germans?" The idea terrified her, and she could barely speak the words.

"I doubt it. Lindbergh's an isolationist. He wants to keep America out of the war entirely. That's what Germany wants too. So they get Lindbergh to tour their factories, put on a show to impress him, so that he'll warn Roosevelt off getting involved. I assume the Germans also wanted an inside man to let them know just how much they'd influenced America. Hap would have been perfect for that job."

Vivian sat back again, her mind spinning. As crazy as it sounded, her uncle's story did make a certain sort of sense. Of anyone she'd ever known, Hap would be the perfect choice to take to spying.

"And he didn't want to do that?" she said. "Spy for Germany?"

Bernard shook his head. "He wanted out of all of it. It was becoming too much. What he'd seen in Spain weighed heavily on his mind. But he couldn't just run away from his troubles. The Germans had him up against the wall. He saw no other way out."

"So he faked his death."

"Yes. They had people watching him all the time, hounding him. He'd come to me, and we'd worked it all out. A plan for his death. An aneurysm, something quiet and simple. To avoid as much mess as possible. I would be the only witness, and I would be the only one who would ever know he was still alive. He wanted to have time to say goodbye to everyone he'd known and loved. That's why he came to the garden party. But then, at the party, Hap saw someone he recognized. Someone from his time in Spain. He knew he'd been found, and he knew he didn't have much time. So he came to me and begged me to let him die right then. What could I do but say yes? He was in a bind. Kill himself or possibly be killed for refusing to cooperate."

"Who did he see?"

"He didn't say who. He just said he'd recognized someone and had spoken to them. That they were here for him, and this was it."

Vivian thought of the party. There had been so many people there, most of whom she didn't know. She needed more to go on. A member of the band perhaps? The staff? There had been the gardener that Charlie had knocked over. Why had a gardener been working in the middle of a garden party on a Sunday? She shook her head. If she followed the rabbit too far into that hole, she would lose the plot entirely. *Charlie,* she thought. *Keep this focused on Charlie, and find a way to get him out of this mess.*

"So how did everything get so mixed up? How did Charlie get involved?"

"We were going to put the aneurysm plan into effect. Hap would go into the game room when everyone was certain to be outside . . . when the band started, perhaps. He would collapse, and I would find him. He would be whisked away to the hospital where he would die without anyone else witnessing or being the wiser. Hap had wanted to add some fake blood from his nose and ears to make it look more realistic to anyone who might see him carried from the house. I thought that was a ridiculous idea, an unnecessary complication. But he must have had the fake blood in his hands when Charlie entered the library.

"Taken by surprise, he broke the package open on his stomach, then faked passing out in front of Charlie, thinking that I would be coming in any second. That things could still be salvaged. But then you came in, followed closely by Constance, and you both assumed that Charlie had stabbed Hap, since he'd been holding what appeared to be bloody scissors. So, what could we do? We pretended to believe that Charlie had stabbed Hap, whisked him away as planned, and he promptly died in the ambulance away from prying eyes. I knew the truth, of course, and I was going to tell the police once everything with Hap was settled."

"But then Charlie escaped custody," she said.

"And Hap came back here."

The voices in Bernard's office, she thought. It hadn't been the radio. "Hap was in your study earlier when I knocked on the door."

"Yes, things had gone awry in his escape plan. His contact for the fake ID and documents needed for his new identity had gone missing. He was unreachable, gone from the face of the earth as if he'd never existed.

The whole plan was compromised. Hap had also heard that Charlie had been charged with his murder. He'd seen Charlie's photo in the newspaper, and he said he couldn't let that lie. He came back to make sure it got sorted out."

Vivian bit her lip. Hap's memory was simultaneously traitorous and upstanding, dangerous and protective, deceptive and honest.

"But Hap couldn't be involved with the sorting out," Vivian said. "He was dead . . . to most people, that is."

"Right. That's what we were discussing when you knocked on the door. Hap hid in the closet. He heard our entire conversation."

So he'd heard her saying that she felt horrible about the way things ended? Things were clicking into place, a timeline for a day that hadn't made any sense before now. "And then he left that note in my room when we were at dinner, asking me to meet him in the boathouse tonight."

"He did? Whatever for?"

"To apologize? To explain? I don't know exactly. He died before I got a chance to find out."

Bernard walked a few paces and then held one finger up.

"Someone else saw that note, or followed him to the boathouse. It must have been the person he'd seen at the garden party. I guess his original death wasn't so believable to everyone."

"Do you really think that's what happened?" She thought of Hap in the boathouse at her feet, his face blank, his eyes clouding over. She hugged her arms to her chest.

Bernard nodded.

"And you cleaned everything up after Adaline took me to the house?" she said.

"Not personally, but I orchestrated the cleanup. And then I came out here to make sure he hadn't left anything incriminating. These papers are old, meaningless. That valise is all I found. Someone clearly got here before me." He shrugged at the paltry contents of Hap's suitcase, at the papers strewn over the floor. They both stared at the open suitcase, the air hot and leaden between them.

"Where is Hap . . . his body?" she asked quietly. The echo of her question earlier in the day gave her goose bumps. Hap had been alive and listening to her ask it the first time. And now he really was dead, blue-tinged skin on a slab somewhere.

"At a funeral home nearby. His body will

be cremated immediately. We can't risk any of this coming out."

"So this, Hap's real death, is a secret?"

"Yes. Until I tell you otherwise. But, Vivian, you understand that I may never tell you otherwise. You may have to keep this secret for the rest of your life."

Vivian nodded. She'd keep Bernard's precious secret as long as she got Charlie back.

"Does the whole family know?" She thought of the pistol lying at the bottom of the lake, and of Gwen. Gwen certainly wouldn't have thrown the murder weapon in the lake if she'd known a spy had killed Hap and not her brother.

"About the spying? Just the two of us. To everyone else, Hap faked his death because of gambling debts, and the underworld figures he was involved in sent someone along to finish the job. That's what I'll tell them."

"Were you going to tell me any of this? Or were you planning on denying it ever happened?"

"No. And yes. But you didn't drink your warm milk and brandy." He lowered his head and glowered at her through red-rimmed eyes.

"I've always been difficult, haven't I?"

Vivian held his gaze for a moment and then shifted her own to the floor. It would take some doing for her to believe the story Bernard had told her. But that didn't matter right now. What mattered was that Charlie hadn't killed anyone, and he needed his name to be cleared.

"You'll tell the police that story too?" she said.

"I'll tell them enough to get the charges against Charlie dropped. Do you know where he is . . . really?"

She shook her head. She wanted to speak and found she couldn't. What she wouldn't give to know where Charlie was right now, to know that he was safe. Bernard nodded at her, and she stood. She smoothed her skirt down over her thighs and then made her way to the door.

As she put her hand on the door latch, Bernard spoke.

"I loved him like a son, you know," he said quietly.

"I know," she said.

The idea that international espionage had reared its head in Lake Geneva, Wisconsin, was outrageous. Yet knowing Hap's personality, Vivian found it entirely plausible that he'd gone to Spain for adventure and found

288

more than he'd bargained for. But the way he'd actually died seemed off to her — a bullet to the stomach? Admittedly, she'd gleaned all of her information on espionage from the movies, but it didn't seem right that a spy would kill another spy by shooting him that way. For one thing, that wound might not necessarily be fatal. For another, even if it was fatal, Hap may have had time to talk before he died. But the thing that bothered her the most about all of it was that someone trained to kill would not have shot once and then run off and tossed the murder weapon in the bushes. That was the mark of panic, as Gwen had said. Spies were trained not to panic.

As Vivian thought of Gwen, the summer kitchen came into view, and Vivian abruptly changed course for it. She paused, hidden from view of the main house, and listened. She heard only crickets. In the dim moonlight, she could just make out cigarette butts littering the ground at her feet. Vivian moved the butts about in the dirt with the toe of her shoe before crouching and picking one up. She brought it to her nose and sniffed. Perhaps Lucky Strikes. Vivian didn't smoke anymore, but she knew from the free cigarettes that the sponsors gave to those associated with *The Darkness Knows* that the quality was only slightly better than that of Sultan's Gold. She dropped the butt to the ground and scanned the remainder. They all looked the same. Then another butt caught her eye. It was wider, blunter. She picked it up, and the tobacco fell out of the end in tiny granules onto her palm. The tobacco was dark brown, almost black in color. She sniffed the butt and recoiled.

She'd smelled that distinct odor recently from the package of cigarettes among Hap's things. The Gauloises. She scoured the ground, but there was only the one. The Lucky Strikes were likely Gwen's, but someone else had been using this secret smoking spot, smoking a distinct French brand of cigarette. Was it Hap? Or the killer?

Vivian stood and pretended to smoke a cigarette. She found the right angle, just as Gwen had said, just as Vivian had done a thousand times in her youth. She could see the corner of the main house, but no one in the main house could see her. Then she mimed dropping the butt to the ground and grinding it out with the toe of her shoe. Vivian's eyes strayed to the bush as Gwen had claimed hers had. It had been an early spring, and the foliage was already thick, the leaves green and lush. Could Gwen have seen the gun under all that in the dark?

She thought back to the gun lying on the bench of the rowboat. The moonlight had been feeble even on the lake with no obstructions. No, the gun's surface had not been polished. It had been a dull brownish-gray. It had not glinted in the moonlight on the bench of the rowboat, and it certainly would not have glinted from underneath that thick mask of leaves. If Gwen hadn't found the gun under the bush like she'd said, then where had she gotten it?

It looked as if someone had been using the game room and just stepped out. The billiard balls were scattered around the table, the cue stick leaning against the side of the table. The radio was on in the corner of the room. Vivian didn't have much time. She walked to the desk and noticed the newspaper clippings were gone. A clock ticked industriously on the desk as she opened the top drawer. It was 11:27 p.m.

She ran her fingertips across the empty desk and reached for the drawer pull.

"It's all right, doll. You see, everything worked out just fine in the end."

Vivian's hand froze. That was Graham's voice. She turned and stared at the yellow dial of the radio, and then she heard herself reply.

"Fitting that the real Kickapoo Lou came through at the end."

Vivian stood, transfixed, staring at the radio speaker. It was the transcription recording they'd made a few days ago. She hadn't stuck around to hear it played back to them after the recording session. It was strange, hearing herself like that. Her voice was higher than it sounded to her when she spoke.

"Yeah, that horse really stuck it to the syndicate, didn't she?" Graham said. "Heck of a girl."

"Mr. Quint got his money," Vivian said as Lorna.

"And I got my girl."

"Oh, Harvey." Then she heard herself sigh — heard Lorna sigh — in that practiced, dreamy way.

The organ swelled, and the ending credit sequence began. "That was 'The Call of Kickapoo Lou,' another thrilling episode of detective muscle on *The Darkness Knows*. Starring Graham Yarborough as Detective Harvey Diamond, Vivian Witchell as Lorna Lafferty, and Dave Chapman as Mr. Quint. This is announcer Bill Purdy, and I invite you to join us again next week for another tantalizing tale of detective muscle in *The Darkness Knows*. This program was transcribed."

The chimes rang in the half hour and broke into Vivian's stupor. No one had told her they'd actually be playing the recording over the air. She thought it had been strictly for advertising purposes — for Mr. Marshfield to sell more Sultan's Gold to an unsuspecting public. She glanced at the clock again. The show usually ran at eight o'clock on Thursday nights. Why play it at this late hour? Perhaps it was just a test of the new technology — to gauge listener reaction to something new. Late in the evening just before sign-off was usually when the station was apt to take risks. And perhaps they had a slot to fill.

Then a voice came over the airwaves that she recognized but had never heard on this side of the speaker.

"Good evening, ladies and gentlemen. This is Morty Nickerson, your host for *Fantasy Ballroom,* the half hour where I spin your favorite dance records." Vivian smiled. Morty wasn't half bad, she thought. His voice was smooth, measured, and at least half a register lower than his normal speaking voice. She still didn't think there was much of a future in spinning dance records on the radio, but he'd been at it for six months so maybe there was something in it she just couldn't see.

The smooth clarinet intro of "Moonlight Serenade" interrupted her train of thought, and Vivian turned back to the desk and the task at hand. She pulled open the top drawer, and the first thing she saw was a key. Vivian stared at it. She had quite a habit of finding keys in desk drawers, she thought. Though this one was certainly easier to find — and hopefully much less trouble. She thought of all the trouble finding that key months ago in her father's study had brought.

She plucked the key from the drawer and turned to the gun cabinet. The lock opened with an efficient snick, and before she knew it, she was staring at dozens of guns: pistols, revolvers, shotguns.

There were rifles displayed vertically, barrels up, at the bottom of the cabinet. For hunting, she presumed. The handguns were hung in an orderly fashion on wooden pegs at the top. There weren't any labels. After all, Bernard knew his own guns, but a quick survey led her to the disappointing conclusion that all of Bernard's guns were accounted for, and none were currently lying under a hundred feet of water in Geneva Lake. She sighed, and then her eyes snagged on the gun on the far right peg — a gun that looked just like the one Gwen had thrown into the lake. Vivian reached out tentatively and removed the small pistol. Bernard's version was shinier than the other one had been. She turned it over gingerly in her hands. It was smaller than she remembered from the boat and heavier than it looked. It wasn't likely to be loaded, but holding it made her nervous. Still, she couldn't help but hold it up in firing position and look down the sight at the far wall.

There was a thump behind her and she whirled, gun still in hand.

"Christ, Viv. Watch that thing." David stood in the doorway, hands raised.

Vivian stood motionless for a few seconds before she realized what she'd been doing. She lowered the gun with an apologetic shrug. "Sorry. I didn't mean . . ."

"What are you doing in here?" David lowered his hands, but still stood stiffly in the doorway. Vivian knew she looked suspicious, standing at the open gun cabinet, a pistol in her hand, Glenn Miller's orchestra playing softly in the background. She sighed and sat down at the desk, the gun cradled in her lap.

"You've . . . heard about Hap? He's really dead." She tried to picture the faces of those she'd passed in the parlor just after it had happened. Had David's been among them?

David nodded. He shoved his hands in his pockets and looked past her. His eyes were red-rimmed, and his lower lip trembled just the tiniest bit. But he masked his emotions with a stern expression. He was his father's son, after all, but he was doing a better job pretending that Hap's actual death hadn't affected him.

"Rum luck," he said. "Hap was something, wasn't he? Always too much. Always doing things the hard way. He couldn't just fly a plane . . . He had to fly it upside down and with a man strapped to the wing." He shook his head. "And he couldn't just gamble, lose a few dollars here and there. No, he had to lose big and get a price on his head."

Vivian furrowed her brow with feigned surprise. "What's that?"

David cocked a brow. "Gambling debts. Big ones. That's why he faked his death on Sunday . . . to elude real death by the goons sent to do him in."

Vivian paused. That was the same story Bernard had tried with her. Did David actually believe it, or was he just using the cover story Bernard had coached him on? She decided to play dumb and let him talk. "Really?"

David nodded. "Father told me. I didn't

know until last evening. Constance came to me and told me some hogwash about having seen Hap very much alive in the guesthouse. Of course, I thought that was some cock-and-bull story. I didn't believe her."

"*Constance* said?"

"Said she was out for a late-night walk. She'd peeked into the windows of the guesthouse and seen Hap quite alive in there after he was supposed to be quite dead." David lowered his chin and looked at her, gauging her reaction to such news, she supposed. But Vivian was focused on what she'd *not* heard in David's rendition of Constance's story. Constance had either not told David she'd seen Hap and Lillian together, or David was purposely leaving that out of his version of events to save face — or cover up a motive for murder.

"Did Hap see Constance?" Vivian asked.

"I don't think so. I thought maybe Constance had had some sort of mental breakdown. She was always very fond of Hap, you know. It really wrecked her when he went off to Europe so suddenly years ago." David frowned and locked eyes with her, and Vivian got the impression that he meant to convey with the dramatic pause that they both knew *exactly* why Hap had gone off to Europe so suddenly years ago. Vivian glanced away and cleared her throat. She pulled the neckline of her dress away from the dried sweat on her chest and pretended that comment meant nothing to her.

"Anyway," David continued. "It's been an . . . odd . . . few days with the murder and Charlie's disappearance, and Father being so tight-lipped about everything. We were all in this strange suspended animation. None of us saw Hap, you see. None of us got to say a proper goodbye. I thought maybe Constance couldn't believe he was really dead. After all, I couldn't believe it either. Not really. Maybe she'd imagined seeing him in the guesthouse. Wishful thinking? So I went to Father. I sat down across from him in his study and said, 'Constance says she's seen Hap in the guesthouse just now.'

"Well, Father is a terrible poker player. The look on his face told me everything. He was so surprised that he couldn't hide it. He knew Hap was alive, of course, but he wasn't supposed to be within one hundred miles of here. I asked Father what was really going on, and he told me everything. That Hap's life was in danger due to gambling debts. He had some hired goons after him, and the only way to get them off his trail was to fake his own death."

Vivian nodded, careful to keep her face blank. So David really didn't know about the spy story.

David drummed his fingers against the desk before speaking again. "And I guess those goons found out that Hap wasn't as dead as he'd appeared, and they came back a few hours ago and finished the job."

Finished the job. The ominous words hung in the air between them.

"I'll admit it makes as much sense as anything else," Vivian said, measuring her words carefully.

"It must have been terrible for you to see that."

"It's a terrible thing for the family," she said carefully.

"For Father especially," David said, a wan smile lighting his lips. "After all, I was the son he had, but Hap was the son he *wanted.*"

Vivian didn't know what to say to that unexpected admission. She examined David's expression, his posture, for signs of bitterness, but she saw only resignation. David had grown up in Hap's shadow. Hap was a ne'er-do-well, but he'd always been a peg above David in his father's estimation.

"I'm just glad Lillian went back to Chicago when she did," he continued. "She was distraught enough about Hap's *fake* death. I can't imagine how she'd have reacted to the *real* one."

Vivian paused and glanced away from him. She knew she had to proceed carefully. Either David truly didn't know Hap and Lillian were having an affair, or he was lying about it. Or perhaps they weren't having an affair at all, and Gwen had made the whole thing up in her attempt at covering something up. *Someone* was lying though. That much was clear.

"But Lillian had only met Hap for a few minutes at the garden party, hadn't she?" Vivian said.

"Lillian is a sensitive soul . . . easily agitated."

Just a sensitive soul, or distraught that she believed her lover had been murdered? But David looked off toward the window, hiding his expression.

"Had you seen Hap much since he'd been back in the country?"

David shrugged. "A few times. Not enough."

"Was he going to stay in Chicago for a while?"

"Apparently not." David gripped the back of the chair and set his jaw. "Apparently, he was planning on *dying.*" His voice wavered,

300

and he put one balled fist to his mouth. He sounded bitter, angry, and unbearably sad. Hap had been around for almost David's entire life. Hap had planned on faking his death, yes, and that's what David meant, didn't he? He'd been his brother in everything but name, and now he was gone.

Vivian looked away, partially because she wanted to give David a moment of privacy and partially because she didn't want to start crying herself. The shock had gone now and left an emptiness in its wake. Hap's real death had yet to hit her, and as long as she concentrated on uncovering the truth, she could manage to stave off the grief. They sat in silence, the clock ticking on the mantel. In the hall, the grandfather clock started to wind up. The chiming led up to the signaling of the hour. There was a single chime. *Someone should stop the clock,* she thought. *There's been a death in the family.* She hitched in a breath and then pressed her lips together.

"Do you even know how to use that thing?" David nodded at the gun.

Vivian blinked. A single tear escaped her lower lashes, and she brushed it away. She looked down at the gun in her lap. She'd forgotten she was still holding it. Her fingers twitched over the grip, and she pulled them

301

away. That gun felt alive, as if it might jump from her hands of its own accord.

"I don't even know what it is. What kind of gun, I mean," she said, staring down at it.

"It's a Luger," David said without hesitation. "A German pistol. Used during the Great War mainly, but they're still being manufactured. It's one of Father's favorites. He likes to tell everyone that it was lifted from the body of a dead German officer at Ypres. Whether that's true or not, I couldn't tell you."

Vivian shivered and stared down at the gun. So the pistol Gwen had thrown into the lake was German and did not belong to Bernard. That made sense if a German agent had come here to shoot Hap. But why would he have thrown that pistol in the bushes? If a spy had shot Hap, he would have kept his gun. He also probably wouldn't have shot Hap in the stomach. But if the murder weapon was not from a German spy, then where did it come from?

Gwen had said she'd thrown it in the lake because she assumed David had shot Hap in a fit of jealousy. It certainly fit that Gwen might do that if she really suspected such a thing. But where would David have gotten the other pistol? And would he be able to stand here and calmly talk about Hap's murder if he had? David had shown no signs of anything but grief over Hap and his death. She'd never known David to be much of an actor. He couldn't even tell a joke without cracking himself up in the process.

"Anyway, Viv. I don't think you need it. Whoever killed Hap was out for Hap alone."

"How can you be so sure?"

David shrugged. "I can't, I suppose, but hired goons usually stick to bumping off who they've been hired to bump off."

She stood and replaced the Luger on its peg. Then she closed the cabinet, locked it, and put the key back in the top drawer of the desk. David watched her, lost in thought. Then she moved to the adjacent wall and made a show of looking at the books on the shelf. She reached out, and her hand hovered over a row of books. She was standing in front of the secret door, and the row she'd chosen purely by chance contained mysteries. Agatha Christie. Her eyes scanned the titles until she found the one she was looking for. She pulled it out and looked at the cover — the man shoveling coal into the fiery furnace of the train engine.

"Have you read it?" She held the book up

so that David could read the cover.

He nodded. "I've read them all. You?"

"Only the first three chapters. I left my copy on the train when I hurried back here."

They stood in silent contemplation for a moment, both lost in thought.

"You want to know who did it?" he asked suddenly.

She hesitated only a moment before nodding.

"Everyone," he said, locking eyes with her. "They were all guilty."

CHAPTER TWENTY

Freddy. The name came to her as she watched David leave the room and head for the back stairs. Vivian hadn't talked to Freddy in what seemed like days — not since she phoned him from the train station in Kansas City and lied to him. Her stomach twisted with guilt. Maybe if she'd called Freddy and told him everything after leaving the cabin, Charlie wouldn't be in such danger now. Maybe she should call Freddy now. Everyone had something to hide in this house, and there wasn't a soul among them she could trust.

She tiptoed into Bernard's office and slid the pocket doors closed behind her, flipping the lock. As she surveyed the room, her eyes lingered on the closet where Hap had been hiding this morning, alive and listening to her express her regret over the way they'd left things. She tore her eyes away and crossed to the other set of pocket doors that led into hall and locked them as well. She sat behind Bernard's imposing desk. The top was tidy, regimented, like the Bernard she'd always known. Her mind flashed an image of how she'd just seen him in the guesthouse — sweaty, disheveled, and red-faced from crying. She shook her head. If she hadn't seen it with her own eyes, she wouldn't have believed it. And she would never have believed that her upstanding uncle had covered up a man's murder if he hadn't told her himself. *You never know what someone's capable of,* she thought.

She picked up the receiver. Freddy had been staying at the rooming house in town, but would he still be there with Charlie on the lam? Probably not, but she decided to try it anyway. What was the name — *Henderson's? Johnson's?* She thought hard. *Albertson's.* Mrs. Albertson. The operator connected her, and an older woman answered breathlessly after seven rings.

"Hello? Mrs. Albertson's Rooming House. Mrs. Albertson speaking."

"Hello, Mrs. Albertson. Sorry to call so late," Vivian said. "But is Mr. Frederick Endicott still boarding there by any chance? It's an emergency."

"Mr. Endicott." The woman pronounced the name as if repeating a word in a foreign language. "Oh yes, he's here, and he told me someone might be calling in the middle of the night, and to always wake him if they did. Lawyer, isn't he? I'll fetch him for you."

Vivian heard the receiver clunk against the table as the woman laid it down.

A moment later, Freddy came on the line. "Viv?"

"Yes, how did you know?"

"What other woman would be calling me in the middle of the night claiming it's an emergency?"

"It *is* an emergency," Vivian said. "The landlady, Mrs. Albertson . . . She's not listening in somewhere, is she?" The woman had perked up considerably at the end of the call. She sounded like the type who loved a good piece of gossip.

"No," Freddy said quietly. "I can see her sitting in the parlor chair, safely out of earshot."

"Good. Because something's gone wrong here. Terribly wrong, and I need your advice."

"In Hollywood?"

"No, Freddy." Vivian paused. She had to just come out and say it. It was the only way. "I lied to you. I didn't get back on that train."

Freddy was silent, waiting for her to

continue. Vivian remembered something he'd told her about his method of getting to the truth of a matter. *Keep quiet and let them talk. They'll eventually hang themselves.* He'd been talking about cross-examining witnesses, but it applied in this situation as well, didn't it? The problem though was she wouldn't hang herself, but she just might hang Charlie. She swallowed the lump in her throat.

"I knew where Charlie was when I phoned you, and I didn't tell you," she said, speaking quickly. "I left the train and went to him, Freddy."

"Where? Are you with him now?"

"I'd rather not say where, and no, I'm not." Vivian glanced around, listening for a sign that anyone might be able to overhear anything she said. She'd assumed David had gone upstairs, but what if he hadn't? The walls were thin and uninsulated. But she only heard the radio in the other room, the muffled dance music playing on. "I'm back at Oakhaven, and things have gone topsy-turvy."

"What's happened?" Freddy asked warily.

"Hap's dead. He's dead *again,*" she whispered. Vivian suddenly felt herself on the verge of tears.

"Vivian, I don't understand."

"I know. I know you don't." She took a moment to gather herself. Tears would do no good now. "But just know that I'm certain Charlie didn't do it. He's been accused of a crime he didn't commit, and now he's running from the law. I need your help to straighten this out. Bernard told me he'd help clear Charlie's name."

"Okay, I'm coming over," Freddy said.

"Wait. No, it's late." Vivian glanced at the clock. It was almost midnight, but that wasn't the real reason. No, the real reason was that there were secrets here, and no one in this family would respond well to a lawyer coming in and asking questions. They'd all need time to get their stories straight. And if that's what it took to clear Charlie's name, she'd give them a little time.

"I don't feel comfortable leaving you there," Freddy said. "You sound . . . Well, you don't sound like yourself. Do you know where Charlie is?"

"No. Has he gotten in touch with you?"

"I have no idea where the fool might be," Freddy said, not hiding the consternation in his voice. "Canada, if he has any sense."

Vivian's heart sank. "Have you heard from Cal, his father?"

"He came up shortly before Charlie escaped custody. I wouldn't be surprised if he put Charlie up to it. They seemed of a kind, if you know what I mean. But no, I haven't spoken to him since. Do you think they're together?"

"I don't know," she said. *I hope so. At least he'd have someone.*

"I'm coming over first thing tomorrow morning," Freddy said.

"Thank you."

"Viv, don't worry. We'll clear all of this up."

"I hope so. Goodbye, Freddy."

"Goodbye."

She held the receiver to her ear for a moment before hanging up, lost in thought. Freddy sounded so sure of himself. She wanted to believe him. The phone clicked as Freddy's line disconnected. Then, moments later, she heard a second soft click, as if another line in the house had disconnected as well.

It was foolish of her to have used the telephone for something so serious, but she hadn't told Freddy anything anyone at Oakhaven didn't already know, had she? Everyone had already known Hap was still alive when she arrived this morning, and now they all knew he was dead. She didn't have time for eavesdroppers.

She stood in the hallway just outside Bernard's office and listened. The house was quiet, but it felt alive, as if it were breathing softly. Something hummed just under the surface, and Vivian had the feeling that the events of the evening had only just begun. Perhaps she should just lie in bed and wait for the sunrise, she thought. Everything would be clear in the morning. Maybe she should have drunk the whole mug of milk and brandy. She'd be blissfully sleeping away, and when she woke up, she'd be convinced none of tonight's events had really happened. But there would be no sleeping tonight for her. She headed to the kitchen for a glass of water and to think of what to do next.

Adaline stood at the kitchen sink, looking out over the darkened lawn. Vivian tried to turn around and reverse course before her aunt noticed her, but the linoleum squeaked under her heel.

Adaline's hand flew up at the sight of Vivian. Her fingertips hovered over her chest and came to rest on her breastbone, just below her double set of pearls. "What are you doing down here?" she said. Then she paused and lowered her hands. "You need your rest." Her narrowed eyes traveled down the length of Vivian's body, lingering on the leaves stuck to her shoes. "Where have you been?" Adaline asked.

"I've been trying to figure out what's going on around here," Vivian said.

Adaline's face was carefully blank, and Vivian was determined to crack that icy facade.

"So you're going to pretend that you didn't try to slip me a few sleeping pills in that milk and brandy and then lock me in my bedroom?" Vivian asked. She was careful to keep her voice even, controlled, matching her aunt's demeanor.

Adaline blinked but registered no surprise at the question. Those Markham women had ice in their veins, Vivian thought. She admired Adaline for that — the steel backbone, the staring down of all obstacles in her path.

"I gave you those sleeping pills because you'd been through a shock," Adaline said. "You needed to calm down."

"Calm down," Vivian repeated. "And you locked me in my room because you wanted to make sure everything that had happened would be cleared up by the time I woke in the morning. And maybe you could convince me that seeing Hap die in the boathouse was a bad dream. Do I have it right?"

"I didn't" — Adaline glanced into the hallway over Vivian's shoulder and then

312

lowered her voice to an irritated hiss — "lock you in your room."

Liar, Vivian thought. She bit her tongue before she could spit the word from her mouth like venom and took a deep breath. She couldn't come at Adaline with fire. Her aunt might respond in kind or, even worse, shut down completely, as Vivian's mother would in a similar situation.

"You knew that Hap wasn't dead. The first time, I mean . . . on Sunday," Vivian said. She tried not to let the anger bleed through into her voice.

"There are so many things you don't know," Adaline said.

"Like about Hap being a German spy?"

Adaline turned her back to look out over the darkened side yard. She was quiet for a moment. Vivian heard the grandfather clock in the hall ticking industriously away. Adaline didn't turn to look at her when she finally spoke.

"You two thought you had the world by the tail," she said. "You really thought no one knew, with you cavorting around like . . . like . . ."

It took a moment for Vivian's mind to catch up to what Adaline was saying. She was referring to that summer eight years ago.

"You knew?" she whispered.

"Of course I knew. All of Lake Geneva knew."

Vivian and Hap hadn't been terribly careful about their carrying-on that summer. Perhaps Adaline had seen them herself. The idea sent a furious blush to Vivian's cheeks. So everyone had known. Hadn't David just alluded to the same thing in the game room? The secret Vivian had carried for years was never a secret at all.

"Why didn't you say anything?" Vivian said.

"I did." Adaline's voice was flat. "I told Hap to put an end to it before your mother found out."

"And that was . . ."

"Shortly after it had begun in earnest."

In earnest. After Vivian had made that fateful visit to the guesthouse. Adaline truly had a talent for saying something without actually *saying* it.

"I thought of warning him off you when I noticed you making cow's eyes at each other across the dinner table that summer. I should have put a stop to it right then, but I hadn't expected that you'd go that far. I had no idea then the kind of girl you were."

Vivian clenched her hands into fists. "And what kind of girl was I?"

314

"Fast," Adaline said. She pitched her voice so low that Vivian almost missed her next words. "You just couldn't keep your hands off him, could you?"

Vivian's mouth fell open. In Adaline's eyes, Vivian had complete responsibility for what had happened. Hap was just a silly playboy. He couldn't be blamed for his behavior. It was expected, after all. Boys were boys, and men were men. They couldn't control themselves in the face of such blatant temptation. It was as if he had played no role in any of it. But he'd answered the door when she knocked. He'd let her in. He'd made her feel as if she were the only girl in the whole world. He'd left her with no explanation . . .

"You sent him away," Vivian said, thinking of how Hap had left so abruptly, without so much as a goodbye. She'd always hoped he hadn't left like that of his own accord, and now she was certain.

"What other choice did I have?"

What other choice? Adaline could have told them she knew. She could have talked to them both about the situation. That was the logical response, but that was never how the family handled things. Unpleasantness was not addressed head-on. No, they let things fester until they exploded.

"You must have bribed him somehow," Vivian said.

Adaline half turned, one eyebrow arched. "Oh, he went willingly enough. After I told him he could never accomplish anything he wanted in life if he stayed here."

"And you told him to just leave — without saying goodbye. To just disappear from my life as if pulling the bandage right off would make it hurt any less. That was cruel."

Adaline waved her hand dismissively, and the gesture was so much like her mother that it made the small hairs at the back of Vivian's neck bristle.

"That's neither here nor there. It was best for both of you, for all of us, if you just forgot each other."

Vivian wanted to scream. Instead, she dug her fingernails into her palms. "And it never occurred to you to tell me any of this in the years since?"

"Why would I? The problem was solved. I'm just grateful that you didn't get yourself in the family way. What would we have done with you then?"

Vivian couldn't speak because of the fury rising in her chest.

"You've always been willful, Vivian. I'm just glad your father wasn't around to see the way you behaved that summer."

"The way I behaved? Like a girl in love?"

"Love? That wasn't love."

"What do *you* know about it?"

"A lot of silly girls thought they were in love with Hap Prescott . . . all of them fools. And when you get a chance to calm yourself and think all of this through, I think you'll understand why I did what I did."

There was a noise at the end of a hall, and Vivian jumped. Someone was knocking on the front door. Vivian turned back to Adaline.

"I understand that you toy with people's lives when it suits you," Vivian said.

Adaline raised an eyebrow. Vivian heard David answer the front door.

"Believe it or not, I was protecting you."

"From myself, you mean?" Vivian said. "From my own *baser urges*?"

A humorless laugh escaped Adaline's mouth in a hiss. "No. I never liked Hap. He was a manipulator, and he had a particular talent for hurting people."

Adaline's eyes shifted to the doorway as David's voice rang out behind her. "There you are." Vivian turned to find David standing there. "Western Union man on the porch for you, Viv."

David's blue eyes darted from Adaline to Vivian. How much of their conversation had he heard?

What had he just told her so gravely in the game room? *They were all guilty.* Maybe he'd only been talking about the Agatha Christie book, but maybe he hadn't. Maybe they were all in on it, she thought. Bernard, Adaline, Gwen, the lot of them. Maybe they were all crazy as loons. Maybe they'd all conspired to get rid of Hap Prescott.

CHAPTER TWENTY-ONE

The young man stood in the open doorway in his dark-blue uniform and flat cap, the triangular Western Union badge glinting in the dim light of the hall. Vivian approached, her pulse thumping. *Charlie,* she thought. *The telegram could be about Charlie.*

The deliveryman straightened and smiled as she approached.

"Miss Vivian Witchell?"

"Yes."

The man held the envelope out to her and she took it, her hands shaking. She ripped it open and read it before she could lose her nerve.

LOS ANGELES CA 830 P JUN 15 1939
MISS VIVIAN WITCHELL
LANG RESIDENCE OAKHAVEN LAKE GENEVA WI

MET MAYER SCREEN TEST COMPLETE STOP
YOU ARE REPLACED IN SUN CC HOUR — NO

Vivian's heart slowed as her brain absorbed the information. How had Graham found her here? She stared at the words. The show would go on without her. It wasn't a surprise, but despite everything else that had happened tonight, it still stung. She'd missed her screen test and had been replaced in the guest spot on *The Carlton Coffee Hour.* They'd have to rewrite the part.

But these were all petty concerns since she still had no idea where Charlie was. She imagined him at this moment, cornered by the police in a rank back alley somewhere. He could be in custody. He could be hurt. He could be dead. There was a dull ache in the pit of her stomach.

"Miss?"

She glanced up and realized the Western Union man was hovering in the doorway. "I'm sorry, yes?"

"Would you like to send a reply?"

"No. No reply. Thank you."

The deliveryman tipped his cap and made his way down the porch stairs. She watched him go, her mind returning to the scant words of the telegram. *Replaced,* Graham had written. Replaced by whom? It hardly mattered. There were a thousand girls always at the ready to take her place if she faltered even the tiniest bit. And this was more than a tiny falter. This was a tumble.

Her eyes fell on the shiny black telephone sitting on the gossip bench. She wanted to call someone. But who? Adrenaline thrummed through her veins. She had to *do* something.

The telephone rang, and she jumped. She shouldn't answer it. No one was supposed to know she was here. She glanced around but heard no indication that anyone else was stirring on either floor to answer. She looked toward the kitchen, but there was no sound. Adaline and David must have left while she was at the door with the delivery-man. She moved to the table, picked up the receiver, and held it gingerly to her ear. She swallowed.

"Lang residence," she said.

"Is there a Vivian Witchell at this number?" the operator said.

"Y-yes. This is Vivian Witchell." Her heart thumped in her chest.

"Hold, please, for a person-to-person long-distance call," the operator said in a singsong voice.

Vivian heard several clicks before the operator told the other party, "You may proceed."

"Yes, hello. I'm looking for a Vivian Witchell. I was told she was staying there." It was a man's voice, one that Vivian didn't recognize, one that was commanding and take-charge even over the miles of long-distance wires.

Were the police calling her to tell her that Charlie had been captured and was back behind bars? That he'd been grievously wounded in a shoot-out? No, she thought. The police wouldn't call her like this — not directly, and certainly not long distance. Perhaps it was Cal, telling her not to worry and that Charlie was fine.

"This is Vivian Witchell speaking," she said.

"Miss Witchell? Louis Mayer here."

She froze, her pulse whooshing in her ears. She craned her neck to get a glimpse at the hall clock. Why would Louis Mayer be calling her at this hour? Why would Louis Mayer be calling her at all — especially after that telegram from Graham telling her not to hurry out?

"Hello? Do we have a bad connection?"

"Uh, no. No." She cleared her throat. "The connection is fine. Hello, Mr. Mayer."

"Good. Good. I was calling to tell you that

322

I'm sorry you missed our meeting yester-day."

"Yes, I'm sorry too," she said. "I had to return to Chicago . . . family emergency." Her mind worked furiously to think of a suitable emergency in case he asked. *My ex-lover's been murdered.* The thought sprang to her mind without warning, and she pressed the back of her free hand to her mouth to stop the hysterical laughter that threatened.

"Yes, I heard," he said. "I hope every-thing's all right."

She cleared her throat and took a deep breath. "Things are improving," she said. *Actually, things are looking worse by the min-ute.* She craned her neck to try to look down the hallway into the kitchen, but she couldn't see anything. Were Adaline and David still nearby, listening?

"Anyway, I'm a fan of your work on *The Darkness Knows,*" Mr. Mayer continued. "And if you're half as pretty as the publicity photos I've seen, you're just the kind of American wholesome we look for at MGM."

Vivian glanced around her. This had to be a joke. Her eyes drifted toward the kitchen and her thoughts to the conversation she'd just had with her aunt. *Wholesome,* she thought. *She* was wholesome? Aunt Adaline certainly didn't think so. Mr. Mayer continued talking, blithely unaware that she was on the verge of breaking down entirely.

"I liked that Yarborough fellow," he said. "But no one we tested with him had any chemistry. He insisted that you were the only actress who could play Lorna on the big screen, and I'm inclined to take him at his word."

Vivian leaned back against the wall and exhaled. So Graham had come through for her again, she thought. She truly didn't deserve his friendship. What sort of alchemy had he worked in his scant twenty-four hours in Hollywood?

". . . make it, won't you?"

Vivian blinked herself back to the present.

"Yes, yes, of course. I'll make it," she said automatically.

"Good. Then we'll see you on the lot Monday morning."

"Yes," she said. "Monday morning." *Monday morning?* Her mind raced to catch up. It seemed Louis B. Mayer himself was offering her another chance at that screen test. Her movie career was not dead on arrival after all. But that would mean she'd need to be on the Super Chief tomorrow evening. How could she ever swing that — with Hap truly dead and Charlie on the run?

"I look forward to meeting you. Good night, Miss Witchell," he said.

"Good night, Mr. Mayer."

Vivian sat with the receiver to her ear for a full minute after the connection cut off. She was stunned, but through the fog, she heard that soft click again that signaled someone somewhere in this house had been listening on another extension. She just couldn't make herself care at this particular moment. Her mind was whirling. She hung up the phone and then stared down at it as if it might offer further clues to what had just occurred. Louis B. Mayer had called her personally to invite her to take a screen test. But how would she ever make it out to Hollywood by Monday morning?

This had to end. She needed to find everyone and gather them together and get to the bottom of all of this. No more secrets. No more fantastic stories. No more suspicion. She walked down the hall to the parlor. The lights and the radio were on, but the room was deserted. She checked every room on the first floor, including the bathroom, and found them all empty.

She'd been stumbling over people around every corner over the past few hours. Now that she wanted them all together, where had everyone gone?

■ ■ ■ ■

The wind gusted as Vivian came out the back door, catching the screen and slamming it against the wooden siding with a bang. The air roared in the trees at the back of the house. Vivian looked off toward the west and saw a flash of lightning illuminate the sky under glowering clouds. She didn't have long until rain starting pouring down, she thought. She didn't know where she was headed or what she wanted to do. So much had happened since dinner, and she needed answers.

She glanced around the yard. The summer kitchen sat dark and quiet a few feet away. The murderer had been there, she thought. Just out of sight around the corner. It seemed ominous, with its blank windows like two unseeing eyes winking in the reflected flashes of intermittent lightning. Then again, everything looked ominous under the threat of a storm. The wind whipped a strand of hair across her eyes, and she tossed her head to clear her vision.

"Psst."

The noise came from direction of the summer kitchen. She stood still and listened. There it came again, barely audible over the roar of the trees. *Psst.* Someone was calling to her from the spot where the murderer had been hours before. Vivian hesitated. The murderer would not go back to the spot where they left the murder weapon, unless it was to retrieve said weapon. In this case, he or she would have quickly found that the gun was already gone, so there would be no reason to hang around. Besides, would someone who wanted to do her harm call to her like a cartoon villain in a Merrie Melodies short?

"Psst."

Against her better judgment, Vivian made her way down the back stairs and inched around the corner. She would be out of view from the house, she reminded herself. No one would see if the killer accosted her here. She stuck her head around the corner and could discern the bulk of a man in the shadows. She saw the tiny orange glow of a cigarette as the man moved toward her.

"Oh, you're not Gwen."

"Who is it?" she said, her voice quavering.

The man stepped forward, and Vivian sighed with relief as his face came into view. She didn't know what she was expecting — a bloodthirsty German spy luring unsuspecting family members to their deaths with a whisper?

"What are you doing out here, Marshall?"

He took a long drag on his cigarette and spoke with the exhale.

"I was worried about Gwen," he said. "She seemed . . . odd . . . when she said good night earlier. I just had to see her and make sure she was okay. She usually comes out here before she turns in for the night, so I decided to wait for her. Sorry if I scared you. You two look a lot alike from a distance."

"You should go," Vivian said. "This really isn't the best time."

"Why? What happened?" He leaned toward her and lowered his voice to a whisper. "Does it have to do with that Hap fellow?"

"No," she lied.

Marshall squinted at her as he brought the cigarette to his lips again. "Her sister Constance then? She's had another crackup?"

"Another?"

"She has them on the regular, I hear. Usually little ones for attention. You know, takes to her room for a few days, then reemerges good as new once the act has worn out its novelty. But Gwen told me she had a big one a while ago, and they sent Constance to some loony bin in Switzerland to recover."

The wind was picking up. Vivian heard

the rowboat knocking against the dock where she and Gwen had tied it earlier.

"A while ago . . . when?" she asked.

Marshall shrugged. "Sometime before my folks bought the house next door."

"And when was that?"

"Well, we moved in five years ago, so she must have spent time in the booby hatch before that," he said.

"I think they prefer the term 'sanatorium' these days," Vivian said absently. She had never heard of Constance spending time in a sanatorium. Then again, that wasn't the sort of news that was distributed in the yearly Christmas card, was it?

"Smoke?"

Marshall held an open pack of cigarettes out to her. She glanced at the brown paper wrapper, the winged helmet illustration on the front, and the breath caught in her throat. "Gauloises," she said, pretending to read the name upside down. "French?"

"Sure sounds like it," he said, turning the pack around to look at the cover himself. "Gwen gave them to me."

"Did she?"

"Sure, she likes to be sophisticated." He smirked. "They're too strong for my taste, but I'm desperate. I ran out of Lucky Strikes."

"Where did Gwen get French cigarettes?" Vivian knew the answer, of course, but did Marshall?

Marshall shrugged as lightning lit up the sky behind him. He cocked his head to the side as he shoved the pack back into his pocket.

"Say, are you all right? I saw you when Gwen's mother brought you back from your walk earlier. You didn't look so good."

"I'm fine, thank you."

"You do look better now. You have more color in your cheeks," he said, motioning vaguely with his lit cigarette. "Gwen told me all about you. You're on the radio, aren't you?"

"I am."

"Gwen thinks you hung the moon."

Vivian exhaled. *That's the problem,* she thought. *If only she didn't, then none of us would be in this mess. And maybe Hap might not be dead.*

"You should go home, Marshall," she said. "Before Mr. Lang finds you and starts to inquire why you might be smoking outside his house in the middle of the night."

"You're probably right," he said. Marshall glanced in the direction of the main house and flicked his cigarette butt to the ground, smashing it out with the toe of his shoe.

"Gwen's fine," Vivian said. "I'll convey your concern."

"Thanks," he said. He turned and started walking away, hands in pockets. In the direction of his own house next door, she hoped. She watched him until he'd disappeared among the trees of the lake path.

Marshall looked awfully comfortable waiting in that hidden smoking spot for Gwen. Vivian was certain he'd done it before — perhaps every night of the summer so far. Had he done it earlier tonight? Maybe Marshall had found the pistol under the bushes — or maybe he'd been the one to leave it there. After all, if Vivian knew where Gwen had gotten French cigarettes, then Marshall might have too and been lying about it. And he might not have taken too kindly to an older man trying to horn in on his girl. That was far-fetched, she thought. But everything that had happened tonight had been far-fetched.

Vivian strode off in the opposite direction from where Marshall had gone. Where was everyone? There were several other buildings on the property, but the most likely place that everyone had gone to meet without her was the guesthouse. Lightning flashed, followed closely by a clap of thunder. She wouldn't make it through the woods before the storm struck. She spotted the odd jumble of angles and sharp peaks that comprised the Siamese pagoda. She'd go there and think for a bit, wait out the storm. Maybe something would come to mind if she had time to think things through.

The wind whipped her hair in front of her eyes again, blinding her. As she lifted her hand to brush it away, strong arms grabbed her around the middle and lifted off her feet with tremendous force. The air escaped her lungs in a whoosh. She tried to scream, but a large hand slapped over her mouth. She struggled, twisting and pushing at the arm around her middle, but the man only tightened his grip.

Marshall? Had he come back to stop her questions? No, that didn't make sense. *Hired goons, then,* she thought frantically as she struggled. *Oh God, David was right.* Hired goons had killed Hap, and now they would kill her too. She bit the fleshy part of the man's thumb and kicked backward with everything she had like an angry mule. Her stacked heel connected solidly with shin-bone, and the man grunted in pain. He didn't release her, but he lightened his grip as he spoke directly into her ear.

"Goddamn it, Viv. Stop kicking."

Vivian's racing heart fluttered at the sound of that voice and the familiar tingle of breath on her ear. *Charlie. Oh God, Charlie.* She tried to twist in his arms, to see him with her own eyes, but he still held her fast.

"Let me go, or I *will* kick you again," she hissed. He released her, and she whirled around when the balls of her feet touched the ground. As soon as she caught sight of his face, she began laughing and crying at once. She reached up and touched his cheek tentatively with her fingertips. Two days' worth of stubble stung her skin. It was really him. He was solid. He was here. She jumped into his arms, latching her fingers at the nape of his neck.

"Thank God," she said between hard, tooth-cracking kisses. "You're okay. Thank God you're okay."

He flexed his arms and pressed her against his chest so tightly she couldn't catch her breath. But she didn't dare struggle again. If she let him go now, she thought, she may never get him back. Finally, he lowered her gently to her feet again. He studied her face, his eyes narrowed, his jaw set.

"Of course I'm okay," he said, studying her face in the dim light. "Something's wrong. What's happened?"

"Hap's dead."

Charlie's brow furrowed. His mouth opened and closed. Then he glanced around the empty lawn and pulled her farther into the shadow of the Siamese pagoda.

"I mean he's dead *again*," Vivian said. "Someone shot him in the boathouse about two hours ago."

Charlie pressed his lips together. "I don't understand."

"Hap didn't die on Sunday, Charlie. You didn't kill him."

"I know that," he said. Vivian couldn't miss the note of frustration in his voice.

God, this is so hard to explain. But she had to try. She placed her palm on Charlie's chest as if she could press the truth into him. "Hap didn't die on Sunday, but someone *did* kill him about two hours ago."

"Who? How?"

"In the boathouse. Someone shot him. He . . ." Suddenly, she was there again, watching Hap fall at her feet, watching the life drain from his eyes. Her voice cracked, and she rested her forehead against Charlie's broad chest. Charlie was here, she reminded herself. He was alive. He was safe. Those thoughts went around and around in her head like a mantra. She slid her palms up his chest to latch around the base of his

334

neck again and gazed up at him. "You're not supposed to be here," she said.

"I couldn't let you do this alone, Viv. Not with a killer on the loose."

There *was* a killer on the loose, she thought. Not the killer Charlie had assumed when he made his way here, perhaps, but a killer nonetheless. How *had* he made his way here? She glanced over her shoulder at the cars lined up in the drive. There were her jalopy and the family's sedan. There weren't any other cars in the drive.

"But you're wanted, Charlie," she said, turning back to him. "If someone sees you and calls the police . . ."

He kissed her quickly again before she could continue with that train of thought. "Wild horses couldn't keep me away from you." Though his breath was warm against her ear, it made chills crawl up her spine. They stood looking at each other, the wind roaring in the trees around them.

"Show me where it happened," he said finally. "Let's figure this out."

She took his hand and led him toward the boathouse.

"We have to be careful," she said, turning to glance at him and then at the house. "Stay out of sight. I don't know where my family is, and I don't know who may be watching."

Charlie nodded and they continued in silence, hugging the shadows and glancing anxiously back at the house. The lights were still on, though Vivian couldn't see any shadows in the windows.

They stopped as they reached the shore side of the boathouse and gazed up at it.

"Where, exactly?" Charlie whispered.

"Inside," she said, pointing up. She headed toward the stair door and then stopped as she reached for the knob, her hand hovering in midair. She'd heard something.

"Viv —"

She turned to face Charlie and held one finger up to her lips.

There it was again. A rustling. She locked eyes with Charlie and knew from his expression that he'd heard it too. He nodded his head toward the front of the boathouse and motioned for her to follow. They crept around the side to the front, where the old-fashioned double doors hung ajar. The lock that held them together was missing. The rustling noise came again, louder this time.

Vivian tiptoed toward the doors. She glanced back at Charlie and shrugged. There shouldn't be anything inside except the old steam yacht. The family took it out sometimes for excursions on the lake. She knew Uncle Bernard wanted to sell it, although Adaline wouldn't let him because of a sentimental attachment. They had a devil of a time keeping it afloat with its expensive upkeep.

They stood still for another long moment, and Charlie motioned toward the side door. Vivian shook her head, but he slipped inside before she could stop him. This didn't feel right. The door opened onto only blackness inside. She listened at the door and heard nothing. Just as she was about to enter, she saw Charlie coming back toward her out of the darkness.

"It's nothing," he said. "Probably a ra—"

He didn't finish. Instead, she heard a meaty thud and watched Charlie fall to the floor, his eyes rolling back into his head.

"Charlie!" Vivian said. She rushed toward him, but stopped as someone pointed a flashlight directly into her eyes.

"Who is it? Who's there?" Vivian asked.

The flashlight lowered and Vivian stood blinking, spots jumping back and forth in front of her eyes. When her vision returned, she saw a woman standing just behind Charlie's prostrate form. She was holding a gun.

Vivian raised her hands reflexively, and slowly the woman's face came into focus.

"Lillian, what — ?"

"Shut up," Lillian said. She squatted next to Charlie and searched him one-handed, keeping the gun, a Luger, trained on Vivian. She pulled Charlie's revolver from the waistband at the back of his trousers, then fished in his trouser pockets. Vivian heard the jingle of his car keys as Lillian stood and dropped them into her pocket. Vivian saw Charlie's eyes flutter open and then close again before the light of the flashlight left his face.

"I don't understand," Vivian said quietly. The bulk of the steam yacht loomed directly in front of her, but she couldn't see anything beyond that. She heard the water lapping gently at the metal hull of the yacht and a lone frog singing somewhere in the darkness.

"There's nothing for you to understand," Lillian said curtly. She took a step toward Vivian, and as she did, Charlie groaned. Lillian stopped and trained the flashlight beam on Charlie's face. Charlie squinted in the light. He pressed a hand to the back of his head and hissed in pain.

"Ah, thick-headed. I knew I should've hit you harder. Get up and stand by your lady friend there." She nudged Charlie with the toe of her shoe. He groaned again, but

338

didn't move. "You'll get up if you know what's good for you."

Charlie's eyes opened slowly, the whites visible before the irises slid back down into place. He squinted at Vivian, and she motioned him toward her. Slowly, so very slowly, he staggered to his feet. He tottered for a moment, leaning drunkenly against the hull of the yacht before righting himself. Vivian watched as he patted his waistband, looking for his gun, and then saw a look of resignation pass over his features when he realized it was gone. He made his way to Vivian's side and turned to face Lillian. Vivian looped her arm through his to steady him.

"What am I going to do with you two?" Lillian said.

"You're supposed to be in Chicago," Vivian said.

She pointed the gun at Charlie. "And this one's supposed to be in jail."

"Change of plans," he said in a quiet voice.

"I can sympathize," Lillian said. "Things haven't gone the way I expected today either."

What was Lillian doing here in the first place? Hadn't David taken her to catch the train to Chicago earlier today? Vivian's mind whirred like a clock that had been wound too tight. Then a gear clicked and released, and things fell into place. There was only one conclusion to make.

"You're the German spy," Vivian said.

Lillian snorted, and her mouth curled up. But there was no amusement on her face, and she flexed her fingers on the handle of the gun. Her eyes were hard, cold, calculating.

"Hap recognized someone from his time in Spain at the garden party," Vivian said. "Someone that frightened him enough to put that silly fake-death plan into play. That someone was you, wasn't it?" Vivian pressed. She had to press. She was so close to figuring everything out. She felt Charlie sway against her. *Please don't pass out again,* she thought.

"I never met Hap before that party."

"Don't play coy, Lillian. The jig is up. If you aren't a German spy, then why did you have David take you to the train station today and then secretly make your way back here? Why are you hiding from your own fiancé in the boathouse? Why are you holding us at gunpoint?"

"Is this twenty questions?"

Vivian swallowed. "You shot Hap."

Lillian stared at her. She shifted the gun so that it pointed at Vivian, then Charlie, and then back again at Vivian. "I didn't have the chance."

"But you came back here because you knew Hap was still alive, and you wanted one last chance to convince him of his place — with the Germans, spying on his own country. You'd convince him or finish the job and kill him yourself. And I'd bet even money that you were standing near that copse of birches around nine o'clock tonight watching the boathouse. You'd followed Hap there."

One of Lillian's blond eyebrows rose.

"I saw the light of your cigarette."

Lillian studied Vivian. "I did follow Hap to the boathouse. I watched him enter from the trees. I was curious what he was up to. A few minutes later, I heard the shot. Then you came along."

"And you didn't see anyone leave?"

"I watched your aunt rush in and then lead you back out again," she said. "No one else."

"Why should I believe you?"

"Maybe you shouldn't," she said. "But why would I lie? Believe me, I'm just as upset about Hap's untimely demise as you are."

Vivian didn't doubt that she was, but for a different reason entirely. "How did you know he was still alive?" she asked.

"Oh, please," Lillian said. Vivian watched the tip of the gun dip as she spoke. "You accuse me of being involved in international espionage and then believe that I couldn't see through that silly ruse?"

"So how?"

"I actually didn't until after I left this morning. I found out that someone of Hap's description was trying to get brand-new identity papers. I made sure those papers were destroyed before Hap could get them. Then I knew that Hap had no choice but to come back here and devise a new plan, or perhaps simply accept his destiny." Lillian paused and cocked her head to the side, a look of mock sympathy coming over her face. "Oh, darling, you didn't think he came back here for you?"

Vivian's face burned, and she felt Charlie stiffen beside her. She squeezed his arm in what she hoped was a reassuring way. "No, of course not," she said, trying not to sound defensive. "But maybe he came back to clear an innocent man's name."

Lillian turned her attention to Charlie, a smile curling the corner of her mouth. "Perhaps. Hap could be quite gallant when he wanted to be." Her attention shifted back to Vivian. "But I suspect he just wanted help escaping the trap he'd found himself in, and you were a gullible person. A secret rendezvous in the secluded boathouse? He wanted to sweet-talk you into helping him out of his jam."

"It wasn't a secret rendezvous," Vivian said quietly. "And it wouldn't have worked."

"Hap was a persuasive fellow, as you well know. But maybe you have matured since he'd seen you last. Maybe you could have turned him away. But no doubt, if you didn't deliver, Hap would have just gone to one of the others he had on a string."

Thunder rumbled in the distance, and they all turned instinctively toward the open door.

"Enough talking." Lillian motioned with her gun out the door. "March."

Neither Vivian nor Charlie moved.

"March, or I start shooting."

Vivian felt the hard nose of the gun in the small of her back as Lillian steered them toward the end of the dock. The rowboat bobbed in the water. Could it only have been hours since she and Gwen had tied it there? It seemed like days. Charlie said nothing as they made their way down the dock, and Vivian glanced up at him every few seconds. She couldn't tell if he was still dazed from the blow to the head, or if he was quiet because he was formulating a plan. She hoped it was the latter.

"Get in," Lillian said.

Vivian hesitated, and Charlie urged her forward as he turned to face Lillian, putting Vivian behind him.

"What are you going to do?" he said.

"I'm going to get away." Lillian held her free hand up and jingled the keys she'd taken from Charlie's pocket. Lillian wouldn't dare leave with Bernard's conspicuous Cadillac. Vivian felt Charlie's reassuring hand on the small of her back. He urged her forward into the boat. She climbed in, and he followed.

They both sat on the bench on the far end facing Lillian. Lightning flashed, illuminating Lillian's face. She wasn't smiling, and she still held the gun on them. Thunder rumbled. "Untie it," she said.

Charlie's fingers fumbled with the rope, and Vivian leaned over to help him.

What did she intend? As if in answer, Lillian stepped forward and, without warning, fired two shots into the hull of the boat near the stern. Vivian jumped, and Charlie reflexively lunged sideways to shield her with his body. But Lillian hadn't intended to shoot either one of them. She put one foot against the boat and pushed. The rowboat slid backward into the water and drifted a few feet into the lake. She trained the gun on them again.

"Now, row," she said.

The wind was picking up and pushing the rowboat toward the deepest part of the lake.

"Row, big fella," Lillian said. "Or I put a bullet in her pretty head."

Charlie pushed Vivian to the other side of the boat and wordlessly picked up the oars. He started rowing with a grimace. Vivian glanced over her shoulder at Lillian, still holding the gun on them as she backed down the dock toward shore. Vivian's shoes were already wet as water seeped steadily in from the two holes in the stern of the boat. She looked around for something to plug them with but found nothing waterproof. She ripped a piece of her slip off and stuffed it in one hole, but it was no use. The water was pouring in now. The boat would swamp in minutes.

Charlie stopped rowing. Vivian caught sight of Lillian running around the far side of the boathouse.

The stern was dipping heavily now; it was almost entirely under the water. They were at least fifty yards from shore. Vivian moved to the bench on the other side, next to Charlie. They'd be swamped soon. Likely, the hull would flip, sending them both into the swirling, pitching lake. The wind was picking up and pushing them even farther from shore. Then it started to rain, big, fat raindrops plunking into the water. A flash of lightning lit the sky above them, and for a moment, it was like broad daylight out there on the lake. In that flash of lightning, Vivian caught Charlie's expression, and she didn't like what she saw. Fear.

"I have good news and bad news," he said, raising his voice to be heard over the thundering of the raindrops on the water. He leaned toward her and continued talking without waiting for which she'd like to hear first. "The *good news* is that no one's pointing a gun at us anymore."

"And the bad news?" Vivian asked, grasping his hand.

He pulled back so she couldn't mistake the seriousness of his expression.

"I can't swim."

CHAPTER TWENTY-TWO

Vivian tried to calm her racing mind. She had to think through what would happen next, and then what they could do to get out of this mess. She'd been in the middle of this lake in a swamped rowboat before. That time, the boat had swamped and flipped, but did not sink. She squeezed Charlie's hand.

It didn't take her long to realize something was terribly wrong this time. The rowboat was taking on water fast — too fast. In seconds, they were both chest deep in the lake. Raindrops drove into the water on all sides, splashing her face and making it difficult to see anything beyond her hands in front of her. Lightning flashed above. The water was cold and black. It stung her fingers and her toes. Then, somehow, she was floating free of the boat entirely. Vivian kicked off her shoes so she could tread water better. She'd lost her grip on Charlie's hand in the confusion and glanced around her in the water, panicked.

Charlie had floated a few feet away, clinging to the hull of the boat. She reached for him and realized that the boat hadn't just become swamped as she had assumed it would, and it wasn't going to flip over and float either. No, the entire boat was sinking. Charlie's eyes were wide as he clung to the last few inches of the boat's hull that were still above water. He hadn't been kidding, she realized. Charlie really couldn't swim.

Oh Jesus.

They weren't far from shore — perhaps fifty feet. But the water dropped off suddenly after the dock ended, and they couldn't touch the bottom here. They'd have to swim, or at least tread water. But Charlie didn't know how to tread water. The thought screamed in her head. She looked around wildly for something that would float. Anything. Water splashed in her eyes. There was almost no light to see by out here. Her mind could not latch on to the idea that the boat had sunk. That heavy box in the stern she'd noticed earlier while with Gwen. It had sunk them. Once the hull slipped beneath the surface, Charlie would panic, despite his best efforts not to. It was human nature. He'd flail out and instinctively grab her in an effort to keep himself afloat. He'd end up drowning them both.

They locked eyes above the churning surface of the lake. Charlie's jaw was clenched, his mouth a grim line. His hair was plastered to his forehead. He reached out and touched her face. His mouth moved, but Vivian couldn't hear him over the pounding roar of the raindrops on the lake. She shook her head.

"Go!" he shouted.

Go? Go where?

"Swim to shore! Save yourself!"

Vivian shook her head. The words stuck in her throat.

"Go!" he shouted again.

She shook her head furiously. Wet tendrils of hair slapped her cheeks. She *could* turn and go now. She *could* swim to shore. She'd done it a thousand times. She could make it, but she could not take Charlie with her. She wouldn't leave Charlie to drown. Never. And she couldn't stay here and watch him drown. This was not happening, she thought. Not like this. This wasn't some sappy daytime melodrama at the radio station. She would not sacrifice him to save herself. She would not have it.

She held Charlie's gaze as she swam toward him. The last of the hull slipped under the water, and Charlie's head immediately dipped below the surface. *No,* she thought. *No!* She reached for him and pulled him into an embrace. She squeezed him to her, kicking madly for the both of them. His head bobbed to the surface, and he gasped. This wouldn't work. No matter how hard she kicked, she could not keep both of them afloat. She squeezed her eyes shut, and when she opened them, she saw a flash of white bobbing on the waves.

Charlie slid under the water again. She reached down for him and caught his sleeve, but he was too heavy and she could not drag him back to the surface. She fought the panic that rose in her throat. Something white flashed in the corner of her eye again. A life preserver! There must have been one under the bench seat of the rowboat that hadn't been tied down. Charlie resurfaced briefly then, and he coughed and gasped.

"Stay there!" she screamed. "Keep your face out of the water! Kick! Move your arms like this." She showed him the motion above the water, but she didn't know if he could hear her, if he could understand. Thunder boomed in the sky as she spoke. Lightning zigzagged almost directly above them, so close she heard the sizzle of the electricity. If a lightning bolt hit the water, they were done for, life preserver or no life preserver. But she couldn't worry about that now. She swam furiously for the white ring as the wind and the waves forced it away from her. She lunged and caught it with her fingertips. *Thank God.* She turned, pushing the preserver in front of her, and saw nothing but the dark, choppy water. Charlie was gone.

Vivian forced the panic down yet again. She swam back to where she'd seen him last, but it was so hard to tell if she was in the right spot. The rain had not relented. If anything, it had increased in its ferocity. She was very close to panicking entirely. She treaded water where Charlie should be. Her eyes darted frantically over the waves, but there was no sign of him. Then her foot connected with something underwater, something soft and fleshy. Without thinking, she dove. The water was like ink. She couldn't see her hand in front of her face. She flailed her arms around and connected with him. An arm. She pulled Charlie to the surface with every bit of strength she had. When his mouth broke the surface, he gasped and sputtered, and coughed a warm jet of water right into her face.

Oh, thank God. Thank God.

"I have a life preserver," she shouted into his ear. "Here. Put your arms over it." She pulled one of his amazingly heavy limbs from the water and heaved it over the ring. He blinked. Then he coughed another torrent of lake water. It streamed from his nose in wild rivulets. His eyes rolled up alarmingly into his head, but he pulled his other arm from the water and threw it over the preserver. He rested his chin on it and closed his eyes.

He'd been a hairbreadth from death, and he knew it. Maybe he still was, Vivian thought. Lillian had given him one hell of a wallop on the head. He probably had a concussion. She had to get him to shore as soon as possible.

She leaned over and pressed her lips to his temple, then said into his ear, "Just hold on to me and keep your head above water. I'm going to tow you to shore."

CHAPTER TWENTY-THREE

Vivian opened the front door and stepped into the foyer. She stood dripping water onto the wooden floor, unsure of what to do next. She was just glad to be in the house and to be safe, even if she was soaked to the skin and even if they'd let Lillian get away.

Vivian blessed every minute of time she'd spent swimming as a child. The rain had lightened by the time she had towed Charlie to solid ground, and they had lain on the shoreline, panting. Vivian had watched Charlie intently, pinching him every time his eyelids started to drift shut. He'd perked up on the walk inside, but she'd still have to watch him.

She reached out and took Charlie's hand. They exchanged a glance. They'd have to dry off, get changed, do something about what just happened, shouldn't they? Then again, maybe they shouldn't do anything at all — just disappear and let Bernard and

Freddy clear everything up in a few hours. After all, clearing Charlie's name did not necessarily depend on pinning everything on Lillian. Not if Bernard went with the gambling debts story as he'd intended to do earlier. In that case, Vivian probably shouldn't tell anyone about what had just happened with Lillian and the rowboat. Maybe they could sneak upstairs before anyone noticed they were here. Vivian took a step toward the stairs.

Then Gwen came out of the parlor into the hall and stopped in her tracks.

"Lands," Gwen said. "What happened?" She took in Vivian's bedraggled appearance, and then her eyes darted to Charlie with alarm. "What's *he* doing here?"

"Almost drowning," he said after a beat.

"Drowning?" Her eyes shifted from Charlie to Vivian. "What's going on?"

Vivian opened her mouth to explain and then closed it again. Where should she begin, and what version of events did Gwen know or should she know? Vivian didn't want to muddle things for Charlie by saying the wrong thing to the wrong person.

"What's that, Gwen? Who's there?" David called from the parlor. He popped his head around the doorframe. "Viv . . . *Charlie?*" He stepped fully into the hall. They all stood staring at one another, unsure where to begin. Then David said, "I think you should come in here. There's someone here to see you."

"Me?" Vivian said.

"Both of you."

Uncle Freddy sat in the chair nearest the radio. He turned his head as they entered the room, and he stood and smiled slightly at Vivian. She had never been so happy to see anyone in her life — barring seeing Charlie earlier in the evening, that is. She ran to Freddy and kissed him on the check.

"I told you to come in the morning," she said.

He shook his head. "That phone call tied me in knots, Viv. How could I sit in that rooming house a few miles away and not try to help if I could? And I'm glad I did." He eyed her all over again, a million questions on his face.

She grasped his hand and squeezed lightly.

He leaned in and whispered, "Has Charlie been here the whole time?"

Vivian bit her lip. So Freddy assumed she'd lied to him earlier on the telephone, and why wouldn't he? She'd done it before.

"No . . . I . . . Well, it's a long story," Vivian said.

Freddy motioned for everyone to sit. Vivian slumped onto the settee facing him, with Charlie next to her. She watched the lake water drip from the hem of her ruined dress onto the parlor rug. *Plink. Plink.*

David leaned over to Gwen and said quietly, "Gwen, find these two some towels, would you? Mother will have kittens when she sees this mess."

Gwen hurried off.

"Where *is* Aunt Adaline?" Vivian asked. "She should probably be here for this. Uncle Bernard too." She thought of the Agatha Christie novel again. Didn't her books always end with that funny little detective gathering all of the suspects in one room to explain his theory of what had happened and to accuse the murderer of the crime?

"I'm not sure, actually," David said. "I haven't seen Mother since you were speaking with her in the kitchen earlier. What the devil happened to the two of you?"

Vivian exchanged a look with Charlie, and he nodded at her.

"Lillian," Vivian said. "She forced us out into the rowboat and then shot it full of holes so she could make her getaway."

David turned his head slightly to the side and regarded them out of the corner of one eye. Vivian had seen that look a million

356

times from David. He'd always been gullible, an easy mark for a practical joke. She'd taken advantage of that gullibility as a child. Unfortunately, this time it wasn't a joke.

"Lillian?" he said after a moment of silence. The skeptical look faded.

David had no idea who Lillian really was, and he had no idea he'd been jilted. That's where they'd have to begin, Vivian thought. She took another deep breath.

"Maybe you should sit down," she said.

He shook his head and set his jaw. Thunder rumbled, but it was far off in the distance. The storm had moved on.

"David," she began, shooting a sideways glance at Charlie. "Lillian isn't who you thought she was."

David glanced at everyone, a half smile on his face as if he were ready to say "I knew it!" when Vivian revealed that it had all been an elaborate prank. His smile faded entirely as he gauged their serious expressions. "What do you mean?"

"I doubt that Lillian Dacre is even her real name." Vivian paused and cleared her throat. "That is to say, Lillian Dacre is a real person, but I doubt that the woman you called your fiancée was that person."

David narrowed his eyes at her. "What exactly are you getting at?"

"Hap and Lillian knew each other."

"Of course they did," he said. "They met at the party on Sunday."

"No, they knew each other before . . . in Spain. Lillian didn't take the train to Chicago today, David. She was hiding in the boathouse. She'd come back for Hap. She sent us into the lake with a rowboat full of holes while she made her escape." Vivian gestured down to her wet clothing and the growing puddle at her feet.

David's mouth opened and then closed again.

"Bernard told you that Hap had gambling debts," she continued. "But he told *me* that Hap was a spy . . . part of Franco's fifth column."

"Franco? Viv, none of this makes any sense. I saw Lillian get on that train." David shook his head. "And Hap was a member of the International Brigades. He was fighting *against* Franco. He sent us letters . . ."

Vivian shook her head. "He was undermining their cause."

David stared down at his hands. Vivian could see the emotions flash over his face — confusion, anger, fear. *David would be terrible at poker,* she thought.

"But Lillian got on that train," he said finally. "I saw it pull away."

"She fooled you, David. She fooled all of us."

He looked up and stared at both of them. His eyes darted over them, taking in their general state all over again. He stared hard at Charlie.

"Lillian did this to you?"

"Yes, and clocked me a good one with the butt of her gun," Charlie said. He touched the tender spot on the back of his head and winced.

David turned away and stalked toward the door. Vivian thought he might leave, that he might have had enough of their unbelievable accusations about his fiancée. But he turned at the doorway and grasped the frame as if for support. Slowly, he turned to face the room.

"So Lillian . . . Do you think she . . . ?" He couldn't seem to be able to finish the sentence, but Vivian could guess what he was trying to say.

"I think she probably killed Hap tonight in the boathouse," she said quietly. Charlie reached over and placed his strong, warm hand atop hers.

"And she's gone?" David asked.

"Yes."

"She took my car," Charlie said. "And my gun."

David looked down at the rug, his jaw clenching and unclenching with unspoken feeling. Lillian had only been using him to work her way into Hap's life. David hadn't known her at all. He'd seen the girl he wanted Lillian to be and had never bothered to look any further.

Gwen rushed back into the room, arms outstretched with a pile of towels. She handed Vivian and Charlie each a large bath towel and dropped the rest in a pile at their feet. "Sorry it took me so long. I had to run all the way upstairs to the linen . . ." Her brow furrowed as she took in the somber mood of those present. "What's happened?"

"You really don't know where your parents are?" Freddy asked.

"In the guesthouse, I think," Gwen said. "Trapped by this storm."

"The guesthouse?" David said.

Vivian paused in the middle of drying her hair and lifted the towel from her so that she could meet David's eyes when she spoke next. "I suspect Bernard and Adaline have been very busy in the past few hours destroying any evidence that might prove Hap Prescott's continued existence after Sunday afternoon."

Vivian watched David's mouth open in question, but Gwen spoke first.

"And they're in the guesthouse because that's where Hap and Lillian . . ." Gwen said. Her eyes darted to the floor, and she slapped a hand to her mouth.

David's head turned sharply toward his younger sister. "Where Hap and Lillian what?"

"Well, Constance told me she saw Hap and Lillian together in the guesthouse on Saturday evening. She told me they were having an affair." She stepped forward and put a hand lightly on her brother's arm, but he shook it off.

"An affair? That's preposterous. Constance never said anything about that to me."

"I'm sorry. I assumed you knew," Gwen said, glancing around at the others in the room in a panic. "That's why I . . . Well, that's why I threw the gun in the lake."

"What gun?"

"The gun I found in the bushes by the summer kitchen. I assumed you'd killed Hap and then tossed the gun in the bushes when your temper wore off."

David stared at his younger sister, his mouth agape, and then he shook his head. "Oh, Gwen."

"So you didn't . . . ?"

"Shoot Hap in a jealous rage? No."

Gwen glanced at Vivian, her eyes big. "If David didn't do it, then . . ."

"It was Lillian," David said before Vivian could open her mouth.

"Lillian?" Gwen said.

"She and Hap *did* know each other, Gwen. From Spain. They may or may not have had an affair, but that's not the real headliner. She'd been playing me for a fool in order to get closer to the man she really wanted. Lillian, or whoever she really was, was here to convince Hap to spy for Hitler," David said.

Gwen stared at her brother, her eyes wide. Vivian nodded at her.

"Poppycock," Gwen said finally. "Knock-her-over-with-a-feather Lillian? A German spy?"

"She as much as admitted it," Vivian said.

"Before she shot the rowboat full of holes and nearly drowned us," Charlie added.

Gwen took that information in silently, and then she dropped into the nearest armchair. "It's just . . . Well, that's just too unbelievable," she said. "Lillian?"

"She was a good actress," Vivian said. "She had me fooled."

Gwen shook her head. "Maybe she was. You know, it's funny. They looked nothing alike, but her act reminded me quite a bit of Constance. So wan and nervous. So easily excitable. Why, when I saw them together at the garden party, it struck me. How alike they were with their delicate constitutions. Maybe it's for the best. She wasn't at all who I would have picked for you, David."

David sighed in response. That's exactly what Vivian had thought upon meeting the girl. Gwen's words echoed in her mind: delicate constitutions. She'd seen Constance insert herself between Hap and Gwen at that garden party. She'd seen the look on her face. Annoyance and disappointment. Heavy on the disappointment.

". . . so agitated talking to Hap and me at the garden party that her hands were shaking," Gwen said.

"What's that?" Vivian asked.

"Shaking, I said," Gwen repeated. "That happens when Constance is starting one of her spells . . . tremors of some sort. Any little thing can set her off. It was always hard to predict what. She wasn't happy with Hap talking to me the way he was, I suppose."

Vivian's stomach turned, and she pressed a hand to it. "And how exactly was he talking to you?"

"Oh, like an oily Continental. Complimenting my dress. Telling me I had lovely eyes. You know Hap. *Knew* Hap," she corrected with an embarrassed wave of her hand. "It was harmless."

Vivian looked down at her own hands, her fingertips still pruney from having been in the lake. Vivian had seen Gwen and Hap talking at the garden party, and she'd thought that too, hadn't she? Hap was up to his old tricks. *Had* it been harmless? Gwen was so young. The same age Vivian had been when Hap had taken advantage. It was a reflex with him — flirt with the pretty, young girl, see if you can get her to take the bait. How silly Vivian was to think she'd been special to him. There had been others before her and others since.

Adaline said Hap had a history of hurting people, Vivian thought. And what had Lillian said? That offhand remark about Hap having others on a string? Then she knew. She was certain. Adaline hadn't sent Hap away that summer to save Vivian or her reputation. She'd sent him away to save Constance, and then she'd sent Constance to that sanitarium in Switzerland that Marshall had mentioned. It hadn't been nervousness that had Constance's hands shaking over Hap's flirtations with her younger sister. It wasn't just a spell to get attention. It had been agitation, years of frustration and pent-up emotion.

No, Vivian hadn't been the first of Hap's

conquests, but perhaps Constance had. Perhaps Constance had the misfortune of caring more for Hap than he'd ever cared for anyone other than himself. Constance had watched Hap seduce Vivian that summer. What would she do if she thought Hap, the man she loved, had designs on her younger sister? What would she do if she'd finally come to terms with the fact that the man she loved would not only never love her back, but never stop rubbing her face in his lack of concern for her?

"Where's Constance?" Vivian asked.

"Sleeping," David said. "Been sleeping all evening, or so I assume since she didn't come down to dinner. She does this sometimes after a spell, hibernates for a week like a bear."

Vivian had seen Constance asleep in her room just before she'd gone outside and found Charlie and been dunked in the lake. Still, Vivian jumped from the sofa. She had time to register the astonished faces of Gwen and David as she bolted from the room.

Vivian jiggled the handle, but the bedroom door was locked. She pounded on the door with her fist. "Constance," she shouted. "Constance!" But there was no response.

She pressed her ear to the door. She heard nothing. Charlie nearly barreled into her as he rushed onto the landing behind her. Vivian looked up at him, panic rising in her chest. She could barely get the words out.

"We have to get in there," she said. "There isn't any time."

Charlie jiggled the handle himself before pushing her unceremoniously out of the way. He backed up and hit the bedroom door with his shoulder, grunting in pain. The door shuddered in its frame but didn't budge. Charlie backed away, rubbing his shoulder, his face a determined scowl. He took a step back toward the door when there came a shout from the stairway.

"Stop!"

Vivian turned to find David running up the stairs, waving something over his head. He stopped at the landing, panting, and held it out to Vivian. "A skeleton key," he said. "Opens every door in the house."

She plucked the key from his open palm and turned to the door. Her hands were shaking so badly that the tip of the key missed the keyhole and skittered sideways on her first two attempts, but on the third, the tumbler turned and the door swung open.

Vivian stood for a moment in the doorway.

The room was dark and still. Constance lay in bed just as Vivian had left her earlier. Her hands were clasped loosely over her stomach on top of the white coverlet now, her pale face a mask of serenity.

"Constance," Vivian said. Her voice was barely above a whisper, but it thundered in the silence of the bedroom. "Constance."

No response. No movement.

Vivian stepped forward into the room. Constance wasn't snoring. She wasn't breathing deeply. She wasn't breathing at all.

Vivian rushed to the bed. She spotted the bottle of Veronal on its side on the nightstand. Vivian picked it up and turned it over. It was empty. The same bottle had been full only this morning. She pressed her hand against Constance's forehead. It was chilled and dry, but not ice cold. She moved her hand to inches in front of Constance's mouth. She felt nothing. She crouched and pressed her ear to Constance's face. A faint exhale tickled Vivian's cheek, and Vivian exhaled herself. So Constance was still breathing, but very shallowly.

She took Constance by both shoulders and shook her. "Constance," she said. "Constance, wake up." There was no response. Vivian glanced over her shoulder at

Charlie, David, Freddy, and Gwen, who'd followed her into the bedroom and hovered near the doorway.

"Oh God, what is it? What's wrong with her?" David asked, pushing past Charlie to grasp his sister's hand.

"She's not breathing," Vivian said. "She's taken an overdose of sleeping pills."

"Sleeping pills? Oh no. Oh no, Constance." David shook his sister's limp form so hard her teeth rattled together. "Constance, wake up."

"Charlie, call the hospital. There's a telephone in a nook down the hall," Vivian said. "And Gwen, go get your parents." Vivian stared down into Constance's serene face. She looked calm now; there was no tension in her brow, no suspicion in her eyes. She looked so much younger with all her hard angles smoothed out. She looked beautiful.

Vivian looked again at the empty bottle and then noticed what was underneath — a sheet of floral stationery. Vivian plucked it from the nightstand and focused on the single line of scrawled writing.

It was an accident. God forgive me. I loved him.

She sat back on her heels, the paper clutched in her fingers. Dimly, she heard Charlie speaking to someone on the telephone. "Now," he said. "Sleeping pills. I'm afraid it might already be too late."

Someone crouched next to Vivian in the dim, silent room and gently plucked the letter from her fingers. She glanced up. Freddy nodded at her and stood. He would take care of it, she thought. *Thank God for Freddy.* She heard David sobbing quietly. He'd stopped shaking his sister and was now kneeling at her bedside, his head in his hands.

Then came the thunder of footsteps pounding up the carpeted hall stairs.

Adaline rushed into the room, followed closely by Bernard and Gwen, all of them soaked to the skin. Adaline stared wide-eyed at Vivian, a wet tendril of hair sticking diagonally across her forehead. Her eyes shifted to Constance unmoving on the bed, David kneeling next to her.

"What's happened? What's she done?"

"I think you know exactly what she's done," Vivian said quietly.

"Oh God. Oh no. My Constance." Adaline rushed forward and collapsed onto the bed on her daughter's prostrate form.

Charlie strode back into the room, pushing past Bernard, who seemed frozen in place near the door. "The hospital's sending an ambulance," he said. Then he gently pulled Vivian to her feet and led her from the room.

CHAPTER TWENTY-FOUR

Imogene looked up from her typewriter and smiled. She glanced from Vivian toward Mr. Langley's closed office door, and her smile disappeared. "Are you sure you should be here? You're in deep, you know."

"I know."

"I mean *possibly fired* deep." Imogene leaned toward her on the desk.

Vivian took off her gloves and folded them. Then she leaned against the corner of the desk, eyeing the closed door as well. "Oh, I know," she said.

"You don't seem very concerned."

"I'm not."

"Why?"

"Because I'm alive," Vivian said with a smile. "And Charlie's alive. It's a beautiful day, and the sun is shining."

Vivian watched her friend's brow furrow. "Did you hit your head or something?"

"I may have, but let's just say I found a

little perspective in Wisconsin. Oh, and I'm here because I have something to share with Mr. Langley. A trump card, so to speak." Vivian leaned down conspiratorially. "I have a screen test at MGM on Monday morning. Mr. Mayer called me himself."

Imogene's blue eyes widened. "You *did* hit your head."

"It's true. I swear it on my mother's name." Vivian held up a pinkie and crossed it over her heart.

"Well, knowing just how deeply you respect your mother . . . Say, why did you say all that about Charlie being alive? Last I saw you, you were crying over him being accused of killing someone. Was Charlie ever in danger of *not* being alive? What happened with all that? How can you just breeze in here as if that never happened?"

Vivian sighed. "I'm still piecing it together myself, but the long and the short of it is that Charlie didn't kill anyone, and now the police are savvy to that too."

"Oh . . . That's good?"

"Very good." Vivian looked down at her watch. "Oh, gee, is that the time? Can you call Langley for me? I'm in a bit of a rush. I've got a train to catch."

Imogene shook her head and pushed back her chair to head toward Mr. Langley's office, but the door opened of its own accord. Morty Nickerson stepped out and stopped short at the sight of Vivian. He smiled at her in surprise.

"Say, Viv," he said. "Aren't you supposed to be in Hollywood with Graham?"

"Yes," she said, moving toward the door. She stopped beside Morty and touched his arm. "I heard *Fantasy Ballroom* last night, Morty. Sounds like you've really got something with that idea."

Vivian smiled at Morty as he blushed from his toes to his hairline. She gave Mr. Langley a dazzling smile as he waved her into his office.

Vivian hurried through the bustling waiting area toward Track Five with Charlie just barely keeping pace beside her.

"How do you move so fast on those short legs?" he asked.

Vivian cast an exasperated look at him and then at the porter lagging behind them. "If he doesn't get a move on, it won't matter how fast my short legs can go."

Charlie put a large hand on Vivian's shoulder, slowing her forward momentum. "Don't worry," he said. "It's going to be fine."

"Is it?"

He squeezed her shoulder, and Vivian slowed her pace. There was something in that squeeze — comfort, reassurance, safety. She was starting to think everything would be fine after all. She knew Track Five and the shiny silver tail of the Super Chief would soon be in sight. She exhaled and looped her arm through Charlie's. He was here beside her. And that's where he'd stay, now that the police were no longer after him. She would make her train. She would be in Los Angeles in forty hours and meeting Louis B. Mayer bright and early Monday morning. And then? Well, then she'd have to work her way up to a whole new level of fine.

"Listen, I know you don't want to talk about it," Charlie said in low voice. "But —"

"I don't," she answered automatically. She started to quicken her pace again, but Charlie tugged on her arm, stopping her outright.

"I know, but I've been going over it in my head, and it's killing me not knowing what happened. Please, Viv?"

Vivian glanced up at him. He was smiling down at her, actually showing his teeth. He smiled so rarely these days, she thought, and God knew she couldn't say no to the dimple in his cheek.

"One question," she said begrudgingly. She hadn't thought it through herself yet. She'd been avoiding it, skirting the events of the past few days and filling her mind with thoughts of Los Angeles and screen tests so she wouldn't have to think of Hap's death and the fact that Constance had caused it.

Charlie leaned down toward her so that they wouldn't be overheard by any travelers hurrying past. His smile faded. "How had Constance known you were going to meet Hap in the boathouse?"

Vivian chewed the inside of her lip in thought. "Well, we switched bedrooms earlier in the day — at Constance's request. When the family was at dinner that evening, Hap must have snuck up the back stairs to deliver the note to my room. Except my room had become Constance's an hour or so earlier. He entered her room by mistake, and Constance woke from her doze and saw him — without letting him know he'd been seen. She hadn't been sleeping well, and she thought she'd been seeing ghosts, hadn't she? She thought she was losing her mind. She got up and followed him."

"She thought he was a ghost?" he said incredulously.

"That's two questions," she chided.

Charlie squeezed her hand, and she sighed at the comforting heaviness of it, the warmth of it through her white cotton glove. She decided she'd let another question slide if he'd just keep holding her hand like that.

"Yes, at the time I think she *did* think Hap was a ghost. Then when Hap left my bedroom, Constance entered and read the note meant for me."

"And maybe then she realized that ghosts don't leave notes to arrange secret rendezvous."

"Exactly. So Constance went back to her room and pretended to be asleep when I stopped by, intending to follow me outside and spy on our meeting. But then my aunt detained me for a few minutes in the parlor, and Constance must have slipped out in front of me. I don't know what happened in that boathouse. We may never know. Maybe she became hysterical, and he pulled his gun on her in an effort to get her to leave. They fought over it. But somehow, she got ahold of it and shot him. Anyway, she claims it was an accident, and maybe it was."

"But why didn't you see her leaving the boathouse? You got there only moments after, and there's only one way out."

Vivian thought for a moment. "My aunt Adaline came out only moments after me.

Constance must have . . . I don't know . . . been crouching on the railing outside, just around the corner? It's crazy, but that's the only place I wouldn't have seen her. There was nowhere else to hide. You know, when Adaline was rushing me out of the boathouse, she waved her hand like she was shooing someone away. That must have been Constance. She must have steered me away quickly so that Constance could make her escape. From there, I figure Constance ran in a panic, and when she realized she still had the gun, she threw it under the bushes. Gwen found the gun shortly thereafter and chucked it in the lake because she thought she was protecting David."

"And then Bernard and Adaline went about trying to cover up everything about Hap's real murder."

"And it might have worked if I'd drunk that whole glass of spiked milk," she said.

Charlie's gaze drifted over the top of her hat as he considered the explanation they'd come up with together.

"You're sure everything's taken care of? Legally, I mean?"

"As much as it can be," she said. "The complete opposite of legally, in point of fact. I assume Bernard has paid a lot of money to someone to keep the details of Hap's actual death a secret. A fudged death certificate, no inquest, cremation, Lord knows what else."

"And Constance?"

"We found her just in time. Once she recovers, she'll be sent back to the sanitarium in Switzerland."

"But why did she do it?"

Vivian shrugged. "The most common motive of all, I think. Love, jealousy. You know, I always thought Constance was a cold fish, but that was just a front. From what I've pieced together in the past few days, she'd been in love with Hap most of her life. I never knew about it, but she and Hap had a fling at some point . . . probably when they were no more than kids. It ended badly, I assume. Things tended to end badly with Hap." She paused, glancing over the faces of the people passing by. "He went away for a few years. But then he got hurt in that plane crash and came back to Oakhaven to recuperate. When he started something with me that summer, Constance couldn't handle it. Adaline saw it happening. That's what she meant when she told me that Hap was good at hurting people. Not just me, but also Constance because of me."

"But Constance was married with children at that point, wasn't she?"

"Yes, but a marriage vow doesn't stop you from loving someone else, does it?"

"I suppose not."

"And then Hap came back again and stirred all those old feelings back up, and Constance was in such a fragile state that she had a breakdown of sorts. Then they fought in the boathouse and . . . *bang.*"

Charlie shook his head, lost in thought. "And all that spy business. Was that ever real?"

"Lillian as much as admitted it herself. She tried to drown us, after all. Is it so far-fetched to believe that she and Hap met in Spain and were both secret German spies?"

"Yes, actually," Charlie said drily. "It's very far-fetched. All of it is."

"If it hadn't actually happened to me . . . to us . . . I wouldn't believe it either."

Charlie smiled suddenly and nodded to the newsstand behind her. Vivian followed his gaze to the *Radio Stars* magazine with her and Graham on the cover. He plucked a copy and stared down at it with a smile, then walked to the counter with it, fishing some change out of his pocket.

"You don't need to buy that for me," she said.

"Oh, I'm not buying it for you," he said, slapping a dime down on the counter of the newsstand. "I'm going to have a lot of leisure time on that train, and I'm keen to find out if this gorgeous radio star on the cover has a beau."

Vivian smiled. "I'm fairly certain Graham's unattached at the moment."

Charlie rolled up the magazine and tapped her playfully with it.

A man's voice came over the loudspeaker above their heads. "This is the last call for Train Number Seventeen, the Super Chief, scheduled to depart for Kansas City."

Charlie held his arm out to Vivian.

The reporters were bunched near the front of the train. One of them spotted Vivian as she and Charlie rushed toward their car, and the reporters all moved en masse toward the couple.

"Miss Witchell! Miss Witchell! A photo?" The calls came from all directions at once.

Vivian paused at the stairs to Car 176 and turned, motioning the porter on ahead with their bags. Flashbulbs popped before she could answer.

"Who's this, Miss Witchell?"

She smiled up at Charlie. "Shall I tell them?"

He was squinting from the glare of the flashbulbs and the commotion, but he nodded and managed a smile.

"My fiancé," she announced, beaming up at Charlie. The flashbulbs lit up the platform of Track Five like broad daylight, and then the train whistle hooted.

"All aboooard!" the conductor shouted as he walked toward them.

"Sorry, boys. That's us," Vivian said. She turned, and Charlie helped her up the stairs. She was looking forward to the forty hours alone with Charlie on this train. No reporters, no questions, no murderous family members, no ghosts. Just the two of them.

She stopped halfway up the stairs, removing her left glove.

"Turn and smile," she whispered to Charlie.

They did, and Vivian was sure to turn her engagement ring out to the cameras as the flashbulbs popped.

ABOUT THE AUTHOR

Cheryl Honigford is the author of the Daphne Award–winning *The Darkness Knows* and *Homicide for the Holidays.* She lives in the suburbs of Chicago, where she enjoys listening to old-time radio, watching classic movies, tumbling down historical research rabbit holes, and living vicariously through her writing.

The employees of Thorndike Press hope you have enjoyed this Large Print book. All our Thorndike, Wheeler, and Kennebec Large Print titles are designed for easy reading, and all our books are made to last. Other Thorndike Press Large Print books are available at your library, through selected bookstores, or directly from us.

For information about titles, please call:
(800) 223-1244

or visit our website at:
gale.com/thorndike

To share your comments, please write:

Publisher
Thorndike Press
10 Water St., Suite 310
Waterville, ME 04901